Under My Skin

NEW CANADIAN NOVELISTS SERIES

The New Canadian Novelists Series from Quarry Press charts new directions being taken in contemporary Canadian fiction by presenting the first novel of innovative writers. Other titles in the series include *Mona's Dance* by Ann Diamond, *Ritual Slaughter* by Sharon Drache, *Thrice Upon a Time* by Genni Gunn, and *The Ascension of Jesse Rapture* by Barry Dempster.

Under My Skin

Mary di Michele

QUARRY PRESS

The author gratefully acknowledges the assistance of the Toronto Arts Council.

The publisher gratefully acknowledges the assistance of The Canada Council, the Ministry of Canadian Heritage, the Ontario Arts Council, and the Ontario Publishing Centre.

Canadian Cataloguing in Publication Data

Cover art entitled "Hommage to Max Ernst I" by Theodore and Esther Dragonieri, reproduced by permission of the artists.
Design by Keith Abraham.
Printed and bound in Canada by Webcom Limited, Toronto, Ontario.

Published by
Quarry Press, Inc.,
P.O. Box 1061, Kingston, Ontario.

Under My Skin

Morally, those of us who have a high opinion of sex cannot accept the idea of passive consent sanctioning all kinds of carnal communication; rather than rely on negative criterion that absence of resistance justifies sexual congress, we must insist that evidence of positive desire alone dignifies sexual intercourse and makes it joyful. From a proud and passionate woman's point of view, anything less is rape.

GERMAINE GREER

There is no female Mozart because there is no female Jack the Ripper.

CAMILLE PAGLIA

```
          THE BOOK COMPANY
   OAKRIDGE CTR. VANCOUVER, B.C.
             264-9245
       GST-FED #: 101048478

SALE    000104  0605 002  00001 94696
           94/07/23              17:27

FICT. PAPER BK. 1550820990 90
 1 @                            16.95
FICT. PAPER BK. 088910476X 90
 1 @                            16.95
        SUB-TOTAL              33.90
   07.0% GST - FED              2.37
        TOTAL SALE             36.27
         VISA                  36.27
780249    9703 4535112567756

PLEASE RETAIN YOUR RECEIPT FOR REFUNDS

          CUSTOMER COPY
```

THE BOOK COMPANY
OAKRIDGE CTR., VANCOUVER, B.C.

SALE 000104 0605 002 00001 94449
94/07/23 17:27

FICT. PAPER BK. 1550820990 90
1 @ 16.95
FICT. PAPER BK. 0889104764 90
SUB-TOTAL 33.90
TOTAL SALE 36.27

PLEASE RETAIN YOUR RECEIPT FOR REFUNDS

CUSTOMER COPY

Preface

Call me Lady Lazarus because I am looking for a friend,
a father, an angel, a lover who can bring me back from the
dead. Most people I know don't read poetry or the Bible.
They've never heard of Sylvia Plath though they recognize
Jesus Christ as a character from a film by Pasolini. But
this is the real world — of documentary, not movies — the
world of credit cards and Black's photography and
Canada and Christmas shopping which begins here with
the first snow, in September. This is not the world of literature, this is not the Holy Land, but the reception area
of a theater in a mall termed a cultural complex, where
tonight I'm stuck, as I am routinely, at one of those deadly
premieres I'm responsible for. Let me tell you I have a
yen to do something else, something vital. Something sig-
nificant. It feels more pressing tonight than ever, the need
to change. But I'm premenstrual and I've forgotten to
take my B-6's, so that must be contributing to the state I'm
in. In this mood I run into my boss, Peter the Great. I've
missed the public screening and if he's not people illiterate,
he'll read the guilt on my face.

   Peter the Great looks down at my five-foot-nothing
frame from his six-plus-eminence, the way you might

notice something shiny on the floor, a bright dime you don't need to stoop to pick up, because you're rich, because you have it all. He pretends he doesn't know me. He's holding his drink with one hand and his elbow with another. He's dressed in a tuxedo with tails. There's a miniature rose in his lapel. It's dark red, moist and dewy. He's a lady killer. He always wears a rosebud in his jacket. Don't think it's a target marking where his heart must be. The rose is what he offers a woman, a real flower, a fake heart.

Nobody else is dressed so formally, but he's not embarrassed. How can one man make a room full of men look wrong?

His curly hair is dark with no visible gray. He must prefer the lie of youth to looking distinguished. His eyes are bedroom eyes with one door half open, one door half shut.

I reintroduce myself, Margaret Latte, from publicity. I do this humbly, without a trace of irony (okay, I try). "My friends call me Rita," I say. After all I don't want to lose my job. What I get in return is a bad pun.

"Oh yes, you're Late, ha, you're the one," he says, sizing me up and down. "Always short on time, eh?"

I titter politely. Unfortunately when I'm nervous I punctuate sentences with a giggle. "If you like, you can call me Rita," I say.

"Rrrrrrita." He purrs the r's in my name. "Were you the one who handled the publicity for our film tonight? Good turn out." He looks around the crowded salon. "A remarkable film about a remarkable man . . . !" he adds, but I can't punctuate that properly (exclamation or ellipsis?) because his voice, which is stainless steel, no trace of irony, is contradicted by his quizzical eyes. So I don't know how he would like me to respond. But I'm smart enough not to confide in any man from the hierarchy in this

8

government-funded arts bureaucracy.

"Yes. Fisherman's best study in the poetic character yet," I concede rather slyly, but only you and I know what I'm really thinking. Good thing too because just then the director approaches us. I smile and excuse myself, making for the ladies' room. Fisherman is too busy to notice me just then. He wants to speak to the big boss, not hassle an underling about not doing enough to promote his latest cinematic oeuvre. Some might call it an oeuf, a rotten one. I'm one of the first to see these films when they're completed so that I can lie meaningfully in the publicity. This particular masterpiece is a literary documentary, a biography of one of the old guys, a poet nobody really reads. He is kind of romantic, you know, the way you expect a poet to be. His hair looks windswept even indoors; he must carry a portable heath and English weather in his pocket. The subject himself, surrounded by women of various ages, is seated on one of the leather sofas placed in strategic corners of the rooms. One of the pathetic creatures is kneeling at his feet holding an ashtray. His cigarette is burning down to the filter as he speaks but he hasn't yet deigned to flick it into the female's proferred vessel.

That is one "Brilliant Corner" — I think in parody of a beautiful and raucous phrase from jazz. I didn't realize until recently what Thelonius Monk, the composer, meant. I was drinking a glass of wine and trying to relax. It was a week night, after too much work, and I lit a candle and put a CD by Monk on the stereo. The music filled the room like light, to the ceiling, enough music to drown in. Then I saw what Monk meant was magic, more than just an ironic inversion of what you expect to find in the corners of dimly lit rooms. Nightclubs were his chambers and music was his brilliance, music flowing into every nook and cranny, into every crevice in every corner, music blinding each ear with its epiphanic glow.

Tonight there's no music, only murmurings. There's a lot of talk and a little laughter, you know, the knowing kind, the kind of laughter that is so controlled it stays in the throat or is released through the nose. It doesn't resonate in the abdomen, it doesn't draw a stitch in your side or effect your breathing. Laughter that makes you feel more isolated at a party than when you're alone at home. Laughter with a head but no body.

I am laughing that laugh with a local critic. I am wearing my violet silk Chinese style dress, slit to the deep south on one side. I am wearing a chiffon scarf in the same hue wrapped around my head. The outfit is modeled on Natalie Wood's costume in some film I can't entirely forget, although I saw it only once as a child. I have forgotten the plot, but I can't forget the color. Violet enhanced her dark hair and eyes; its elusive sheen seemed to be the first vestige of light, the first trace of sun on the horizon. Or the last.

I am waiting for someone to notice my new outfit. The dress is not cold, it's hot. And I am waiting for someone to notice. I wonder if I can get away with this getup with the harshest critics, with other women, with the feminists. I worry about what my female friends will think. I worry about stuff like that but at the same time I'd never sacrifice looking good. No "fuck-me heels" though. I keep my balance. In fashion. Instead of killer pumps I'm wearing dark plum silk slippers embroidered with a phoenix, the head on the right foot, the tail on the left; I have to keep my feet primly together for you to get the whole picture. I like flat shoes so I can walk that walk without tripping, without practically keeling over *in high heels. Walking in high heels makes you feel as if you're climbing the tower of Pisa, as if you've just caught the flu, as if you've been wandering around all day in a Pop Art gallery, as if you've got new glasses and the prescription is too strong, as if you've just watched Hitchcock's* Vertigo *for the seventeenth time and still can't remember which blonde is which — and you're the blonde.*

I'm spending the whole time in my head or by the bar because the reception is proving to be an even duller event than I expected. I catered the affair myself, so I'm responsible for the indigestion. Wine and Swedish crackers and various ripe and moldy cheeses. I try to eat some of the food but a little of the brie on crispbread tastes like polyfill on sandpaper. I'm doing some minor repairs to the walls of my house. I recognize the taste.

There isn't much food left to go around anyway. Luckily there is lots of wine. It's Bordeaux, dry and good. I slink over to the bartender, a young man I know. He works our functions pretty regularly. I am getting into the habit of taking him home. Or maybe it is he who takes me home; it's hard to know when you get as drunk as I do. I keep drinking and looking into his beautiful gray eyes at the same time. It's hard to tell which is more intoxicating, but if I had to choose, I'd always choose the man. John keeps refilling the wine in my glass. As the liquid pours, the bottle makes little gulping sounds. As if it too were drinking. The wine I want is white. When I sniff to judge its bouquet, it smells golden, like a peach when the first fruit flies hover around it.

I almost drain the latest glass too. Then I cross that invisible line which separates us. To get closer to him I move behind the serving table. The elbow of the arm holding my wine glass is snuggled into my hip. It's an art making time without spilling a drop. I stop drinking long enough to whisper in his ear. I nibble the full fleshy lobe. It sparkles with a diamond stud. Obviously there are others who appreciate him even more than I do.

"Can I see you later?" I ask.

He gives me a little push at my chest. This hurts my pride. But he adds a sly smile to the rebuff; he peeks up at me over the frames of his little round wire-rimmed spectacles. Then he bends to fill more glasses with wine, red and white, lining them up into neat rows on the white linen cloth of the table. John himself is dressed in white like the table. He's dressed to serve. There's an aura around him and in his skin from all that white. He's so young, I think, half with pleasure, half with envy. I take another sip from the thin blood of the grape and walk away.

I am getting drunk, but not too drunk. Drunk enough to try to do what I need to do, corner the big boss again and convince him that I have a good idea for a film and that with my experience I should join a studio and direct. I have ambitions to be a Von Trotta but I don't have the political savvy. What I do have is an unpublished novel I've written myself. Right now it's stuffed into my briefcase which I checked with my coat for fear of appearing ridiculous, for fear of appearing as if I actually did some work in this organization. The case is bulging with the bulk of my manuscript like a pregnant woman way past her due date.

So I sidle up again to the head man, Peter the Great, acting cool and friendly at the same time. The only time I can pull it off is when I'm drunk; otherwise cool gets the better of me.

I don't know how to begin so I raise my glass to him as if in a toast and I smile and then I sip the wine.

How to get his attention, how to get him interested in my book? I have four years of my life, my weekends, my restless nights in my portfolio. Those years, all that work, give me the courage to try.

"*I'm a writer too, you know, as well as a publicist here. In fact I've had a novel recently accepted for publication by the best literary press in the country. But it's more than a book, it's easily adaptable into a screenplay. I can see how the camera will move for every scene.*"

"*When will it be published?*"

"*Oh, not for some time I'm afraid. They're booked for the next two seasons. Are you at all interested?*"

"*A novel! How unusual!*" *he says.* "*I wouldn't have expected that from one of our staff. Literary ambitions. What's it about?*"

"*A serial rapist who is a Dr. Jekyll and Mr. Hyde type character. And a heroine who is a young filmmaker. You get to know and like her but she becomes his last victim. My idea is that the blondes knocked off in thrillers are always anonymous and disposable. Yellow kleenex, if you know what I mean. They leave decorative corpses, that's all. I want the film, this book, to force the viewer to feel the violence in the genre. If you identify with the woman, it happens to you. If you love the woman, it happens to your lover.*"

"*Hummmmph. Sounds as if it might not be uninteresting. Tell me more.*"

I ignore the ironic hedging in his response. I know he wants a plot that's really original, a sequel for a film about to be made.

"*Think of it as a feminist* Crime and Punishment,*" I say.* "*Not, of course, so intellectual. More like uh . . . Margaret Atwood writes Mickey Spillane.*"

He laughs through his nose and shakes his head at the same time. He takes a drink from his wine and runs his tongue over his top lip. Then he says, "You're a funny girl" and "yes, perhaps the novel is amusing." He checks out the slit along the thigh of my dress.

When he says, "Let's have lunch and discuss it some more," I respond, "Great, fantastic, when?" "Tomorrow," he says. "Wow," I say, "you're a fast reader!" I can be incredibly naive at times. I just assumed that by "discuss" he meant that he would read the manuscript. There's the slightest change in his expression, some sort of clarification in the mental processes, the portent of which eludes me; but it looks like the shift in the sharpness of the image on the screen of your TV when you switch from a regular broadcast to the video of your VCR.

"Just a sec, I'll be right back," I say. And I'm back with my briefcase and I pull out the manuscript before he can change his mind gracefully, and I hand it over to him.

He feels the weight of it, moving it up and down, the way you estimate the cost of a melon in the supermarket. Then he flips it open to the first page and reads the title, Many Small Deaths, out loud. "Not too thrilling," he says. "We will have to find something catchier than that." Then his eyes are moving so rapidly back and forth across the page that he looks more like a dreamer in REM cycle than a reader. Dreaming with his eyes open.

By the time I get our drinks refilled, he's stopped flipping through my novel. I'm afraid he's not interested. But he tells me that he likes what he's seen at a glance and he's even read a few of the pages! He would like to take the manuscript home; he'll let me know what he thinks of it tomorrow. Since it's close to 11:00 p.m., I wonder if he's going to skip sleeping. But he is a fast reader, he *tells me that he once read* War and Peace *in two hours.*

The film version takes longer. I wonder why anyone would want to do that. I believe that a book is like a world and if you love the world you want it to never end. Although I have to admit anyone would want to exit the world of my story, anyone would have to breathe a sigh of relief when it's over, anyone would be glad that it's not their real life, that it's just some dark form of entertainment. That's part of the intention of the book, if authors are still allowed any intentions.

"You should have skipped the novelization and just written a screenplay, Rita. It's a waste of time." Pausing meaningfully, he burns me with the statement "It's not literature." He smiles as he says this, to let me in on the compliment.

Then Peter the Great moves in on me, so close that my nose is rubbing against the starched stiffness of his tux. His scent makes it hard for me to breathe; his scent suggests musk and spice and cigarette. And then he briefly places his hand at my waist. His hand slides down the curve of my hip. Silk is slippery like that.

"Tomorrow, my lovely Rita, remember we must meet to discuss things. Call me first thing in the morning. If this story is as good as it looks, then I may be able to help you. Imagine, you can move out of that dingy little cubbyhole, your post, and into a more creative role. Wasn't it Flaubert who said that the artist must be comfortable in his life so that he can take bigger risks in his art?"

"Who am I to argue with Flaubert?" I smile . . .

1
The Journal

I kept the details on three-by-five file cards, wrapped simply in a rubber band, and stored in the glove compartment of my car. I filled in these cards immediately after every incident, sitting in my car in the garage, before going back into the house. They are reports, not diary entries. There is nothing personal or self-indulgent in them. Everything is empirically observed and noted. I abstained from all rationalizations. These cards may be useful in understanding my case. A case where I was completely in control, the proof in the minutiae and accuracy of my reporting.

I could say I didn't know what made me act as I did and you would accept this, in fact, perhaps prefer it. We would like to attribute the darkness from which these actions, not I, sprang, not to the demonic, that mixture of myth and the will, but to psychopathology. In the story of Dr. Jekyll and Mr. Hyde you are shown the truth that Robert Louis Stevenson discovered, between the observation (or the scientific) and the narration (or the fiction), the truth, or those entertainments some call literature. I know you would prefer to have these events explained in this way and perhaps you could, if I had not recorded all the details meticulously, with the keen observation and accurate memory that has made me an excellent diagnostic doctor — one who can detect, in advance of signs of bleeding or the results of x-rays, the cancer in the patient who, walking into my office for the first time, sits down and before he can open his mouth, wraps his arms around his chest like a mother who needs to quiet her child so that she can speak. You or someone like Stevenson could make a parable of this part of my life, a fable to warn away good citizens from the consequences of violent lust. But here I present to you the facts — in the cards. I remove the elastic and hand them over to you, both evidence and confession. Thirteen cards in all, thirteen women — the where, the how, the who, the when — detailed and dated.

By reputation, indeed by occupation, I am a philanthropist, and my humanism is rationally based. Mine is an exemplary life. And as you may know, I have been a happy man. A man to whom nothing is given, by whom all has been earned. There is much satisfaction in that. I have two children, a daughter and a son, who excel at everything they engage in; I have a wife, who is both social and discreet; and I have all the material comforts. My house, on its cherished plot in the city, backs onto a ravine, so that it seems a country estate. Indeed, I have more than I allow myself time to enjoy. I love my work and know full well its importance.

I am not the sort of man who underestimates himself. I am not the sort of man who is not tender towards his wife. Those other women helped me to preserve that tenderness.

You will call them my victims and think my wife wronged. The truth is, they were actors in a drama where the crucial scenes are improvised. They cued me how to act, they led me to an interpretation of my part, one I hadn't fully intended to play. This is not a confession. This is a testimony.

I saw the first one close to home, the one who undressed with the blind half way up. I was driving back late one night from the hospital. I had to stop and watch. The heat and moisture of the summer night was like a pall. I could tell I had too much valium in my bloodstream because my body seemed to keep drifting forward even after the car had stopped. The shirt under my suit jacket was wet and clinging. I loosened my tie. It was hard to breathe. An odor of magnolia, like the sweet and musk of the female sex, saturated the atmosphere. The sensuality of the deep South growing here in Ontario, though on thin, dwarf saplings. It seemed half comic, half provocative; it made me think of little girls in high heels.

I could see the distant headlights of cars from St. Clair. But no sound of a motor penetrated the sleepy crescent, muffled in shrubbery and the cathedral-like arches of shade maples. Her window was the only light on the street. I watched the scissor-like action of her legs as she moved across the room. I found it hard to breathe but lit a cigarette anyway, my first in days. Inhaled deeply. I smoke infrequently, in order to savor the nicotine. Her hips and buttocks shone like chrome distorted as in a convex mirror. The slim waist, the ribs that support the breasts, the clearly defined pectoral muscles, the obliques, as she turned. The white blind that blocked out the rest of her upper body. I felt my penis stiffen and find its way past the elastic of my jockey shorts.

For several nights, sitting in the dark car, I kept watching her. I kept watch over her.

After that I came prepared. After that I felt compelled

to act. Compelled by the stifling heat perhaps, by the sudden tropics this winter-weary city serves up as summer weather. Or by some small thing, a mosquito trapped with me that night, a needling irritation, its insistent whine, silence, then whine again. I clapped and caught it between my spread hands. A little oily smear of an insect gorged on blood.

I picked her lock with a surgical probe. For a mask, I used an old nylon stocking of my wife's that I had pulled out of the wastebasket in the bedroom. Thus the doctor is fully disguised.

That first woman, the woman of the half blind, lived only a few blocks away from our home. Months later, I spotted her while shopping at Loblaws. She was looking rather haggard as if from too much dieting. Or as if, living alone, she often forgot to eat. Though I saw once more that she was attractive, she looked jaundiced in the fluorescent lighting of the supermarket, like someone who takes tablets to simulate a suntan, the orange tones of carotene giving away the illusion she wishes to conjure, the fantasy of the luxury of sun and beach and idleness. Although I watched her closely, I feigned the detachment I might have given the tomatoes in the fresh produce section when I observe the pyramid of their fruit, their brilliant color, without hunger, without need to buy. I noticed her sidelong glances at me and I enjoyed the oblique flirtation in them. I caught her gaze and held it briefly, as one holds a bus transfer, accepted automatically, before you crumple it and throw it away.

On that first night, I had kissed my wife goodnight and waited, reading in my pyjamas, for her pills to take effect. Then I slipped into my jogging clothes and quietly left the house.

I let myself in through the kitchen as easily, as fluidly,

as a Siamese slipping through its cat door.

She was still awake, lying naked on the bed, the sheets turned back. Her hands held up an issue of Vogue in the circle of light from her reading lamp and she turned the pages slowly.

From my pocket I pulled out some cotton strips. I crushed them into a ball in one hand. In the other I wore a roll of surgical tape, like a bracelet that doesn't quite fit, that won't slip past the knuckles and onto the wrist.

Though it was only a few feet to the bed, the distance felt like miles of black tunnel, as if connecting England and France under the channel. My feet were soundless, cushioned by the deep pile of her wine dark rug.

Her body was golden in the tungsten light. Her face was blocked out by the magazine; her face was June's covergirl, the smiling face of Harry Belafonte's daughter. When I leapt onto the bed, she dropped the glossy smile.

I stuffed her mouth with cotton strips. I sealed those lips with adhesive. I taped her blindly flaying, ineffectual arms to the bedposts. Her skin felt like gauze. I took the magazine, which had the weight of the Bible, and set it face down by the clock-radio. She made muffled gasping sounds, like some sea-creature, breathless and beached. I whispered no threats, just began the touching, the touching that comes naturally for a man with a woman, comes naturally when he doesn't have to worry about what's gentle, what's rough. When he doesn't have to think about pleasure, her pleasure. When he feels desire travel through his loins like the blue shuddering light he once felt as a boy touching what shouldn't be touched, the prongs of the radio's plug as he pushed it into the electrical socket. The exhilarating release when a man's escape from a woman is calculated. From the start.

She didn't fight me. She seemed paralyzed by the

weight of my body bearing down on her chest, as if I were a nightmare that rode her. Struggling through the gag, a muffled sound, not a voice, an inarticulate murmuring, as if through the throat of an animal. An engine, a purring, the roaring of the lesser cats. As if human speech alone could not free her. As it cannot free anyone.

Then as she drew back, almost swooning, like a young girl for her first kiss, that narcotic mix of anxiety and romance, she asked me with her eyes what would be left to her if I were going to kill her. I did not want to disappoint her, or the others later, but my business is to save lives. Still I saw the excitement that distorted her face, as if she were a witness to an accident, drawn to the spectacle, as if the body of the victim thrown out onto the road were not her own. So I took her as I later took others, to the edge. I showed each of them how to act out their deaths. An expert in resuscitation techniques, I would almost kill them, but could stop at the point where I had the power to bring them back. For that first woman, I showed her a soft death, what it is to be smothered by a pillow. I said, "You're dead." Then, "You're dead if you report or remember any of this."

Then I left.

I left them all. Like fish that had been hooked, then tossed still alive into a bucket of water to keep them fresh. Left them with death assigned to them like widows' plots, marked with their names on the plaques beside their husbands' decaying mounds, the dates to be filled in later. Left them all with a death to tame their dying.

2

Rita

THE morning was fresh. After a night of rain, the grass was brilliant with moisture. Fragrant. Rita opened the front door to bring in the morning paper, wondering where she would find it this time. It seemed to her that the paper boy bundled the news into blue elastic bands and then ten times out of ten missed the front steps. Rita had called the office to complain once, but later she had learned from her next door neighbor that the paper boy was actually a twelve-year-old girl being raised by a divorced mother on a secretary's salary. She could never bring herself to complain about the service again. After that, discovering the paper soaking under the lawn sprinkler she'd left on overnight, she found herself, as she picked up the phone to call *The Globe* office, imagining instead the young girl's early morning routine, her need, and the pittance she would be paid for her work. She was, she told herself, a woman of too much empathy and too much imagination for her own good. She ended up blaming herself for forgetting to turn the sprinkler off.

Though Rita was an early riser, she could picture how, before she had even had her first cup of coffee, that child would have bundled the papers, loaded them into the basket of her bike, and thrown them onto all the lawns along her route. Rita saw her once just before dawn, a thin girl almost invisible in her dark blue windbreaker. At last the paper was always there, even though Rita often had to hunt for it. Always somewhere in the shrubs or among her flowers, or under the Holstein, the lawn ornament Rita kept as a gargoyle on her front yard. But today was better, she thought, today the paper had luckily landed on the walkway to her steps. Rita wouldn't have to hang the first section up to dry on the bathroom rod before she could read it.

It was Saturday morning. Though it was only seven-thirty, she could hear the TV in the house next door blaring the chaos of cartoons. The knock'em-out action and violence-without-consequence would last for hours. In the back lane a couple of dogs were barking for their breakfasts. Somewhere down the street somebody was awake enough to attack the hot and humid heat wave's growth of lawn. The lawnmower's engine blended with the muffled rattle of guns on the TV.

These sounds of domestic life pleased Rita. Her own home was cool and dark. To fill the emptiness she kept the radio on whether she listened to it or not. If she had been Joan of Arc, she sometimes thought, she wouldn't need the radio. There would always be voices all around. Well, thank goddess for airwaves. Those other kinds of voices always get you into trouble.

When the radio was off, her house was as quiet as a tomb. But the word tomb seemed melodramatic. As she told herself that, she recognized the voice of the censor long ago internalized, her mother. Turning forty was beginning to seem like a problem.

There *was* a marriage certificate, a piece of paper in a

24

metal file cabinet, but she was not really married. It was not the proof that she had been searching for, proof that her Greek lover loved her. Although it was only a notarized document, it was an integral part of her history. Nikos, the man she had been living with, had been about to lose his landed immigrant status because of his radical politics. Rita had married him to help him stay in the country. But also unfortunately, because she was in love with him.

That was ten years ago. Though they were still married, she hadn't seen him in the last seven of those ten years. They had written letters after he'd returned to Greece, to a mother in Athens, and to the cause. But after a while, her letters had gone unacknowledged. She felt hurt, then alarmed, then hurt again. But what could she do?

Nikos was the only man she had ever loved so passionately. He was the kind of man who makes you forget you're also intelligent, who makes you forget it even while he's politicizing you. Because he's politicizing you. If she had had his children, she would have stepped back into the house on mornings such as this and begun her day of making breakfast for the family, handing over the newspaper to him, taking gulps of coffee between cracking eggs, buttering toast. Then, if she had kept her job, she would also have had to clean the house on the weekends. And her kids would have complained about the sound of the vacuum interfering with their cartoons.

Such is the service for which a woman is supposed to be expert! So what would be the good part, if that wasn't it? Desire not dead, but aged and enriched, like a good wine, the complexity of flavors, experience on the palate, that was Rita's fantasy. In the evening, after putting the kids to bed early, they would have sat on lawn chairs in the backyard, with a bottle of chilled retsina, Ella Fitzgerald singing some

Cole Porter softly in the background: "I've got you under my skin . . ."

In the heat of the humid summer evening, Rita would wear shorts to get some sun on her legs. In those endless evenings when the light never quits. Nikos would have worn a white cotton T-shirt, an undershirt actually, deeply scooped, his smooth bronze chest picking up the warm tones of the setting sun, his dark eyes, deepening profoundly, shaded by long lashes, those same lashes curled in sleep over the eyes of their children. Remembering his eyes made her breathless with desire.

She would have watched her weight very strictly through the pregnancies. She would still be Rita with long slim legs, the kind he so appreciated in North American women. She would touch those legs there on that lawn chair as she massaged cocoa butter onto her calves and thighs and then slipped her fingers up the back of her shorts to adjust her panties. He would watch through eyes narrowed against the glare of the sun, and then he would put his wine glass down to kiss her. His lips would be fragrant with pine needles. But they would taste something like turpentine. From the retsina. She never could stand that stuff. She used to drink it to please him.

She knew how rare such evenings would really be. In fact, Nikos would condemn her little fantasy as bourgeois. Actually he would have spent evenings out with his comrades, debating Greek politics, cursing the *junta*, postulating a paper revolution, affirming good left-wing democracy, concerned about the Middle East, Nicaragua, American imperialism. And about how they were made exiles from their own culture, these men who called Athens at least once a week to see if their mothers had starved to death on their widow's pensions. Rita would have had to stay home with the kids. But some women might come to the meetings. Young women, politically correct, whose pelvises had not been stretched by childbirth. Or young Greek women who continued to live at home, with whom the men must become engaged so that the girls could attend meetings without their chaperones. Rita's piece of paper came in handy whenever she reached this point in her reveries. At least in Canada that possibility had been eliminated. She had no illusions that it had stopped Nikos from doing whatever he wanted to do in Greece.

A pebble which had worn itself loose from the concrete of her porch intruded sharply into her consciousness. As she shifted her weight onto her right side, it had worked its way into her instep. She kicked it away, her bare feet beginning to feel numb from the chill damp that lingers in concrete. Painted pink like the front door, the color looked so warm that the cement fooled you. As Nikos had fooled her. He would not feel bound by western imperialist contracts. She could see him marrying in a church. He was always able to reconcile being a Christian with being a Marxist.

Rita plopped herself into the director's chair that occupied one corner of the porch, its taut canvas also pink. It was a gift for her last birthday from Margo, Margo's far from subtle attempt to encourage Rita to go back to making films.

But Margo detested pink because it was emblematic of traditional femininity. "Weakness, sweet syrupy weakness," Margo called it. "Color the conspiracy that keeps women little girls pink. Even old women are compelled to wear two inches of pancake powder on their noses and a grease slick named something like 'tender pink' on their lips."

Rita stripped the rubber band from the newspaper. The sharp scent of ink testified to the freshness of the print, if not of the news. She turned the pages of the Entertainment section, scanning the film reviews.

She had been prepared to give it all up — ambition, independence, idleness — for the one man who wouldn't ask it of her. Maybe Barry — the guy she'd been seeing for several months, ever since they had met through a promotional tour she had done in the schools — was right: that she clung to her obsession for Nikos because it limited the power of other men in her life. Barry told her that she played the role of bitch, dating men, sleeping with them sometimes, but giving them no real place in her life.

But she didn't think love possible again for her. Not because love is rare, no, not rare, but because it leaves scorched earth when it fails. Love for Rita had become some sacred animal, an albatross, a white whale, she had to kill.

She still felt the loss physically like a sharp pain in the side of the chest from running too long and too hard. Oxygen debt. She still had to run to forget that man. For the drug, for the sly endorphins the body releases as it consumes itself. And she liked the sensation of her pulse at her throat, at her brow, wet and radiant with perspiration. As in the night of a spring long ago after which she had never been so happy.

Because her innocence had been the base for that happiness. So what if such innocence wasn't fashionable now. It hadn't been fashionable even then, in the early seventies, in the age of Aquarius. She remembered, with ironic tolerance, her shame then at being so square, at her twenty-four-year-old and virgin self.

But her life began to change radically in an European history class, "Revolution and Counter-Revolution," where she had met a young man. She was drawn — all the more powerfully because it was in spite of herself — to his intelligence and intensity and the beliefs that challenged, that eclipsed, her own Catholic family values with Marxist revolutionary ones. That young man had been Nikos, a foreign student with sculptural beauty and an exotic accent, a young man who had insisted their relationship be on his own, enlightened terms, the terms of the times — open relationships, free love.

All Rita had ever wanted was to be safe and to keep her young man safe in his fierce battles with injustice. Her moral qualms about getting sexually involved made her feel priggish and petty. Nikos insisted they were. To change that judgment she found herself approaching, uninvited, Nikos' room one afternoon. He was very poor and oranges were expensive that wintery spring. She could still see the gift she offered, the large navel orange in her hand, how its leathery skin glistened with fragrance and moisture. The weight of the orange, her doubts, the weight of her world, slowed her steps, made her hesitate a long time outside his door before she could find the courage to knock.

Nikos was on his way out when he opened the door. All Rita could do was offer the fruit. Feeling very foolish, she smiled at the brilliant orange in her hand. She rubbed its skin with her thumb releasing some of its oily resin as she stuttered incomprehensible phrases to explain her presence in his residence. Rita could not remember what she said. She remembered what she had imagined would happen, how she would peel the fruit for him, releasing the fine spray of oil from its rind, the white phosphorescent scales which would make her fingers sticky with the bitter sweetness of citrus, how she would feed him sections of the orange, how his lips might accidentally touch her hand, how he might suck the fruit, suck her fingers.

Nikos took her by the elbow and pulled her into the room. When he threw her onto the bed she must have dropped the orange. When she talks to women friends and they exchange anecdotes about the first time she always draws a blank here. Her friends think she's shy about it.

Folding up the newspaper, Rita dropped it onto the pink cement, her fingers smudged black from the newsprint. She made an effort to get up and go back into the house, wondering how long she had lingered, not fully dressed, on her porch. *Making a spectacle of herself,* her mother would say. Rita looked down at her white cotton nightgown. Under a fitted bodice, her nipples stood erect in the cool morning air, chafing against the texture.

Back inside, the coffee smell spreading through the house had turned from the rich and tantalizing odor of fresh roasted beans to something slightly burnt, the smell of reheated coffee she despised. She would have to start fresh.

She had used up the last of the Colombian beans. All she had left, stored in the freezer, was a Brazilian blend, the beans larger, the body coarser tasting. She had made the mistake of buying them, the monthly special, two months before in the market. It would have to do. She ground the coffee and filled the basket of her automatic coffeemaker and sat at the kitchen table with the radio playing Bruce Springsteen's *Dancing in the Dark*: ". . . start a fire sitting 'round crying . . ."

In contrast to her image of Nikos, which had the thick and furious brush strokes of a Van Gogh painting, she could visualize Barry as accurately as a black and white photograph. A slight man, a little shorter than herself, Barry had his hair permed into an Afro, though that hadn't been fashionable since the sixties for a white man. Maybe it was to give him a bit of height, or else to try to disguise the fact that it was thinning. He was a teacher in a technical school. He was not an intellectual, but he was a thoughtful man. He was a good man, as such, a rarity.

A good single man at that. A dying breed, like those whales killed to make cosmetics and perfume. She imagined herself a female whale, warm blooded, huge, blue, adrift, combing the icy depths of Arctic oceans for a mate. Try putting *that* in the personal columns of *The Globe and Mail!*

Barry was there for her. For a while longer perhaps. He had said that "dating" was not the thing for grown men and women to do for more than a year. That was his position on the relationship.

The problem was that she found it impossible to make decisions, emotional decisions. At work, it was easy. On paper, within the compass of an hour and the white rectangle of words, on the page, she felt a sense of control. Snap decisions on what didn't work, what wouldn't go over were easy for her compared to the question of whom she should share her bed with. At work nobody could get to the point faster. She knew how to find what she needed. When she had a story to tell, she got the facts, established a point of view. Her emotions were there, but controlled. Even in the film she had made where she had interviewed twelve-year-olds turning tricks on the streets to survive, she had been in charge, composed but not without compassion. A fucking lot of good it had done except shake up a few liberals like herself.

Perhaps that was the best she could do. Inform. But once informed, people had to see what ought to be done. She could only describe, not change the way things were.

She tapped her fingers on the table as she waited for the coffee to brew. Since giving up smoking during her winter doldrums, she had not yet found out what her hands should do instead at those moments during lapses in a conversation, internal or otherwise, as the angel of silence had once manifested itself in white rings of smoke. When the phone rang, she grabbed the receiver with a sense of release, jerking it across the table. It slipped from her hand. Even as she picked up the phone from the floor, she could hear Barry's voice, shrill with alarm.

"Rita, Rita, are you there? What's wrong?" he asked.

"Nothing. What do you mean what's wrong? Hello is the traditional salutation."

"PMS. Is that what's giving you such a lovely disposition?"

"Fuck you."

"Don't mind if you do."

"Is this a conversation or what? Why did you call, Barry?"

"It seems beside the point to talk about it now, with you in this mood. Let's just chat. Tell Pappa what's wrong."

"Nothing. I was just having a nicotine fit when you called. And it's not fair, it's been bloody years since I quit."

"It's been two weeks."

"Bullshit, it's been months and you know it!"

"The physical addiction is gone after three days. It's psychological dependency you have to deal with."

"Knowing that doesn't help." She still felt irritated but determined to be more pleasant. "How are you?"

"Great! Great to talk to you. I'm excited. When I'm not teaching, I'm house hunting. And I've found this terrific place on Albany. It's huge, and divided into three apartments, a good income property, will practically pay for itself. And there you are right where you want to be in the Annex, a walk to work." He knew they both loved the area with its shaded residential roads giving way to commercial streets with a cinema and book stores.

"The Annex is getting too trendy for me. I miss the goulash restaurants."

She felt herself growing impatient. This was something she had outgrown: house fever. She became as determined to be difficult as she had been a few moments ago to be sweet.

"You love that stuff. All that street life is exciting for a good middle-class boy who grew up in Etobicoke before the Italians moved out there. You're everything your parents would have been if they had given birth to themselves and grown up in the sixties and become professional in the eighties."

"Very cute. I'll let that pass. I could dish it out too, if I wanted to. But I don't want to. Think about that one for awhile." There was a long pause. Rita did not respond. "Rita, honey, listen to me, this house would be perfect for both of us."

"But Barry, I love my house. I've been living here for eight years. I hate moving."

"You like your freedom!" He made it sound like a dirty word.

"And you hate it, I suppose! Give me a break, Mr. Forty and Never-Been-Married."

"That could change very easily, you know, if *you* wanted it to. I'd like to talk about that again tonight over dinner. There's a new Malaysian restaurant I want us to try. Hot and spicy. The way it always is when I'm with you."

She quickly invented an excuse. "I can't tonight. I

promised Margo that I would help her sink rushes. When she says that she wants my editing expertise, she means that she needs free labor. You know how Margo is. I can't get out of it." She knew that Barry had been expecting to see her that night. And she had been looking forward to it herself as little as ten minutes ago. But she didn't want to have to listen to another marriage proposal as she indulged in the peanut sauce.

"Well, after tonight I have a lot of preparation to do for my summer course. I won't have much time. Have fun. Bye."

The dial tone sounded ominous. Men. Why did they always look so good from the back? Walking out the door. That's when she wanted them not to leave her again. She clasped her hands together to keep herself from grabbing the phone. It was anxiety she was feeling, not love. She knew so much about what was *not* love.

"Let it go," she said out loud, as she tried to calm herself by breathing deeply. She changed into leotards and moved into the living room to try to regain her detachment through yoga. The domestic sounds of the morning world outside had retreated, as if to some great distance. The lawn mower might have been the drone of a mosquito trapped by the screened window in another room. She felt the cool stillness of the house around her, the knobby weave of the wool rug under her thighs and buttocks. She breathed deeply. Gravity was pulling her down, tugging most insistently at her shoulders, the back of her neck.

Rising slowly, she went to the front of the house and opened the door again, surprised to see that the light had changed from the blue of early morning to yellow and orange. Before the street had seemed merely empty, but now it seemed mysteriously evacuated.

How to re-enter the morning, she thought? How to become part of life, like other women, in its dust and drama? She felt like Alice in Wonderland looking through the door to the garden, the wonderland on the other side, the door the size of a mouse hole. She would have to shrink to walk through. She would have to shrink.

3

The Journal

THE ferns were losing their leaves so I knew they had to be real. The ferns were runaways from chichi restaurants which serve such delicacies as oily croissants and onion soup au gratin, made with Oxo cubes and processed cheese and onions in the form of soggy white chips. The onion feels gritty against the teeth, like sand from improperly cleaned mussels or clams. Eating such things elucidates why the term "organic" is necessary in the local dialect to describe food. At *Le Magot*, around the corner from my clinic, even the prints on the wall were predictable: the queen riding a moose, a yellow bicycle with the blue sky in its spokes.

I found nothing in the papers again. Two weeks have passed since the Melrose woman: May 9, 1989 at 2:10 a.m. I checked the date and time last night in the file cards in the glove compartment. Of that much I am sure. Of the facts, I am sure.

Each day I have searched methodically through the papers: *Globe, Star*, and the *Sun*, which specializes in the more sensational aspects of the news, misnamed human interest. The *Sun* would be the most likely source. At a box on the street corner I slipped a quarter into the ragged red metal slit, reminiscent of something equally cold in the mind. At 40° below, freezing metal feels like burning to the hand: icy fire, at 40° below love is Petrarchan. It's still summer.

I opened the trap door to draw out a paper which I folded and stuck under the arm of my suit coat. *Le Magot* is a restaurant for the blue-jeaned and the young, for the gourmand in a hurry. My silk suit made me feel conspicuous, so I went to sit at a table for two in a remote corner.

The Sunshine girl was wearing a bikini which looked as if it were made of crinkled paper. Pink crepe paper like the streamers decorating the cars of a bridal party. Or like the toilet paper in cheap European hotels. Culture is also something that grows in septic tanks.

I gingerly spread out the paper on the high tech surface of the table. Then I thought better of it and held it up, a mask for my face. The details of scandal and grisly accidents were printed in bold type. A man had killed his five-year-old daughter, accidentally, backing up his truck in the driveway of their condominium in Rexdale. Another man, from the Windsor area, had murdered his mistress. She was a musician with the symphony orchestra. He dismembered the body and packed it into her cello case. He threw the case from the Ambassador bridge into the river. He threw the cello after it but the cello wouldn't sink. The tell-tale cello. The killer bee has crossed the Mason-Dixon line and is expected to continue migrating north to Canada.

I drank more coffee and perused the room from behind the paper. Nobody from the hospital I could recognize. No one would expect to find me here, reading a tabloid. Not at this or at any hour. I have weighed the risk against the convenience. Convenience decided for me.

As far as the papers were concerned the woman on Melrose did not exist. So had she not reported our little encounter to the police? I marveled at the efficacity of my dark threats. Threats seem to work better than prayer.

But when someone files such a complaint with the police, how long does it take to become news? Or did the papers think that there was nothing worth printing?

I work in a pattern. More than their bodies, the patterning satisfies my aesthetic sense through an ordering of accident. No, through an ordering of incidents. I do not wish to leave *no* clues. Nor do I want to get caught. I want some sense of sport in it. I want the satisfaction of a game well played. Girls are easy. But the police? From them I expect more. All my deliberations, all my reconnaissance is to avoid detection by them. The women I can have with impunity, but in my own way I also want to have the authorities.

There is nothing to connect me to the woman. Even though there is an obvious and identifiable trail. The perfect crime is not without clues. The perfect crime teases the brain, a jigsaw puzzle where the completed picture must be visualized to be solved. They have all the pieces but I withhold the portrait, my face. It seems to take no special talent on my part to outwit them. Only that I not be observed. The car I always park miles away from my intended. I wear the contact lenses, a gift from Lily, that I have never used in my diurnal life because I prefer the sober frames, the structure, of my glasses.

In the dark I don't need glasses. In the dark I use a nylon stocking over my face.

I have rehearsed my part at home, locked in the bathroom, watching my altered mien, the good doctor, a hangman. The stocking is excellent cover, easy to slip on, easy to see through. A flesh-colored pair of support hose that

belonged to my wife. A snag, a ladder running to the far corner of my right eye, looks like scar tissue. Because the
stockings are elasticized, they fit well and flatten my features.
I become a stranger, my face pressed against the window
glass of a dining room where there is a large table prepared
for a feast. I am hungry. I dine where I am not invited.

I knotted the legs of the hose into a pony tail at the
back. A detail that I felt to be both sinister and playful,
appropriate to the nature of the act. A small crime, if not a
petty crime. After all, I do not harm the women. I would
not, will not, harm any woman. I remember their bodies
shuddering with pleasure.

I think I provide a more interesting drama than what
can be found in the singles bars. After the sexual revolution,
the ease of contraception, of abortion, how is what I do a
major crime? When the woman is not harmed?

I suspect that she has not called the police. It was
just something that happened to her, it was something that
left her more alive. An anecdote for the cafés. An anti-
dote for boredom. Allowing her to be consoled by friends.
To be envied the adventure of it in a way that brings you
closer to them. The way success never can.

More than fear or curiosity, an artistic interest has led
me to keep up my daily scouting of the papers for news of
what perhaps I may otherwise have dreamed. That night, a
dream.

I would like to read a report of what happened, from
another point of view. From that of the woman? The journalist? The police report? In order to experience it again, in
order to know it from every which way. I would like to
be more than a protagonist, yes, to be my own dramatist, yes
to be both male and female.

I began to enjoy being out of place, feeling superior to

my environment. That feeling is familiar to me.

A woman walked in and chose a table in the center. Did she want my attention? There was evidence in the studied manner, the calculation she took to sit, if not next to me, but still well within range of conversation.

But at first the only thing which openly absorbed her was a rather large hamburger. She picked up the thing from her dish and began to eat it. Onion and tomato spilt from one side. She gathered up the stray dressings with her fingers and slipped them back into the sandwich. With her tongue she licked up a trace of green relish from the corner of her mouth.

Meat-eaters! They carry the smell of the slaughterhouse with them. I felt an acute distaste that was not *not* sexual.

The woman had short blonde hair which darkened visibly where it was parted in the center. She was dressed in pants, a printed cotton, with a matching jacket. The fabric had a black background and was decorated with large cottage roses in red with green. A design more appropriate for upholstery, I thought, but apparently the height of fashion that summer.

Watching her, I thought she might do for my purposes. But to have been seen in the same restaurant with the woman might be the sort of clue I could not afford to provide. After all I was merely trying to ease the boredom of it all, not to get caught. I might of course act in a more conventional fashion, suggest a drink somewhere. Elsewhere. She was making such a fanfare of eating her food, I thought she wanted me to notice her, to approach her. But when I thought about afterwards, after our sordid business, of things she might expect, frankly I couldn't abide it. It was not conversation I desired.

I checked my watch. It was 23:10. She must live in the neighborhood, this must be a working girl's stop before going home to an empty apartment, an empty refrigerator doing its bit to edge us back into the ice age.

She wore high heeled sandals. A single thick woven band formed the top, which was embroidered with rosebuds. They had no back straps. They were designed to be easy to kick off, and designed to allow the ankle to collapse when running. The shoes were my allies, or perhaps in themselves a provocation. I liked the shapely ankle and the round muscle at the back of her calf.

My car was still in the parking lot at the hospital. I heard the dragging sound as she sucked through her straw snorting at the dregs of her soft drink. As if that were my cue I exited quickly and smoothly, crushing in my hand the empty styrofoam cup and disposing of it. I didn't allow myself to give her a second glance, although I observed in the periphery of my vision that her head turned to watch me go. She must have been disappointed.

Unlike the dim interior, the outside of the restaurant was bright, to attract customers and repel holdups. When I reached my car I paused briefly to check my watch again. Not my pulse — I was perfectly calm but alert, balanced on that nice edge of expectation. The parking lot was unlit but it was easy to see the green glow of the numerals, of time luminous at my wrist, 23:25.

I drove my car without turning on my headlights to the southern extreme of the parking lot where I had a clear view of College Street. The attendant who supervises the lot until eleven had shut up the hut and gone home for the night.

I waited. When I saw her walk out the door and head west along College, I pulled out of the parking lot and drove

along College west for a block. Then I turned north. I circled the block and left the car on the side street. I waited until
she was well past and then followed her discreetly on foot.
She had the unhurried, deliberate steps of a woman going
straight home by a very familiar route. No looking into
the darkened windows of the shops, no interest in the small
patchwork of urban sky. The constellations hint at other
dimensions she must have ignored as useless or unchartable.
I suspected her reality was a dull one, the life of a girl working in the hosiery department of Eaton's, perhaps newly
broken up with her boyfriend, comforting herself with a
late night snack, going home alone. She turned a corner
onto a street lined with low rise apartments. She approached
the entrance of the second of these.

I lit a cigarette in the shadows and sucked on it hungrily.
She fumbled in her purse for her keys. Through this not
unpleasant wait for her to enter the building, I continued to
enjoy my smoke. The place was not properly lit. One of
the torch-shaped lamps above the door was out, the other
couldn't have held much more than a forty-watt bulb. Barely
a candle against such darkness, the darkness in which the
smoke thickened and curled invisibly from my cigarette.

The lighting inside the vestibule was better. It silhouetted
her when she opened the front door and leaked through the
glass panels on either side. I could see her through one of
those panels; my back was against the brick. She was opening her mailbox. I could even make out the number in orange
neon dynamo figures: 39. She pulled out some leaflets and
a brown envelope and proceeded to the stairs.

I slipped back into the street. On the third floor a
light went on. Every other window was in darkness. I knew
it must be number 39. I knew enough and I could guess
the rest.

I had to calm myself by breathing deeply until I could stroll very casually, in control, back to where I'd left the car. I had no fears for myself and no scruples about what I was planning. Again the familiar tension of my need, its urgency, made my clothes feel tight, made my clothes feel like a cage. But at the same time, another part of me was engaged by something cooler, the kind of interest, the personal disinterest if you will, of the chess master plotting his next move, assessing an opponent, assuring her defeat. Or her surrender.

Then my thoughts filled with the shoulders of the woman from Melrose. I recalled the way she pulled them back, making her breasts thrust forward more, opening herself to me, her vulnerability, her back against the headboard of the bed. I thought of the tremor, the white speech in those shoulders, which seemed to ask whether I intended to kill her. Which seemed to ask for it.

That made me angry. I was insulted. Didn't she realize that she was begging for death from a physician, a healer? I knew that I had every right to be angry because I hadn't harmed her in the least. At that point, what was it? Just a little sex. For such peccadilloes the angels shrug.

Without violence! Without violence outside of my form of persuasion. She must have known that it had never crossed my mind.

No, she had planted it. She had wanted it. I recognized in that trembling, in the curve of her white, white shoulders, the desire to get it over with. Taking the nipple of her left breast I began to twist it as if it were a radio dial and I were searching for some station, as if I were searching for music as I tried to decide what to do with her. The nipple naughty, thickening, primly pouting in my fingers. I pinched it until she gasped. Then I knew just what to do.

Lily

SOMETIMES a woman doesn't know that she's happy. She focuses on little complaints, irritations, what fails to satisfy in what is largely good. As she made her way through the living room gathering up dirty mugs to carry into the kitchen, Lily convinced herself that she was that kind of woman. Discontent without just cause. Discontent where another woman would be satisfied. Well, if not satisfied, certainly grateful, pleased with her good fortune: to be affluent and comfortably married, to have children both healthy and bright. But as she washed the cups and cleaned up the left-over crumbs from their bedtime snacks of Ovaltine and cookies, she thought the success of her marriage seemed to depend more on her husband's tolerance than on anything she did. Lily was ashamed of her secret grudges.

Her brooding was woven into the routine of her days. Where was the housewife humming as she worked? But that's what it used to be like, her happiness, when the children were younger, when she hardly had a minute to herself, before they started school. Or at least that was how she remembered it. Now this self, this drudge, this *hausfrau*, seemed such a burden. She was afraid it would one day, like a doberman, in a fit of jealousy or temperament turn on its master. Or eat the baby. Ruin everything.

Had she in some way stopped really loving her husband? Was she merely a self-absorbed and idle woman? Or did she love him too much? Was it love or obsession? No, it must be possession! She still wanted him. But he had her as part of the lock, stock, and marriage barrel. And how can a man continue to want what he already has? What he has almost forgotten he has, like a beautiful painting by a young artist purchased many years before, accruing value on the living-room wall, its hues, its textures, forgotten, even though the walls were originally tinted and the furniture purchased to showcase the piece. In time, domestic background becomes foreground.

So familiarity, through years of marriage, had submerged Lily in the domestic household and rendered her invisible to her husband. No, that was not Lily's problem. That was how she rationalized her husband's indifference. The problem was that she did not know her husband, that their years together had brought only greater distance, deeper mystery. She lived with a man of surfaces, complex and civilized surfaces. A man who was secretive without working at it. Even his altruism just led attention away from himself to others.

She was like a Victorian wife, married to a man whose body she hadn't seen, having made love and conceived children only in the dark. Or had she not dared to look?

But of course it was not his body that perplexed her. She knew his every mole. No, not the body, but the mind, that language of neurons. His spoken words seemed as remote as fossils pointing only to where life has once been.

At times her husband would address her as he might

a servant with whom infrequent and furtive couplings were never acknowledged during daylight hours.

As usual Lily was up before the rest of the family. Even when, as today, she spent it doing a bit of early housework, she needed some time just to herself, before the teasing and bickering of the children, before Michael's aloofness invaded her.

Michael and his work were connected with matters of life and death. That explained his gravity. But he was not a healer, of this she was convinced: his hands were too cold and analytical. He was perhaps a great detective of disease with extraordinary insight and deductive powers. Then he passed his patients on to the specialists.

In Michael's study Lily found another used cup; the coffee remains had evaporated staining the bottom. She did not touch the book on his desk, although it bothered her to see it open on its face that way, the spine stretched. She knew this annotated text of *Paradise Lost* better than she knew the man. He now spent most of his nights in the study, saying that he did not wish to disturb her in their bed, with the light, with the quickly turning pages, with the restlessness of his mind. But she was sure that it was to disguise the tension in his body, and the way he avoided touching her.

Lily felt like an intruder in this room. Michael had accused her of snooping at his desk one morning last week. He had made a point of showing her that his irritation was controlled. He was cool to her. Squinting his eyes, he examined her for an interminable minute, like a man in a foreign country inspecting a glass of water for impurities he's convinced are there.

Pulling the door quietly shut behind her, Lily left the room. When Michael came down she would be in the kitchen, preparing a pot of coffee. Its aroma would drift up the stairs, fill the house. She watched her hands work as if they were mechanical, separate from herself. She had become a robot, the small, domestic kind, the model wife.

Her kitchen was full of light, painted a soft yellow, glowing with it.

That morning Lily decided to make pancakes, buckwheat pancakes with buttermilk and the fresh blueberries she had purchased at their local greengrocer, The Cornucopia. She mixed the batter in a large earthenware bowl. She washed the blueberries, which were wild, very sweet, very small, the size of dried currants. She drained and placed them aside, ready to be turned into the batter when the children came down for breakfast.

After she prepared three place-settings in the breakfast nook, she opened the back door, sliding its glass panels aside and stepping out to look at the garden. She wanted to breathe in the freshness of the June morning. This summer her flowers and herbs were thriving. Even the French tarragon had taken well, and her rosemary had grown into a robust bush the size of a small Christmas tree. It was blooming in tiny exquisite flowers. The blue blossoms were very fragrant; their woodsy scent seemed a hybrid of evergreen and flora. And her chrysanthemums were tall with stunning platinum heads. She thought they looked like Elizabethan women, faces dwarfed by immense and ruffled collars. No, like Vogue models on thin tall stalks, female bodies evolved for the fit of designer clothes.

Lily was a small woman, who, aware of her own body's failure to conform to the standards of high fashion, had learned to withdraw into a secret beauty, like a night-blooming flower in a neon city. So she believed that she was lucky to be married to a man like Michael because she had less to offer, because she was older than him and not truly beautiful. They had met when he had been a student in her American Literature class, a brilliant student headed for a medical career, but also interested in the arts.

She still remembered the essay he wrote on Poe. It had helped her understand a writer she had previously disliked. She had preferred Henry James, and — drawn to Michael and expecting some sign of intellectual correspondence — she had thought he would want to write on James. Instead, he had given her an essay on Poe that had transformed the tales for her. Michael had argued that Poe was a psychological expressionist, a precursor of Kafka, an artist keenly aware of how too sharp an interest in art leads away from life and to a kind of necrophilia. It was the best kind of criticism. It was like literature itself: visionary.

And so she got to know some of his thoughts, if not to understand his thinking. He became more comfortable around her, and at times she could ease the stiffness in his shoulders. That summer he wrote to her while traveling in Europe, letters filled with details of cities and museums.

What was he, a man who forgets his history trying to find one? Before his fourth birthday, Michael's family had been killed in an accident. He had been lying down, curled up in a blanket with his teddy bear in the back of the automobile. His brother had been leaning forward into the gap between the bucket seats up front, talking to their mother. Tony was hurled out the window. The shattered glass showered Michael like confetti, the European variety made of hard candy and dry rice. The glass left fine scars on his face, lines like signs of premature aging. But his body was unmarked.

After they married, Lily found a photo in the back of his well-worn Concise Oxford Dictionary, a family snapshot, taken when Michael was a baby. All members of his family appeared natural, unposed in front of the Chevrolet sedan. The parents were laughing, the child looked as if he were struggling to get free of his mother's arms. Wrapped in a blanket, baby Michael, the features of his face indistinct or blurred by the camera, was held up like a parcel for the photograph. The picture was wrinkled badly and creased. It looked as if it had been wadded up to be thrown away — and then smoothed down again.

It was not jealousy that made Lily lethargic. She did not suspect that Michael loved someone else. But she had become a melancholic woman. Yes, melancholic was the most precise word she could think of to denote what she felt. She preferred the literary, the Renaissance associations of the word to the imaginative bankruptcy of *depressed*. "Depressed" made her think of solutions in the form of pulleys.

Something was wrong with her. Michael only stayed with her because he was so inflexible about changes and she was part of his routine. Or Michael stayed because of the children. Because he felt guilty that she had given up a career to raise them. Or he stayed with her because the house was in her name. Because she had met the mortgage payments out of her salary, pregnant and teaching while he was going to medical school. A litany of reasons made up her daily marriage mass.

Lately she found him sleeping beside her in the morning, though she had not felt him slip into bed. With his glasses off he looked like one of the children. He liked to lie flat on his stomach, his face turned towards her. His freckled lids rolling in a dream cycle. That face, half smothered in the pillow, was sensitive, gentle. Why did she sometimes imagine him as a character in Dreiser's *An American Tragedy*, pushing the superfluous and pregnant girlfriend off the rowboat?

Lily was staring into the pancake batter as if it were a crystal ball. Not until he touched her arm, his fingers cold on her skin, was she aware that Michael must have silently pushed his way through the swinging door and into the kitchen. His hand felt damp, and his beard had round perfect drops of moisture suspended in it like dew.

"Good morning, Lily." He bent down to kiss her cheek as she turned her head to look up at him. The kiss was deflected, and he did not try again.

"I was just going to make pancakes. Would you care for some, Michael?"

"No, none for me thanks. I'm sure the children will want them though. I'd just like a cup of coffee." He inhaled the aroma and looked around for the newspaper.

"It's on the counter, still rolled. News before breakfast puts me off my food. Do you think that's maybe why you eat so little, Michael?"

Dazzling sunlight flooded the kitchen. "It's a glorious morning," he declared, ignoring Lily's question, turning his attention to the patio doors, more apparently addressing them. When they were pulled open, it seemed to remove the entire side of the house; the garden became simply a verdant extension of the house.

"What's the idea! You mustn't leave the door completely open this way. You're inviting intruders!" He pulled the screen portion shut, locking the light in mesh.

But Lily had always felt both private and safe in their house bordering on the ravine. Although, on the one hand, she found his alarm absurd, on the other, it pleased her to see him react strongly to something. His shouting felt more real than the clipped routine words and gestures which he immediately settled back into.

Michael poured his coffee and picked up the paper.

"I'm going to my study." He glanced at his wrist watch. "Isn't it time to wake the children for camp?" Taking a sip from his cup, he added, "The coffee is excellent as usual." Then he turned quite briskly away from her, a man with a purpose, a man in a hurry to get somewhere.

She looked at the space where his body had just been, searching for traces of him, of something. She could no more follow Michael into his study than into the men's room.

5 Rita

I T was not the set for fairy tale theater, but it was once upon a Monday morning in the realm of grim reality where beauty meets beastly bureaucracy. At the switchboard, the receptionist was a creature of unearthly delights. Her earphones were almost invisible in the thicket of her permed curls. A speaking mike, suspended by some invisible device, hovered around her bright red lips. But the mystery was not in the technology, the mystery was in the young woman's hopes. Lana, the receptionist, who moonlighted as an actor for a small theater company, worked for more than pay. She sat at her post expecting to be discovered by one of those directors who breezed through the portals to this northern Hollywood. Not missing a beat in her speaking, the woman nodded and smiled at Rita. That morning Lana was affecting the nasal twang Lily Tomlin has made famous. Her energy and her style made Rita smile. I like women, Rita thought. She did not mean I like women as opposed to men. She did not mean that she did not like men. Although it was true that there, at headquarters, the women were in another class than the men. And Rita's nature was such that she always sided with the underdog. The "underbitch" grumbled the men in the office who were mysteriously beginning to suffer from the effects of an employment equity program which was always being discussed and never being implemented.

The female staff members Rita knew excelled in intelligence, dedication, and energy and yet were constantly overlooked for promotion. But they were not disgruntled. That was the problem, or part of it. Not assertive enough. Slave mentality. While people like Frank kept their jobs, Frank who came into the office every morning, shut the door, and was never heard of again until he left for lunch, or at the end of the day. Missing in inaction for the last nine years. Nothing had been generated from his office in all the time that Rita had been with the Board, not even, to her knowledge, the ubiquitous interoffice memo. Frank. Francis. Forget to dot that i and imagine the change in roles. Frances drowning in the secretarial pool. Like Celeste, Rita's secretary, who was bilingual, quick, and not uneducated, such a Frances would keep typing and filing for him. For them. For men.

Celeste was a single parent who was supporting two children on a secretary's income. She could not afford to stop working to look for another job. She commuted each day from Scarborough, where the rents were cheaper, where she lived in hiding from an ex-husband who used to beat her. When he started to threaten the children, she found enough courage to run out. Leaving with nothing, a worn suitcase full of clothes, a few toys.

And why on earth had Rita hired her? At the interviews there had been many applicants, experienced, some even more qualified, and in most cases more presentable than Celeste, certainly more confident. Although Celeste had been good at answering the questions Rita had posed, her responses came out too quickly, like someone who has been holding her breath and so has just enough oxygen to complete an entire sentence before gasping for more air. The young woman was gaunt, trembling. It was apparent that she was desperate for the job, and Rita, against usual hiring practice, which seems to consider need as a primary kind of fault, gave the position to Celeste. It had been the right decision. Celeste was both congenial and hard-working, and fiercely loyal to Rita. She had relaxed and bloomed in the last year, confident in her new ability to earn her own living and no longer terrified of going out for lunch, of walking out in public where her husband might be lurking to drag her back home with him.

Rita was always happy to see Celeste, who was a classic secretary, a hybrid of a clerk and a mother. Sometimes Celeste would surprise her with some flowers for the office. "To brighten things up!" These words were spoken with a kind of sweetness and simplicity, a vitality which belied her hard life.

Rita liked women, women like Celeste who took on responsibility with love, because loving is a spontaneous gift a salary can't simulate. Only a 'mother' could give human warmth and depth even to a bureaucracy. Thinking of her early that morning, Rita had picked two bouquets of fresh flowers from her garden.

"I'm learning from you, Celeste. Even funeral homes sport a posy or two. These dahlias, aren't they magnificent?"

"Why yes, Rita madame. They're exquisite." Celeste, although she had agreed to use Rita's first name, always added the "madame" afterwards, ran it in as if part of the name. Rita was not sure why. Perhaps some exaggerated sense of politeness, which turned "madame" into a suffix

like the "san" in Japanese. Perhaps because of the age difference between them, for Celeste with all her children and
tragedy was barely twenty-six. Rita knew it was meant as a
sign of respect and not distance, because Celeste pronounced it as if it were an intimate or a pet name, with velvet in her voice.

Celeste gave Rita the morning mail, sorted and dutifully
slit open, and Rita went into her office to see what she could
come up with to promote the season's crop of overbud-
geted and dull films. She threw a loose bundle of envelopes
onto her desk. It slid across the smooth hardwood top and
the letters fanned out like a deck of cards.

Celeste walked in with an old — although antique
might be the more accurate word — milk bottle, half-filled
with water for Rita's flowers. Rita smiled her thanks,
unwrapped the flowers from newsprint, and slid their long
and supple stems into the water. She had gathered a mixture of different kinds of dahlias from her garden that morning. Some of the blooms had round, flat heads. They were
purple, bordering on magenta. Others were white, but her
favorites were the salmon pink ones with spiky heads. Rita
kept touching and rearranging the flowers as she sorted
through her mail. Her skin glowed, reflecting the warmth of
their colors. Distracted she kept fingering the petals, as a
woman with a new hairdo, fresh from the beauty salon,
will constantly reach up to touch her hair because she can no
longer feel anything up there and she is uncertain whether
she is beautiful or bald. Rita spread the head of one of
the flowers tenderly, with her thumbs, and looked into
its center, its insouciant heart, without seeing anything.
Unsurprised.

Then Rita turned away from the flowers ready to
work, as if she had gathered some inner resolve from the

blossoms. Certainly in the corolla of that flower the question that recurred to her was how much of life was spent wished away or waiting: as an adolescent for romance and "real" life, as a middle-aged woman for romance and retirement. She should have entered a serious marriage. That surely would have killed it for her, the myth of romance. Or did marriage just make the gorgon sprout new heads elsewhere? In extramarital affairs with your best friend's husband or the mailman. Everything is risked but nothing is ventured, all for the thrill of "in love" and new sex. She felt that she herself was not like *that*, but she had yet to prove it. There were more burning issues in the world, more vital concerns. When she was with Nikos they were political, but they were his concerns.

Rita went through her mail, much of which could be dealt with through memos and the odd letter she scrawled in the form of a few notes for Celeste to type up. Then she made some phone calls to set up publicity and possible reviews for a film festival of thrillers directed by women: *Mama Noire*. Among the movies was a new Von Trotta picture she had previewed. When the shot rang out at the end of *Sheer Madness*, Rita felt as if she herself had pulled the trigger.

The intercom buzzed. Celeste gave her a message from Pierre Bilodeau, Rita's boss. He wanted to see her sooner than possible. Whenever he called Rita into his office, he had his secretary make the call to her secretary. He called her in often and on the slightest pretext, but he used a formality which belied their intimacy. Pierre was a married man. Pierre was a careful man. At the office. He did not thumb his nose at his wife with his affairs. This in itself was remarkable because he seemed so ruthless and self-absorbed, the kind of selfishness that usually doubles with a relentless kind of honesty. If someone had told her a few years ago, when she started working for the Board, that she might become involved with Pierre, she would have been outraged. They had hated each other at first sight. Rita saw him as the enemy, the epitome of male power and misogyny. It made her blush to remember this.

Rita preferred not to recall those first months at the Board where she was the only female executive. Bilodeau chaired all the meetings. It was not merely Roberts' Rules of Order which so effectively silenced her. Her welcoming to the job had been a humiliation. Pierre had introduced her as one to add flesh to their department, sculpting in the air before his chest the shape of huge breasts.

Certainly she felt marginalized at the Board, invisible as a person, but a target for sex, for shaming. Her anxiety was such that her tongue became too thick to speak. It felt like a wad of cotton rammed down her throat.

So Rita's lips had been sealed. Or gagged. She dared not say anything, afraid to attract Pierre's attention. But in whispered asides he might make some comment about her appearance. Once the hemline of her skirt had ridden up to mid-thigh. Leaning over, closer to her, he had hissed the s's in "Such charming kneessss." His breath smelled of tobacco and brandy. Rita used to rage against him in the privacy of her office or among her friends. At the sexual decoy Pierre was an expert.

As a peevish and perhaps cowardly form of rebellion, Rita deliberately delayed a few minutes more before going to Pierre's office that morning. She sorted out the little jobs she would give to Celeste. When Rita stopped at her desk before leaving to see Pierre, she found her feverishly typing up the copy for *Mama Noire*'s publicity.

"There's no rush on this stuff, Celeste. If Bilodeau

buzzes for me again, tell him I'm on my way." Pierre's office was in another wing of the building, where top level executives were enshrined. There the offices were luxurious, completely self-contained rooms, suites in fact, not the hasty partitions in an open area which characterized her work space. The support staff, even worse off, had no privacy at all, they were exposed to constant supervision in an open and central pit area, as if they were still children sitting at desks in a classroom.

But Pierre's office was private and spacious. From the twenty-first floor he had an exquisite view of the city. Adjoined to his office was a room with a long oak table in the center and a built in bar and kitchenette at the back. Meetings were held there.

Rita walked into the reception area and greeted his secretary, with whom she was not on friendly terms. Rita didn't like her because she was the officious sort, the kind who make the most of whatever authority a position affords, nursing a penchant for tyranny without the power. "Mister Bilodeau is waiting, Miss Chiddo, please won't you go straight in to see him," she enunciated in a rather weary voice as if straining for patience. Giving Rita permission for what she was about to do anyway.

Rita knocked lightly and without waiting for a response turned the knob. The brass of the doorknob felt cold and slick. She realized then that her palms were sweating. She wiped her hands against the hips of her designer jeans, the label making them acceptable for office wear. Then she stepped inside the private office of *Mon sieur* Pierre Bilodeau and pulled the door shut behind her.

Pierre was sitting in the swivel chair behind his desk, swinging back and forth, apparently hard at work looking at the view. He had a silver case in his hand and was tapping a cigarette against the monograph embossed on the front. Placing the cigarette between his lips without lighting it, he turned to greet her.

"It's been a lonely weekend." His cool detachment contradicted his words.

Rita strode over to his desk without commenting, she pressed the tips of her fingers firmly down on the edge of the desk, and looked at him for a long moment. An acute sense of unreality seized her then. She found herself torn between anger and desire. When she felt so divided she had a sense that she was merely observing herself, as if through the eye of a distant camera. It was difficult for her to respond to the challenge, to that irony in his eyes, when she felt it herself so keenly. Every word and feeling seemed to be held at arms' length. Her heart was a hand puppet she could watch perform, as if she weren't manipulating it herself, as if it had taken on a life of its own. At such times she did not believe in her own pain nor in her ability to love any man.

From Pierre's desk she picked up a little wooden box of matches which had a view of the cathedral at Chartres on the side facing up. She pulled out one of the slim waxy matches, struck it and lit the cigarette for him. Pierre inhaled deeply from his cigarette. His eyes narrowed as he looked her up and down through exhaled smoke. Then, with a flawless sense of timing, he pulled the cigarette out of his mouth, leaving it to burn in the ashtray, as he rose and drew Rita to him, taking her in his arms, nuzzling his nose into her ear, her hair. He kissed her deeply so that she ate small particles of turkish tobacco from his mouth.

"Rita, Rita," he repeated, the sweet nothing of syllables given to us at birth. He stroked the back of her neck with his fingers and with the richness of his voice, with the rolling purr of his r's, from deep in his throat like a cat, from deep in the diaphragm where breath begins. What did it matter what she had thought of him as little as five minutes ago? She felt the familiar weakness in her knees, the knock, knock contradictions of her heart and head.

The affair had cooled in the last month, certainly since Rita had learned that Pierre's wife, Kathleen, was pregnant. Not because Pierre was spending more time with his spouse, but because Rita had found that the woman began to intrude into her consciousness — or was it conscience — more and more.

In the spring it had been easy enough to arrange a business lunch and go instead to her house for a couple of hours. They would drive over in his Mercedes. He would park a few blocks away from her place. They would forget to eat. The affair had made her slimmer, tenser, more angular. The bones in her hips emerged like fins breaking through the surface of water. His body was dark and tanned and hard. Their hips had ground against each other, throughout those months, several times a week, rendezvous for lunch Chez Rita.

His mouth sought hers again and she found herself responding, receiving his thrusting tongue, searching with her own the double arched dome of the roof of his mouth, as sensitive as fingertips. Sex with this man gave her vertigo. She could barely see his face, his features obscured as if viewed through smoke or the heat and moisture that makes air in summer undulate like water.

"Today, we will have lunch again. Rita, don't argue with me." He placed his fingers firmly against her lips to keep her from speaking. "Meet me at the car, the west end of the lot, not my reserved spot, at one. I will have left shortly before you. Perhaps you can concoct some outside business, an appointment, so you will not have to return for the rest of the day. I want to spend the whole afternoon with you."

And she wanted it too in spite of the chorus of inner voices chanting in protest, a censorship chorus which failed to overcome her more powerful and physical need for the man, his iron hard body and will. Will is the primary seductive force. His ability to make her obey. It was his will and his classical male assumptions that made him so irresistible. It made her feel weak. It made her feel *so* like a woman. Yes she felt safe in his arms, but what was she safe from? Where do these dreams of rescue lead a woman? His lust had no real concern for her welfare. She was fuel, sugar in the bloodstream. To gratify him became a kind of drug for her. It was hypnotic the way her desire, bonding with his, became as much for herself as for him. "This is not love," she thought feebly, probing, with as much distance as she could muster, the nature of her obsession, like a child poking with a whittled branch at a snake, a poisonous snake, half asleep, sunning itself on a rock.

For the remainder of the morning she was agitated and restless. Her clitoris ached like a tooth cavity; it throbbed with piercing pulsations. Rita often looked to sex the way some people look to alcohol or drugs: to obliterate consciousness. But not every man had the power of this drug to give her. That, she felt, was the pity of it.

To kill time and as the closest equivalent she could get to taking a cold shower, she called her mother in Detroit.

"Darling." Rita didn't even have to say hello most of the time. Her mother seemed to recognize her breathing over the wire, claimed she could detect from the way the phone rang who was calling.

"Yeah, you guessed it. It's me. How are you, Mum? And Dad, what's he up to?"

"I'm very well, thank you. I'm glad you called. Your

father is in the garden, which is doing very nicely this year. He planted this wonderful basil, a small-leafed kind from Genoa. You know it's supposed to be the best. According to Marcella Hazan that is, you know that New York cook your father swears by. And I'm already convinced that this kind is the most fragrant we've grown. These days it's pesto with everything, pesto with pasta, pesto with fish. I think your father may even put on a little weight this summer, which may be hard for you to imagine."

With a pang Rita visualized her father, his small wiry frame, his tanned smiling face. Her father was the eternal optimist, always buoyant, running on apparently boundless energy. He was never ill, he was always keen on some project, he always made things grow and flourish.

In most ways Rita identified with her father. She thought of herself as ethnic because her father had been born in Italy and immigrated to the States as a boy with his parents. She wanted to identify with her father, but was aware that she was becoming more and more like her mother: a bit of a depressive. What did her mother believe in, outside of her father, Rita wondered? And maybe that's what she wanted too, somebody to believe in life for her. After struggling to make films and then to merely promote them, she wanted somebody to think for her. She wasn't satisfied with what she had come up with for herself. She heard one of her inner voices, in a mocking tone, echo a speech from *Casablanca*: "I'm tired, Rick, and I can't think. You think for me, Rick." All she needed to complete the picture was the Ingrid Bergman cheekbones.

"What did you just say, dear? I couldn't have heard that right. You are a beautiful girl, Rita. You're better looking than Rita Hayworth. There's nothing the matter with your cheekbones!"

"I'm blonde, Mum, I'm not a redhead. What were you thinking when you named me?"

"Why, your father said that you were the prettiest baby in the country, and should be named after the most beautiful star around at the time."

"Okay, Mum. Let's put the blame on Mame. I miss you both."

"When are you coming home, Rita?"

Rita always went home; her parents had never visited her in Canada. Her father wanted to but her mother was a hypochondriac and couldn't be left alone. She could not endure the strain of a car trip which lasted more than an hour and she refused to fly. So Rita went home to see them, rented a car or took the train when the weather was bad. They had not even come to her mock wedding, although the fact that Rita only really told them about it afterwards was a legitimate excuse which she unreasonably could not accept. Rita blamed them. It would have been real, a real marriage, if they had made the trip to bless it. Her mother had been happy that Rita had at last done something serious with her life, her films having failed to impress her. After all they didn't play at the Roxy. They weren't distributed by Twentieth Century Fox. They didn't star Paul Newman. Because they weren't entertainments — the kind of film everybody her mother knew saw — they couldn't be real. It suddenly occurred to Rita that her mother might be partially right, that what she needed to do next was a story of sorts, perhaps something from a novel. She felt the rightness of this idea like a match struck in an imperceptibly darkened room, because of the sudden and extraordinary sense of illumination it provided.

Her mother was talking about something else, about the canning she wanted to do at the end of August. She would like Rita to help. But Rita had missed most of her mother's extended monologue while following her own line of thinking.

"I'll try to make it down for a visit real soon. I want to see Father. I mean to see you both, of course," she added quickly.

"Your father misses you. There's not a time when we sit down for a meal that he doesn't set a place for you. Your father's love is superstitious. He seems to think that a place-setting can protect you or preserve you in some way. He knows you're not coming home for dinner. Shall I call him in? Here I've been very selfishly monopolizing your time. He's still in the garden, I guess. Setting the tomato plants up on stakes is a big job."

"It's okay, Mum. I'm calling from work but I'll call back from home in a couple of days. Just give him my love, will ya? And keep well, Mum."

"Take care, darling, goodbye."

Rita felt tranquilized by the call. She was an only child, not spoiled by her parents, she thought, but altogether too dependent on their love, or perhaps too dependent on love in general.

6

The Journal

I overheard the receptionists talking about me as I went in to the clinic on Wednesday evening. I paused in front of the dark heavy oak door to listen. I turned my ear to the frosted glass, its surface embossed with the practitioners' names: mine, the first of two, in gothic lettering, no abhorrent abbreviations, Doctor Michael Skelton, followed by the name of my associate, Doctor Gerald Guttman. Usually when I give the door a little push to open it, the women are alert enough to notice and fall silent immediately. With their finely tuned instincts these women shy at my approach. That evening I detected a faintly black smell in the room. Sulphur. The constant chattering of the women and the isolation of their shift work has brought them closer together, their menstrual cycles falling into sync.

The blowsy one, the one with the Vachon sweets in her drawer and crumbs of cake at the corner of her mouth, offends me the most. Her personal hygiene is less than adequate. She would never work for me. How Guttman tolerates her is a mystery. Such a woman would never have made it past the application stage to an interview for a position as my receptionist. In the file I saw her resume, soiled by coffee.

Her touch is *magical*, it turns the crispest and most succinct record or document into a soiled serviette.

That evening they were too busy gossiping to pay attention and my entrance caught them by surprise. The fat one was describing me to my secretary as I walked in: ". . . cool as a cucumber that one, you know the kind they call English. Wrapped in plastic. Tight as an erect cock about to burst its safe. But nothing for a good girl to worry about because he's the seedless kind," she snorted.

My own Miss Haskell is like a child; what she feels is always plainly written on her face, whose features were freezing into an expression, half horrified at the crudity of her colleague's remarks, half delighted at her daring when I walked in.

"Good evening, ladies." I addressed them in a rather formal tone, elongating the syllables in ladies and raising my voice on the final inflection as in a question. I was very early. The patients I knew would arrive all at once and have to wait their turn according to luck as Miss Haskell fumbles to find their files.

There were several messages for me that would require phone calls in response. My secretary gave the memos to me, neatly typed on pink paper. Then I walked very briskly into my office and closed the door.

When I work I think of nothing else. I forget who I am, my children, my home. The picture I have of Lily and the children smiling, though I shot the portrait in the garden myself, the picture framed and sitting on my desk in plain view, retreats from my consciousness almost immediately. I hardly give it a glance. I know that it's there but in my mind the colors have faded to the sepia tones of life from another era.

And I look forward to nothing at the end of my shift,

not even the end of my shift. I look forward to nothing. Not food, not sex, not sleep. I study the files of my patients. I learn who they are very quickly. I remember who they are and they come to me as to a doctor in the fullest sense. A healer. A priest. I have an uncanny ability to diagnose illness far beyond what the textbook of symptoms can supply. They come back again and again whether they like me or not. The women who are uncomfortable when naked for examination, bare themselves for me repeatedly. They are like those of little faith who manage to walk haltingly over burning coals. Their feet are charred. They smell of barbecue.

I would like to reassure them that when I am at work, these hands are not a man's hands that touch them. These hands are appendages as remote and as clairvoyant as the mechanical arms developed for research in outer space.

Nervously, the women grasp the open back of their white smocks, sitting on the examination table, on the fresh paper that protects the couch from disease, sitting with bare legs primly together at the knees, the short ones trying to touch the stepping stool with their toes. None swing their legs with the abandon of children. Children who are not afraid. Children before they know what it is to be exposed. Children who learn another's lust before they understand their own.

By seven the waiting room was completely filled with patients. I walked out to pick up the first file. The room smelled of newsprint and perfume. Then a few minutes later I returned. I opened the door and signaled to Miss Haskell to send the first patient in. I felt the eyes of the waiting patients fixed on me; through the back of my shoulders I perceived the intensity of their gaze.

Human beings communicate more subtly without technology. On such instruments as the telephone they pass their messages accurately, but without depth. And I too am guilty of sacrificing depth for accuracy, with my accountant, with my wife. But with my patients, I sacrifice nothing.

I tried to avoid their collective eyes, as if they were the organs of sight of a single and dying animal. The animal destined to consume me in the end. To deflect the powerful anxiety of their watching, their need, I made all my actions, every movement controlled and methodical. They have confidence in the method, in the white lab coat. The more camouflaged in the role of doctor, the greater the security they feel. I acknowledged the presence of no individual patient in the room. I turned the corner precisely, back into my office.

But that evening I felt restless and strangely disturbed. The image of the waiting room filled with patients interfered with my study of the files, the work I must do for them. Imprecise impressions flickered around my eyelids like hypnogogic images. The images were unfocused, as if peripheral. This made them doubly disturbing for me.

I tended to my first patient, a sore throat case, strep I guessed. I am invariably right, but I always insist on a swab test in such cases. I wanted to determine whether the infection was bacterial or viral. I send the samples down to the lab before I prescribe any medication. A waste of good money and a good drug if an infection is viral, but more importantly, when unnecessarily prescribed, the future effectiveness of antibiotics will be undermined for the patient.

As a doctor I am somewhat brisk, but deeply dedicated. The dullest among them seem to perceive that and come back again and again. My practice is overflowing. Miss Haskell double-books all the appointments and still there are more waiting. But I am merely a general practitioner, a slight tremor in my hands having ruined a potentially brilliant career as a surgeon.

The room remained crowded all evening, crowded and restless with waiting and the pages of stale magazines. One man made a display of his impatience, pacing and smoking in the hall. I caught the depth of the first inhaled breath of a chronic smoker, someone who has waited seated on the vinyl couch, rubbing the armrest deeply with his thumb, watching the other patients as if he, himself, were there for some reason other than illness. As if he himself were not also a patient.

But he was not the source of my agitation. The source was sitting in a single armchair reading, wisely having provided herself with her own book. A literate woman in my office is a rare animal. Most of them move their lips as they read thick, paperback potboilers.

I did not recognize her except in a figurative sense. The déjà vu of a powerful attraction. It is not the woman, but the drowning, the power of the undertow from those deeper currents of sex that makes it all again too familiar. Experience as if from another incarnation. I must remember that she is not a person; she is a trigger.

The woman was a new patient, I had no file for her. Clipped to an empty folder was a slip of paper with her name and hospital insurance number along with the name of her referee. Back in the office I found myself fingering the memo like a scrap of paper with a girl's phone number on it in the hands of a teenage boy after a dance. Again I tried to concentrate on my work. I had to cruise on automatic for the rest of the examinations. Luckily they were mostly follow-ups. Otherwise I would have been forced to take some Dexedrine to manage.

Where on this planet did she come from? I felt it immediately with the woman, that sense of recognition, of destiny, if you will. She was slight, but athletic in build. The muscles in her legs, legs dressed in cropped pink knit pants, were defined clearly. Sitting with her legs crossed at the knee, she was unconsciously kicking one foot back and forth as she read, as if keeping time to music. Her white Scholl sandals were wooden soled and high heeled. What contradictions in the design! Obviously she was a woman in principle determined to dress according to health and comfort, but who couldn't resist the higher heel to show off her well-turned calves and the corded angular muscles of her thighs. A runner. Over the pink pants she wore a loose shirt with a tropical print, whose predominating tones were also pink. The shirt was oversize, yet of a soft and shiny material that clung to her breasts, like surf over some luminous rocks on the beach, just before the green foaming spills away to reveal them. The shirt was patterned with outrageous magenta ferns, their fronds like well-placed palms. A provocative modesty.

But I was lingering too long, almost like a patient myself, waiting. Lust radiating from the loins interferes with electrical impulses from the brain. I realized that she must be about to perceive my attention and look up. When she did, I was already turning the corner. She could not know the source of what she had just felt. I was the physician. I was simply looking back to see if my next patient was attentively following me.

But actually I was imagining her unnerved. I was imagining her in the privacy of my office. She did not know she was communicating with me or with anyone keen enough to understand it.

No mystery, memory and musk.

Most likely she blamed the smoker in the hall, his good inches of belly hanging over his belt, his palpable pleasure in sucking on his cigarette designed to be misinterpreted. But she would not be attracted to that herself.

I was anxious to observe her more closely, to hear her speak, but I preserved the chronological order of patients. So Mr. Tendrell, the man who had been pacing in the hall, was next to be called in. His problem has been chronic bronchitis, which was near pneumonia in the spring. Yet he continues to smoke. He is a journalist living on coffee and midnight donuts and cheese sandwiches from dispensers. He has no time to eat properly, although he has time enough to eat too much. He has no time to finish his novel, no time to exercise, he has a phone and a small TV in his car. He dreams of being transferred to the Paris office. He has been offered a post in Winnipeg. But he is biding his time, what little of it he has left. I told him bluntly what he must do. Either/or nothing, premature death, heaven for those simple enough to believe in it, but even then, who is innocent enough to deserve it? No one. Not even a child. I know and they know because they all rush into my office, not to the cemeteries to buy their plots, not to lawyers to write their wills. I laid out the facts of the case to Mr. Tendrell. So much I can do, and mostly superficial. For his body to survive he must will it. I warned, then dismissed him, knowing that I could not work against his will, his secret will to suicide. It is a complicated impulse, whose strength primarily rests on not being recognized, in that way bypassing the immune systems.

But I was most anxious to meet Ms. Rita Chiddo. I fingered the pink note. She was next. I imagined her jumping up when Miss Haskell finally called her name, carefully marking her place in the book, tossing it into her basket. The bag was woven of natural hemp and purple in color. She kept it by her feet as she read. I imagined her striding across the room. Energy, sometimes called grace, animating her every move. I know that much about her, without having seen her move, without having met her eyes. I try to imagine, before I see her, how she will sit in the chair by my desk and then disrobe, her sandals like toppled Lego bricks in one corner of the examining room, by the fragrant heap of her clothes, swinging one leg again over crossed knees as she waits. Impatient, I felt delirious with impatience.

When I actually walked into the examination room, she started up instinctively, as if to bolt out the door. I adjusted my glasses as if to adjust my vision. For her I did not have to fake warmth, I actually experienced something, a burning sensation around my temples, a tensing in the stomach for this woman, for a body defined by muscle and bone. Such glorious architecture of the skeleton. Her clothes were like so much distracting gingerbread.

I pretended to look over the blank form for medical history again in her empty file and then asked the routine questions. To fill in the blanks.

My voice seemed strangely faint and shrunken, like a child dressed in an adult's clothes. The voice no longer seemed to belong to me, but seemed to be projected from the overhead lamp.

I gave her a fresh smock and asked her to undress while I left the room for five minutes. My hand brushing hers set off brief sparks of static electricity. The slight shock made me pause and her laugh.

When I returned, her alert face was ready for me. She was sitting on the examination couch, the gown tightly wound around her body. The air conditioning had rendered the room too cool, the skin of her arms goose-fleshed.

I examined her breasts for lumps, massaging them in a circular motion. I am exactingly professional in my manner and my method for any such examination. The woman who excited me in the waiting room is suddenly elsewhere. I examined her with the same disinterest I afforded the first female cadaver I worked on as a student, performing an autopsy with no trace of loathing or lust. Desire is elsewhere, driven from the brain and into the spine, stiffening with tension there, the serpentine complex of the spine. To release is to strike like a cobra.

The nurse I called in — not to assist, I need no assistance, but to satisfy legal requirements — was invisible. She handed over the instruments I needed, anticipating my requests, efficiently and smoothly, and best of all without a sense of presence except in utility, like the disembodied servant hands in the fairy tale of Beauty and the Beast.

Rita's complaint was chronic and incapacitating dysmenorrhoea. For this a pelvic examination is necessary. I examined first her abdomen, massaging it, checking for pain and lumps around the ovaries. Her belly was lean and flattened completely by gravity. I decided to do a pap smear and asked her to slide down with her feet in the stirrups and ease her legs open.

"Relax and breath deeply," I instructed, and when I noticed the white of her knuckles as she gripped tightly at the sides of the couch, I said "relax" again as softly as I could. Then I heated the metal of the sepula under the warm water tap to ease the shock of metal against the delicate and inner tissues of the body, and to facilitate the penetration of my gloved hand, the interior search and then the snipping from the cervix for a culture sample. I pressed her knees down and apart gently. "Relax," I said exhaling as if deep breathing and again, "Reeeeelaxxxxx." I waited until I heard her own breathing begin to correspond to mine and her legs slumped back. Then I did the necessary probing, scientifically and efficiently, having prepared her in a humane manner. I tried not to notice the scented talc dusted on her inner thighs, lingering in the creases of the flesh.

After the examination, after I returned to the room to find her fully dressed again, I was surprised to hear her thank me with such openness, such candor. She hated "internals," she said. She found them both humiliating and painful.

"But that was not at all painful," she said.

I wanted to reassure her and found my hand had strayed to her knee; my own earnest words of comfort were distracting to me. I withdrew my hand too quickly. I could see that she noticed its withdrawal before she had noticed its pressure and warmth.

7

Rita

RESTLESS from one too many cappuccinos, Rita had no hope of sleeping, not with that much caffeine in her system. So she went to look for something to read in the overflow pile in her study where recent acquisitions and gifts were dumped. Nothing seemed to interest her that night. Gathering some extra dust was a beautiful cloth bound book, blank. It was a notebook, a "Happy Tuesday" gift from Margo, Margo who was ever ambitious *for* Rita and wanted to lure her away from the Board and that job "pushing paper" and back to her real work, making films. "Write a screenplay," Margo had ordered. "You write it and I'll produce it."

"The fuck I can. How come you've got all these brilliant ideas for *me*?" Too much bourbon at a premiere for a Board film fostered this particularly 'amiable' response to her friend's good intentions.

That was several months before, but that evening, alone in her study, Rita caressed the mottled surface of the book. The edges of the paper were gilt. The book had a blue ribbon insert dividing the pages, holding a place in a volume that had never been touched. For the first time, Rita, with difficulty, cracked the book open. It resisted lying flat, so she had to write within the crook of her arm as she held the pages down. The thickness of the pages made the book seem designed for quill, but she only had a rollerball pen.

At that moment Rita felt the impulse to organize her thoughts, to try to understand what was happening to her. A project always forced that on her. She had kept a journal through the worst time of her life, her early teens, when she felt similarly confused.

Dear Diary. (Overly cute perhaps, the address, but let me start with the convention, with what is already known and try to work my way from there.) I am now over sixteen. Surprise, surprise, I am forty. No, the language is wrong. I have forty as the French would say: j'ai quarante ans; *it is not what I am. When I was ten I didn't think I would ever make it. To be that* old!

I would like to glorify you, diary, right from the start, say that you are on the level of a Camus notebook, but who would I be kidding? At worst you're going to be a grown-up version of my grade one reader. Remember what Jane wore, what Dick said, how Spot surprised everyone and had puppies.

But what I want you to do for me is to order my existence with something more than chronology. Like a good novel. To point to whatever else a life might mean. To look for those correspondences and coincidences something in the mind finds so satisfying. Like for Thomas Aquinas, proofs of the existence of God.

I am a middle-aged filmmaker who has not made a film in over five years, not since the child prostitution documentary, Younger Than Their Lies. *After that I decided to play it safe. I saw that opening in the publicity department* at the Board and I went for it. I was burned out by the years I had put in as an independent filmmaker, working on shoe string budgets, with such long gaps of time doing nothing except living on peanut butter (even that I had to share with the cockroaches). All I wanted to do was to make honest films, solid films, films that thumbed their nose at the big budget spectacles, films that wanted to say that art is even a single life understood. Not the fantasy that has everything solved by god or the moviemaker, or worse the expediency of the producer. I am not one of those who think there's a mystic order or a formula to explain it all away.

I run every day, one day of rest, clock enough miles to qualify as a marathoner, but I can't catch up with myself, the self that might have the guts to stop and turn around and face whatever has to be done.

I'm still plagued by adolescent problems, menstrual cramps among them. I went to see yet another doctor trying to find a cure, not wanting to lose days out of every month of an increasingly abbreviated life. They say I have menopause to look forward to. Or hysterectomy.

I think I've been on the wrong track anyway, in the films. I've been trying to explain life in social terms, in terms of the class struggle. No more Marxist analysis of the migration of salmon spawning for me! Of course, we have tried as a society to determine our character in purely sociological or political terms, or in those purer, but equally opaque, biological terms. Sometimes we (meaning males) want to reinforce those prerogatives of the blood (meaning females) with a notion of biological destiny. Woman as nature. As if men didn't have bodies of their own, as if they fell out of the body, female, at birth and dreaded the return. As a woman I'm not prepared to live in or with two thirds of my brain, the primitive and mammalian, to reinforce their myths, to *placate their fears. In the meantime men concentrate in, or is it consecrate to, technology all activity from the neocortex. In technology the primitive manipulation of their sexual organ merges with an intelligence preoccupied with how to direct that stream. Semen and urine. Manna. Money and rain.*

Margo had recommended her Dr. Skelton for me when she found me curled up on the couch in the restroom, too dizzy and weak to move. Not only do you feel physically sick, you also feel demoralized when you've been examined by the doctor and you have been told that there's nothing irregular with your internal organs. Then there must be something wrong with you. I feel that. Even my regular gynecologist, a woman herself, does a thorough exam and shakes her head, as if somehow disappointed in me, certainly, I suspected, disappointed to find no disease (that's cynical), nothing to give me reasonable cause for complaint. I know what I have. Dis-ease.

Margo is the kind of woman who shops around, gets the bargains in food and clothes, is never passive about her health care. But I'm a defeatist. I figure you've seen one doctor, you've seen them all. They've all read the same, one book, the book written by a human without a uterus. They work from those pages by rote.

But Margo is indefatigable. She discovered this guy. She told me that he seems as conservative, as controlled, as unimaginatively repressed as a New England puritan minister. Even his speech resonates in bell tones. But it's uncanny, she continued. He may be some sort of a witch, with some extrasensory way of reading symptoms or he remembers them all, how they work together to alter the body. Anyway, a few minutes in his office and you'll have the sense that you've become as easy to figure out as connect the dots, your skin see-through as cellophane.

And I agree with Margo that there is something gothic about the man. It's hardest to see sometimes what's most plainly in front of your nose. No disguise is the best disguise. What's behind those glasses, their Harvard shape, tortoise shell frames, and the perfectly clear plastic lenses (must be the latest), invisible? I thought I could poke my fingers right through. You want to look behind the frames, or beyond them, but they shape your perception of him. What color were his eyes?

Unusual the way his face seemed bleached, his hair and beard blond, or was it gray? Platinum or gold and if gold then white gold, the metal without the warmth. I think Margo is dead on about him. But I wasn't prepared for how disturbing I would find him. Perplexing. His face is full of light, yet he has the opposite effect. What I usually associate with light: clarity, openness, rationality. He seems to be cryptic, to speak with words, logical, direct, carefully considered, but not to communicate, rather to camouflage the deeper speaking of his eyes as they ignite the room. They seem so distant behind his glasses. Their color the diluted blue? green? of blown glass. Of the invisible dye in milk. His eyes were like creatures housed in a display case, moving slowly in the artificial night created by a zoo for its nocturnal fauna.

The destructive powers we associate with darkness — I get that sense of power from him — but not evil. Evil seems such a simple thing, easy to define and recognize. The destructive power of light may be even more potent, but too cagey to fingerprint. Amoral rather than evil. An iceberg or a white whale. With a double valence, a universal double valence. Like lasers which can be used in surgery or as weapons of war.

That's a considerable word count for a man I don't

know. I think that he's not a man, I think that he's a fantasy. A sexual one, my favorite kind! I guess I'm intrigued. I wonder if he's married. Must be, all the good ones are!

I felt confident in his professionalism, but at the same time appalled by his inscrutability. I suspect that he can do very little for me. One visit so far. No answers. Some more bloody useless tests to go through. It'll be five weeks before I can know the results and they can't schedule a follow-up appointment for another two months unless it's an emergency! But the good doctor is not expecting any, he says. If any new or distressing symptoms should crop up, call him, he says. More distressing than the fainting, vomiting, and diarrhea that I'm getting now when I menstruate.

It'll be three months before he can see me again. Somebody could be dead in that time. I could be dead. Collect call from purgatory for Dr. Skelton.

"See-ee you in September, see-ee you when the summer's through." I should draw some musical notes here to indicate that this sentence is sung vibrato.

Hallelujah, I think I'm actually getting sleepy writing this. I know why I've never been able to keep a diary for more than a few days. Because it forces a great discovery on you which the movies like to disguise: that life is mostly uneventful. A diary is about everything that ends up on the cutting room floor for a film.

Th-th-that's all folks!

8

The Journal

NOTHING is pure chance. Not even lust.

My victims were not chosen entirely at random, although I refrained from selecting them from among patients. Unnecessary risk is a prerogative of the fool. It was enough for me to know that I had broken the law, that the queens were mine and the authorities checkmated. The women were little more than pawns. I had no compulsion to confess to the police, deliberately leaving or phoning in clues, like the Yorkshire Ripper mailing his notes to Scotland Yard from different parts of the country. But I am nothing like the Ripper, a psychopath with a screwdriver where his sex should have been. I have hurt no one. I am not a murderer. What I did to those women was a fantasy and not a fantasy I invented alone, but one that I interpreted. Their deepest desire. Dread.

No charges, no complaints, no headlines, this city continues to be safe at night for women.

The police should have a recognizable pattern to work with by now. If they were pursuing these cases, that is. It's obviously the work of a single man. An unusual man. A careful methodical man. Not at all deranged. A gentleman.

Not at all malicious. I imagine they have guessed that and concentrated their efforts at detection on real crime. A pity, it deprives me of stories from the papers to titillate memory.

But I have been so cautious, careful to choose women who live alone. I have used the files in the medical library of the hospital, secretly of course, after hours, the psychiatric cases, the neurotic women are of particular interest to me.

I chose single women. I staked out their homes. I often checked, phoning in the middle of the night, to see who would answer and how. My preference has been for affluent women in large residences with grounds a discrete distance from their neighbors. Their bodies are well cared for. Their neighbors are old and hard of hearing. I etherized their dogs.

Medical assistance I can provide myself, when I am through with them. Their ennui was halved. I shared that much with them. So really, in a rather convoluted but quite fundamental way, you might say that I had compassion, even empathy, for them.

Of course my method of choosing my victims was not without its exceptions. A few random women I have discovered on the streets, strolling through the rich moist fur of summer darkness or in fast food places, their skins tasting of tobacco and rancid oil. Or as I jogged late at night.

But what I saw late at night in the parks was mostly other men. I remember one, running, completely in the nude, his body the brilliance of birch in the moonlight. Few women risk seeing such visions. Few women risk any kind of vision at all. I was waiting for one who would.

My wife was brooding senselessly over what she thought she knew of my activities. Nothing. A mania for cool night air and fire in the lungs. A new phase. Through another cycle I've pupated. Something winged darkly emerging.

My fitness insures for me a long life and for my family greater security. I have reassured Lily with that. I need little sleep. This has always been true, as if my biological clock were set on another planet. The running has made me more alert, has kept me alive, has kept active my excuse to be outside. When I returned home I would do the reading that makes me cultured or keeps me keen in my profession. You have to understand this, the importance of it, and that I am a civilized man. I also read to expand my consciousness which is only partially cloaked in darkness, that part, like the far side of the moon, perpetually hooded. Don't think that you can guess at my motivation from some point in outer space, or inner, for that matter. There are no clues to be had. Keep it simple, your analysis, what it can discover and predict: lust, blood, hormones, too sensitive receptors in the brain for a single enzyme that alters the mind to schizophrenia. If you can believe that given a bottle of vitamins I might have left those women alone, believe it. But if I believed that, I would have buried those vitamins.

Excellence in many areas, the Renaissance ideal, is what I admire deeply. Excellence in mind and in body. Such superiority is quintessentially male. The genius of Mozart is male. If my wife nods as if to music, as if in agreement, it is not because she understands. Her head bobs, flushed and red, an apple in a barrel.

On that blistering hot night, the fourth of August, I decided to complete my pursuit of a woman I had observed for several weeks. I knew the number of her apartment and her name, written on her mail box: C. Hansen. A wise precaution, the bald initial, not to give away her gender. I looked up her phone number, C. Hansen on Euclid. I tried calling her at different hours, several times, once in the middle of the night. I did not so much as breathe over the receiver. But she most likely guessed it was a man calling. Still a case cannot be made on a dial tone. But I did not want to frighten her. I did not want to find her door double bolted. Don't worry, lady, it's only a wrong number, it's someone too rude or ashamed to apologize. It's nothing to call the police about. I left no voiceprints, as unique as fingerprints, and more easily identifiable outside the laboratory.

Hot humid nights, when the heat seems most oppressive. The air is cloudy with moisture, with the decaying smells of garbage left out for the next morning's pickup and with the exhaust from inner city traffic, the exhaled burning of the buses and the Porsches mingling through an inversion. Overcast sky, with its invisible stars like black carbon, heated and organic; their obscured diamond brilliance formed under some tremendous pressure. That pressure is bearing down overhead and against my solar plexus.

This heat makes women restless, fitful in sleep, but it also makes them careless, lazy.

Should my wife have any questions, I have prepared rationalizations: I took the car to drive down to the beaches to jog, the distance driven worth the coolness of the lake breezes, the spring of wood under my feet, the boardwalk ideal for running. The ravine would have been a cauldron, good enough reason to bypass that. Nothing to make one raise an eyebrow, a questioning eyebrow, a female suspicious eyebrow, whether real or penciled in, the kind of look that never comes out in the open and fires with a direct question, but prods with hushed, concerned queries, and the occasional and dull needle of sarcasm, her facsimile of wit.

I pulled on my gray jogging pants and a T-shirt of the same shade. I kept the nylon panty hose along with a pair of surgical gloves and some fine instruments (although my fingers are wily enough to pick a lock with a hairpin) in an inside zippered pocket of my gym pack, which more obviously contained, for any prying eyes, a towel, a dark blue nylon wind breaker, rolled, and a can of unsweetened apple juice. I was confident in my ability to perform. I had yet to make a slip of any kind, but that did not make me arrogant or careless. Such success is based on intelligence, and discretion, and patient perseverance.

But C. Hansen, the blonde I first detected at *Le Magot* wearing a cottage rose pant suit, was not at all aware of my pursuit. What I was engaged in was a larger and somewhat primal drama. I would overcome her feeble resistance and outwit the social complex, the city with its yellow police patrol cars, the jealousy of other men, the hum of telephone wires, the many voices all talking at once, as when the heat of summer sings with the technological music of cicadas.

I listened for a few moments to the sounds of the house, my family asleep, all of them. Their respiration as if the bricks themselves were breathing. The jump start of the refrigerator, its motor working overtime in the summer heat with a subdued roar, like a rather large cat purring.

I was satisfied that they were all asleep after I picked out and identified the gentle snores of my son, my daughter's light sighs as she turns in her sleep, and the deep and rasping breath of my wife, as I can distinguish which phone is ringing in a busy office by the slight variance in their frequencies. I made my way out the side door through the kitchen and into the garage. I threw the gym pack into the front of the car with me. I would need its hidden contents shortly. It was 12:46 a.m. By that time, on a week night, a shop girl must be asleep. So I had time, time enough. Affecting European habits, taking a half hour nap in mid-afternoon, enables me to subsist very nicely on three or four hours of sleep a night. In summer, it is a sensible routine, to avoid the worst heat of the sun bouncing back from the concrete, the steaming asphalt, looking newly made as it melts, catching at your heels like fresh tar. It was well worth going back to the hospital or the medical center in the evening, to get away from the worst part of the day when the traffic thickens and tempers flare.

Those private hours of daylight were most precious to me. The only time I could be alone at home, when the children were at school or at day camp, and Lily did her shopping. I would leave again just after supper, the only meal I shared with them in a quiet and dignified formality. No gossip or chit-chat to give me a headache. I have tried to teach my children to speak up, not to be afraid, but to choose their words.

I hate that pollution of the airwaves the twentieth century calls communications. My wife has weakened her once fine mind with talk shows and the pseudo-information of the news. I like to hear the music of silver against china, the rich ring of silver against silver, when the knife strikes the fork.

That night my wife had poached a large trout. I prefer the cool white flesh of fish, flaked like its scales, in tiny feathers, that light. I deboned the fish and served portions to everybody. In that way I show them that I can provide and care for them. I am somewhat distant, but not without love. I think of love as what is understood between us, what is taken for granted.

I like the way silence amplifies the other senses. At such times I feel that I can almost watch my children grow, flowers under the light, through the eye of time-lapsed photography. Such moving pictures do they make.

I had eaten very lightly. Lily had made some elegant

dessert — pears, poached in wine then set in a chocolate mold — which the family ate greedily.

"I used very little sugar, Michael, and no cream." Lily tried to tempt me.

"No thank you, dear. In this heat sweets make me feel clogged."

"But, Michael, as I've just explained, I adapted the recipe. It's really very light . . ."

I had to cut her short. "I said no, didn't I? Do I have to spell it out for you? You need to cross out the word dessert and replace it with the word no in your lexicon. Metabolism slows by about 1% each year in middle age. You need less food. Those white slacks you're wearing fit fine last summer. Now you're bulging out of them!" That was effective. That silenced her. She did little more than pick at her pears.

It was my evening at home, so I looked over the academic work of the children. With little Sophia I sat at the piano and we played a duet. Sophia also sings very sweetly, so we often choose choral music, light modern pieces, perhaps something from Gershwin. That is most affecting, the comradery I sometimes have with my daughter. She tends to chatter, has an animated face, full of light and motion. With me she calms right down and behaves sensibly. We play together creatively and intelligently and sometimes our performance is even witty, the bravura of a Liberace without the sequins and greasepaint. Lily usually sits in the living room to listen, smiling quietly throughout our concertino. Perhaps those moments fit her sense of family best, with me at the center, and my small mirror image, the daughter, blessed with my coloring of a Swede, the dour Swede that Lily thinks me to be, and she observing and silent, her hands with palms turned upwards in her lap, as if accepting a gift from heaven.

All that time Thomas would be upstairs doing his calculus, not needing me in the same way. I understand him better.

Sophia is much younger than Thomas. And she is female. It is already apparent that she is not as independent as Thomas was at her age. Girls' brains are smaller. It seems odd to see my face in a female's form, as shepherds must feel who have fathered some hybrid for their flock. Still my Sophia is a charming and lovely creature. She is like a painting of myself, executed by a student, not the master.

I shook myself from my reverie. The meal by then digested, why had I been wasting time thinking about it? Miraculously, the spine of the fish, head still intact, was lying on top of the garbage, like the bust of a composer under which is written the score of his best music.

It was late. I pulled out of the garage and drove south. There was very little traffic on Spadina. The milk trucks were starting up their late night run, huge sixteen wheel trucks, thundering down the almost deserted thoroughfare. In the quiet of the night, it seemed deafening, but was not without aesthetic appeal. But then I wasn't trying to sleep.

Casa Loma loomed to my left, sterile and pretentious, a castle in a postcard. It stands as an anomaly in our modern urban landscape. It looks like a Disney fantasy, clean and kitschy. I was driving south, my windows rolled down to let in the night air.

When I reached College Street I turned right, but soon turned north again because I decided that it was safer to park on a small street parallel to Euclid. I was lucky. I had to be. I parked my old Volvo, a dark blue and inconspicuous car, our junk car from my days of internship, which I've kept for what Lily ascribes to me as sentimental reasons.

A very reliable car, finely made, and without display. It has served me well. I do not like unnecessary notice and that night I wanted absolutely none. The natural reserve in my character, that too has served me well. I parked behind another car, a Volkswagen Rabbit, also apparently dark blue, pulling up so close they formed one long shadow. Then I drank the apple juice and eased the pack onto my back. After rolling up the car windows, I slipped out quietly, leaving my door unlocked.

There was a single light burning from the second story of a house half way down the block. All the other windows were dark. I jogged lightly up the street, taking a circular route from the car to the apartment. It was easy. I found myself at her building before my heartbeat went up.

The humidity of the summer night made the air thick. I felt as if I were running in slow motion. Underwater. The air suffocatingly sweet with the fragrance of flowers. White blooms glowed like the ghosts of flames from some bushes. Mock orange.

It was 1:02, August 4th, my fortieth summer. On a Monday night, now more correctly a Tuesday morning, I imagined her going to bed spiritless, a long tedious week ahead. Her life must seem to be a commodity measured in mere units of time. By a stop watch. I almost felt sorry for her, for what I imagined her life to be, for her lack of ambition. I would enter her routine like that pink and sparkling wine or light beer she must keep in the refrigerator. Refreshing. Intoxicating, but just barely. Surely my ability to excite would be more interesting than those thin alcoholic beverages. Unexpected recreation. How little is left in a life that is truly surprising. Death and accident are predictable for others, shocking only for ourselves.

Anticipation, more than exertion, was causing my

pulse to speed up. I jogged past the building and into a lane that ran parallel and behind the housing on that street. The back entrance was unlit. I stopped at a low-rise building, quite old and shabby, with some battered aluminum garbage cans framing the back steps. Several of the bins lay on their sides, the contents and their stench spilling onto the lawn. I was not used to the smell of garbage. It made me feel a slight nausea, with a bitterness like the taste of tin from old canned goods filming my tongue. For the first time that night, I hesitated, not out of scruples or fear, but out of some vague repulsion I was beginning to experience. The heat, the garbage stench, and I could visualize her again with her hamburger, pushing the pickles back into the bun, the greasy meat, the slippery dressings spilling out. Mustard and ketchup. Excrement and blood. I did not know at that moment whether I really wanted the woman. Just for that moment.

Then I pulled the probe out of my pocket and worked, crouched in shadow and close to the wall. The lock gave no resistance. My hands are expert. My hands are the hands of a surgeon and pianist. The ease, the expertise, was hardly at all surprising. It would have been surprising had I had difficulty.

The door opened outwards. I parted it just enough to slip through and smoothly pulled it back shut, soundlessly. The stairs were immediately to my left. I went up two steps at a time, on the balls of my feet, working the muscles of my thighs, seeing them clearly outlined in the knit fabric of my pants. Tensed thighs.

The windows of the landings were narrow and gray, with cobwebs gathering rolls of dust, as if they had not been washed in years. Flies flourished. I heard an occasional angry buzz, but nothing else. Two large black beetles, back to back, copulated on the door to the third floor level under the light, the red light of the exit sign.

Opening that door slightly, I looked down the hall. There were little individual lights by each suite: ornate, synthetic gas lamps on wrought iron with hourglass shaped fixtures. Even in the dimness of their light I could see that the carpet covering the hall was soiled and worn, in some spots to the sticky tar beneath. I cautiously made my way down to the end of the hall, to Number 39 and I picked open the lock in a matter of seconds. After stepping inside, I slipped the stocking over my head, my back against the door.

In the darkness of her entrance, I waited to accustom myself to the greater darkness of the unlit apartment, until the shapes of furniture began to emerge like pale mushrooms from black loam. I knotted the legs of the stockings and tossed them back over my head, more to get them out of the way than for the sinister, cultish effect they must have created, and which, if unintended, might nevertheless prove to be useful.

I stood in the dark entrance listening for several minutes. A radio seemed to be playing faintly from somewhere down the hall to my right. I tried to gauge the source. There was no sign of light leaking from anywhere within the apartment. I moved to the right twisting the gag I had prepared for her mouth, tightening it firmly into a roll.

I eased my way towards the music, its synthetic big band sound giving me a sense of time outside of time. My eyes had adjusted to the dark. Not pitch, never dark enough that darkness of the city, where at night, light is ever fugitive, yet numinous. I could see clearly, as in a charcoal sketch, in various densities of line.

I disconnected the phone, easily following with my fingers the cord to the jack. But I did not anticipate much of a struggle.

The door to her bedroom was halfway open. I didn't make a sound, moving like a glider on a current of air.

The radio was by the bed on a night table, a clock radio, the light from the dial casting a lurid green aura. Its music played very faintly so it still seemed to come from elsewhere, as indeed in a sense it did. But I don't mean that, I don't mean the broadcasting studio, but an unearthly elsewhere. I could make out her form, the silhouette of her body sleeping prone, the bedding tossed aside. She was wearing some sort of fluffy nylon gown, which was twisted around her waist. Her white legs were cast in the greenish glow of that room's sense of timelessness. They gleamed.

I stood there watching, listening to her breathing for what seemed like a long time, the eternal moment, the countdown in split seconds that it takes the bullet to enter the brain of a suicide.

I could have been her mother, I was that patient and that attentive. For a moment I forgot myself in the role or perhaps you think I was merely prolonging the game, postponing the enjoyment of what was inexorably in my hands. Perhaps you're a greater cynic than I am. I bent over her gently as if to kiss her, like the prince about to waken Briar Rose, the sleeping beauty, from her century-long dream.

I thrust the gag into her mouth instead. Then I pulled her around and tore her gown off. The material gave way easily, sticky and frail as cotton candy. She made some strangled sounds, syllables as they are formed before human speech. I thought of what I had read of the Boston Strangler, how he would climax with the death shuddering of the bodies of the women in his grip.

Her eyes were staring at me, wide with terror. It almost made me smile, knowing she had nothing to fear, however convincing the game might seem. The poor child. I was more than her mother and what I was about to offer her was far better than the gift of life. It was experience.

9

R*ita*

THE landscape of the city is no more natural outside than inside, so stepping out of an office building is bound to be a disappointment. It was a brilliant and searing day, heat radiating from both sky and concrete. Rita thought of it as the urban double broiler effect. She imagined her body barbecued, for what? A pterodactyl swooping down from its nest in a neighboring skyscraper, desirous of her? What was this thing she had for reptiles? A taste, a predilection, acquired from visits to the museum as a child, where she would allow herself to be led by her father, her small white hand fitting snugly into his large tanned one.

She used to love to linger at the dinosaur displays, and her father always tolerated her fascination. He would settle down on a bench nearby and smoke a chain of cigarettes until she was ready to go on to the next thing. But she had been often happy enough to stay until closing time, mesmerized by their glittering scales, until the smoke from her father's cigarettes became thick and seemed part of the tropical rainforest atmosphere of a primordial earth. Recently she had read that scientists now suppose that the blood of those dinosaurs was actually warm, not cold, that they were more closely linked to mammals than had been previously speculated. As an adult she learned what she instinctively knew as a child, looking at those gigantic ancestors.

Rita had not forgotten her rendezvous with Pierre for lunch. He was *not* not on her mind, he was the subtext for her musing. Absorbed again in the exhibits of memory's museum, she had automatically wandered out the exit to the main street. Instead of retracing her steps through the labyrinth of halls to get to the parking lot, Rita circled around the block of the building complex. Pierre was not to be seen, but when Rita walked up to his car she found him inside, his seat reclined, smoking. Soft music leaked from the vehicle like carbon monoxide gas. His windows were rolled up. She tapped on the glass. He looked up leisurely and as languidly. As if falling in slow motion, he leaned over and opened the car door on the passenger side for her.

She got in and sat down beside him. The air inside the vehicle was almost crisp enough to fog her breath. The cooling system was operating full blast. She shivered. He continued to smoke. With men, it is important never to apologize, she thought. They almost respected a woman that way. She herself could not tolerate men who shuffled and sniveled and lied. Wimps. Rita was very tired of those pseudo-liberal men with their closet macho fantasies, who currently seemed to compose the male majority among her acquaintance. Those men got you to trust them, giving you the feminist line, well rehearsed, and then whammo, that not unforgotten chromosome, with its perpetual questioning of the world (Y oh Y wasn't I born a woman not among those questions), reasserted itself at the first opportune moment. She had begun to believe that the only relationship that was likely to work for her would be with a truck driver. Truck drivers or Tarzans, the nature boys or their opposite, the sophisticated and ironic, the suave Pierre, so brutally honest in his manipulation of her. But then, she must like to be used in that way.

"I like a man with confidence. Never been stood up in your life before, eh Pierre?" Rita was the first to speak. Pierre looked at her briefly, into her eyes, then scanned the length of her body.

"*Mais, oui. Certainement,*" he said with his charming half smile, fully conscious as he was of its charm, and inhaled deeply from his cigarette. "It has yet to matter."

The smoke was making her feel lightheaded. She wanted a cigarette, she thought, more than she wanted him. Pulling the case out of his pocket, she stole one of his Marlboros. Pierre had a taste for American tobacco, American jazz, and American film. He indulged that taste along with his contempt for almost anything Anglo-Canadian. He liked Clint Eastwood and Marlboro cigarettes, a man's man and a man's cigarette. He was a cowboy riding the hills of Montana in a parking lot behind an office complex in downtown Toronto. Riding as free as any cowboy.

That freedom in their relationship was intoxicating. An affair with Pierre was an affair with few expectations. He was solidly married. He was taken care of in that way. His freedom from such needs was her freedom. She couldn't quite remember when she started seeing it that way, but the kinds of services that men required in their established relationships were more than she had to give to anyone. She never wanted to see them as children, as boys, who needed their meals prepared and their cleaning done, whose needs must be anticipated in every way. That was love: domesticity. She had voided that ticket or allowed it to be canceled for her.

So what she wanted and what she had was something

entirely different. The sort of thing 'good girls' had been taught to deplore: sex without love. As Pierre turned the key in the ignition and started up the motor to drive to her place, she knew that she had *it*, what she thought she wanted. For another afternoon anyway.

They parked and walked a few blocks to her house, the streets cooling by about ten degrees in her neighborhood because of the shade, because of the hushed air, rich with oxygen from the breathing of trees growing along both sides of the avenue. They were big old trees whose branches seemed to be prototypes for the flying buttresses of the gothic cathedral, embracing silence and at the same time suggesting a presence, in the way that churches do, but with that bitter green incense of chlorophyll. It was a street luxuriant with maples and horse chestnuts. The couple walked in its deodorized silence.

At the house, Pierre stepped into her garden while Rita mixed drinks, gin and tonics with fresh lime slices. She talked to Pierre through the open glass door, pausing over and punctuating what she had to say with the slamming of trays and the tinkle of ice cubes. She just had to complain about the lack of cooperation she had from the press in covering her feminist film festival: "I thought if I played down the word 'feminist' and called it *Mama Noire*, gave it a jazzy, sexy sounding title and associations with the kind of sex-role playing we used to like and understand. Well, I thought I might just get them hooked. But in this town, Mel Gibson, that Aussie actor, gets more publicity for a speeding ticket! That's what gets reviewed in our papers."

Pierre gave no indication that he had heard her or was interested at all in her complaints. He was close enough for her to hear him drag on his cigarette. Rita grimaced at his unresponsiveness. She held the two drinks she had finished mixing to the light to admire them, then took a deep and appreciative tipple from the one that was then meant for her. It was cold and delicious. "Better than lunch," she said, thinking out loud as she stepped out into the garden to join him.

"Your many talents continue to astound me," Pierre said, gesturing around the court at her dahlias and the box of mixed flowers near the back of the house. "What are those small flowers among the primrose? So many colors, could you not decide?"

"That's nicotiana. A tobacco flower. My father always planted them at home. They bring out the hummingbirds. He also filled a feeder for them with sugar and water solution, that's what you put in a hummingbird feeder. Not honey. Honey is poison for them."

He picked a blossom, entered with his thumb the deep throated corolla of the flower, ripping its delicate pink silk to the calyx. "They're very fragrant and exquisitely shaped. Tobacco flowers, did you call them?"

"That's right, tobacco flowers. Shall I send some to your funeral? After you die of lung cancer, that is. *Très apropos*, don't you think?"

"Aha! And you're not also mortal, I suppose, Mizz Jogger, Mizz Health Food Nut. But this is the health food I prefer! The vite-amens," he said saluting her with his glass. "A tonic, is it not?" he crowed. Then he pulled her over to him. "And what is this that I taste on your lips that is not lipstick?" he teased as if he did not know that she had 'borrowed' one of his cigarettes in the car.

They continued to kiss, their icy drinks balanced precariously against each other's spines, deepening with chill the shudder of sexual desire. He slipped his free hand into the back pocket of her jeans.

"But let's go inside, shall we?" He was the first to pull away from the kiss and they went back into the house, he stepping aside to let her enter first. His continental manner was a courtesy, but she felt it to be both controlling and distancing.

He followed Rita into the living room. There she deliberately selected a single armchair near the window where the light was filtered by an overgrown Boston fern, making her seem even paler than usual. She had light, sensitive skin. She tanned, but almost inconsequentially, to a gold and pink color. The closest thing to peach ever synthesized by human skin, a lover had once remarked. She sat apart from Pierre because in his breaking up of their kiss, she had felt too much his calculation, his control of the situation. She resented the distances that he imposed, not because of those distances, but because they insinuated potential and unreasonable demands on her part. She resented it when she suspected that he was behaving as if she were a mistress, when he seemed to be a man who must repeatedly assert that he wants no entanglements, as if he were constantly expecting them, a convoluted action like that of a man in a car driving around imaginary barriers when there is no work being done on the road. He must think her no different than the others. She knew in detail from office gossip about those others.

Almost as soon as she sat down, Rita drained her glass and jumped up again to make another drink. "How's yours?" she gestured with the empty tumbler, held upside down. "Good to the last drop."

"Another, please, for me, but less ice and more gin. The lime is very good. Refreshing," he said, biting the wedge of citrus fruit and pulling, with his white even teeth, the flesh off the rind to eat it.

The drinks were excellent. They were cold in her mouth, frosty in the glass, and spreading warmth inside her stomach. Pierre sat back, his arm across half the length of the couch, his drink in the hand resting on the single carved wooden arm of the divan. He had not removed his jacket. He undid a button and let it fall open, which it was tailored to do in a dramatic fashion. He sat with his legs crossed at the knee, sipping his drink, giving her his half smile, unhurried and confident. The afternoon, unlike their bodies, seemed to promise to be forever young. It promised to lead upstairs and into the bedroom, to Rita's rumpled bed.

Pierre noticed Rita's eyes looking up the stairs and couldn't resist making sly remarks with that wry and playful smile he knew women found so disarming: "Well, your thoughts at least seem to be leading in the right direction," gesturing at the same time with his drink towards the bedroom, "or are we to drink all afternoon and just talk? Delightful conversation, no doubt, but not, Rita, at all what I had in mind this morning. However, what I had in mind might be accomplished here as easily, on your lovely, if somewhat worn, Indian rug, or even on this sofa, should you care to join me here at some point. But that I am afraid is the sort of thing that only a more primitive type than myself could enjoy. Like that scene you so love in the remake of *The Postman Always Rings Twice* in which Jack Nicholson makes love to the exquisite Jessica Lange on the table where she has been kneading bread. All flour and stickiness and rising! The buns all too human! (Rita groaned at the awful pun. Pierre had a wry penchant for them. He claimed that it was his revenge on the English language for being made to speak it in Canada.) Yes, a more primitive or perhaps, and I hate to add this as a qualification, a younger man than myself might relish the inconvenience for the unconventionality of it. My appetite for sex has diminished very little with my middle years, but my enthusiasm for comfort has grown immeasurably. I have never thought of you as coy, Rita. You don't have a flirtatious or silly bone in your body. And that's what I love about you. That body," releasing a snort of laughter. His laughter was like a secret blurted out that he had not meant to share.

At age forty-six, Pierre was not much older than Rita. His slight frame, his Gallic leanness, his nervous intensity, contributed to an air of youthfulness. Most extraordinary were his eyes which were uncannily both dark and bright at the same time. To Rita they suddenly seemed like Nikos' eyes, not Nikos' eyes blazing with righteous anger, with political causes, but Nikos' eyes warmed by summer and intimacy and retsina. A very painful knot constricted her throat as she fought back tears. Pierre noticed the moist light in her eyes, brimming, although not spilling over, and he began to relent somewhat on his irony. So much of their sex together was a kind of sparring, trading in wit or power. He walked over to her and took her in his arms, embracing her very gently. Tenderly.

"It's been too long for us. We do not get together often enough. I did not know that you could still be shy with me."

Ashamed, Rita caught herself up, brushed away her tears and smiled as if they had been tears of laughter.

"Shy, sugar? I don't know what you could be thinking of. As if you didn't know little old me," affecting the southern drawl and style of Blanche Dubois of *A Streetcar Named Desire* as if she were being played by Mae West. "I sound like a schoolteacher, honey, but what I do to those traveling salesmen. Oo la la! Me shy? No, sugar, I was just thinking of something else, something rather sad."

"Something else or someone else? But then I suppose I have no right to ask."

"That's right. You have no right to ask." Rita protected the privacy of her thoughts more jealously than the favors of any lover.

"But enough jokes. Let's retire to the bedroom. The best home for one's old age!" Pierre rose decisively. He pulled her roughly out of the chair and began kissing her. Lingering, prolonging the moment for the pleasure of it, the keener pleasures that postponement brings, sharpening the senses. Rita freed herself from the embrace and turned around wordlessly to make her way up the stairs. Pierre followed closely behind her, his hands on her hips.

Rita undressed quickly. She threw her clothes on a chair in the time it took Pierre to take off his jacket. He found one of her padded silk hangers and fitted his jacket over it, then after pulling off his pants, he folded them neatly along the crease line and placed them with the jacket. Unbuttoning his shirt he made his way to the bed where Rita lay, propped on several pillows, clothed only in her pink silk panties and matching brassiere. Her arms folded back, with her head resting on her hands, she was watching him intently as he disrobed.

"Not exactly a Las Vegas act, are you Pierre? Why don't you take off your socks and stay awhile."

"A funny girl. But, I like that," he said as he tried to unhook her bra, pawing at the front of it where a rosebud applique separated the two spheres of the lace cups. She led his fingers to the back. Pierre stopped smiling. He wanted to take that smirk off her face; he knew how to undress a woman. He started to kiss her passionately, to caress and probe the body he had come to know so well, until he had her where he knew she would be thinking of nothing else. He knew, or he thought he knew, how to make *une fille méchante*, a smart-ass woman, shut up.

The coffee was very good. She must remember to pick up another pound of that blend, she thought. They obviously kept it very fresh. Roasted on the premises was no idle claim. Walking into the shop was enough of a sensual experience to placate a sultan for the loss of his entire harem. No drink had more texture than coffee for Rita. She liked it prepared in many ways, in the 1001 ways of the Kama Sutra. Thick and muddy bottomed demi-tasses of Turkish coffee she had learned to appreciate with Nikos, semi-sweet, and the most exquisite of these blends which she drank was made from beans ground to a fine powder and laced with cardamom. Regular American brew, perked, home style. The Java of a Chandler mystery, mocca. The drip method with Melitta filter adopted in college. The sun in dark espresso, the Roman way, with a twist of lemon rind. But it was the Melitta she chose that afternoon to make coffee for Pierre and herself.

Waiting upstairs in bed for her to return, propped up on his side by a pillow, Pierre browsed through the assortment of books Rita had on top of the little night table beside her futon. She liked to read before sleep, liked to have books within reach during the night, the comfort of familiar fictions, the volumes, however often hugged or read, opened worlds for her, all the sweeter, all the more desirable because they are only within imaginative reach.

Naked, Rita carried the coffees up the stairs on a tray. She got high on the odor of freshly brewed Columbian from the steaming cups. Placing the tray precariously on a pile of books, she addressed Pierre playfully, as if he were a sultan. With a sweeping gesture she performed an elaborate bow, fingers touching forehead and lips and chest, a salaam, her right palm on her forehead. Bending very low, she was flexible enough to kiss the rug.

They both laughed, feeling light after love, younger, playing truant from their jobs and commitments. For Pierre it was also an escape from vows sanctified in church and biologically ratified by his wife's pregnancy. Their first child. He had begun to realize that he would start to age in a different way, in a more marked way. This perception made him need his affair with Rita even more than his simple lust for her in the spring. His fear of aging compelled him to reinitiate something he might have otherwise let cool because of pride and forced indifference. Indifference came so easily, became natural soon enough. But now he found that he needed the lightness of her touch, her humor. She was not young, but young women, the hot twenty-year-old secretaries he had easy access to, just made him feel older. He had tried it with them. They made him feel wise and jaded. They made him feel like their father. He was no fool. He knew how other men looked, how he had also appeared, men his age with women who could be easily mistaken for their daughters. It emphasized rather than camouflaged the age difference, solicited unwelcome attention and speculation. Moreover, the girls had always exhausted him with their demands. They did not have the perspective and independence he wanted in relationships. He felt it a clear sign of his intelligence that these callow young women did not make him feel expansive. His decidedly superior knowledge had nothing to play with. No balls served. Just serviced. Those fluffy young girls made him want to go straight home and write his memoirs.

He needed Rita to make him feel young, an affair with

a woman the same age as his wife, who was not his wife. An affair with a woman who shared his knowledge and experience and with whom he was not bound, like a lover in college he had picked up after a class. A woman both casual and fun. A woman who was not part of his routine life, not found among the household accounts. A woman who was still more than a little mysterious to him.

Rita stretched out in bed with him naked, drinking coffee. "The way you caress that cup, the way you savor each sip, almost lap with your tongue that dark beverage, makes me jealous." He offered the remark with a vague challenge on his smiling lips.

"No more than I do you, darling. You're the same kind of drug. Strong and dark. A few drops injected under the skin and instant death. A most *potent* poison. My handyman, my sweet fix."

He caressed her body, rubbing her belly in a circular motion until he noticed the raspy coarseness of shaved skin around her navel.

"You used to not shave there."

"I know. It's a drag, but this summer, for the first time in my life, I feel thin enough to wear a bikini and I've been taking full advantage of it. I'm not ethnic enough to show off my excess body hair. So I'm as shaved and smooth as the belly of a fish. The roughness due to the scales belies the impression of smoothness. But then how many fish do you feel up in a day?"

"You should try waxing. Kathleen has been having that done for years and now she says it's almost unnecessary."

"So stick with your wife, why don't you!?"

"Don't be difficult, *ma cherie*. I'm here with you in spite of her, not because of her. I told you that right from the start."

10 The Journal

THE bruises on her neck were dark blue. They were ink prints. It almost went too far, the game. As if in thinking about the Boston Strangler, I had conjured him. It was the Strangler who tightened fingers around her throat. It was the Strangler who created those purple welts. The dark velvet ribbon from which hung the white cameo of a woman's face.

The deepest impressions were made by the thumbs, where they almost succeeded in breaking the neck; fragile as the chicken bones we crack to suck out the marrow, the juices. We crack. It was the Strangler who climaxed with her sputtering breath. It was the woman who cracked.

Then I came back to revive her. I gave her a little water and some sleeping pills. Her body shook violently. Her teeth rattled like ivory dice. Her skin felt chilled to the touch. Her eyes were wide, yet vacant. I made sure she was asleep before I left. Not dead. I made sure she slept.

Sex for the Strangler must have been his way of denying death, of denying his own death, as he snuffed out those housewives one by one. I am not like that. Of my own death I have taken the measure. Yes, even today to be calcium phosphate might be enough. I preserve what I can for life.

It was 3:28 a.m. before I returned home. I sat in the

garage for some time with my thoughts, reluctant to enter without the transition provided for by this little pause in time, this enclave in space. I felt like a transatlantic traveler deplaning in a foreign city. His psyche has not yet arrived. His psyche's in bed with his wife in Toronto where it's 4:00 a.m., but his body is picking up the luggage at the airport in Rome without him.

I switched on the overhead light, opened the glove compartment, and drew out my file cards, idly flipping their corners like a poker player with a hand dealt by another. A hand he knows to be unlucky. I pulled out a blank one. With my blue and yellow, fine point Bic, as anonymous a tool for recording information as I know, I filled in a report. I created a new file for her:

> *C. Hansen, Apt. 19, Euclid & College, August 4*
> *white, caucasian, blonde, about 25 years of age*
> *5'2" and at least 120 pounds*
> *identifying marks: prominent scar from an*
> *appendectomy across her abdomen*
> *experiment: death by strangulation*
> *condition on leaving: revived & calmed, deep*
> *bruises around the neck*

I filed the card chronologically.

Memory cannot be trusted. It is important to keep a record, to be armed with the facts. It will render me more resilient should a crisis occur, should I be apprehended. I know exactly what I've done, without embellishment, or the hysteria with which these events may be discussed in the future.

Yes, for some time I sat in the car in the garage, flipping through the cards idly with my thumb, as if mesmerized by my manicured nail, its natural gloss, its inbred clarity, its full moon brilliantly rising above the cuticle.

Rita

BLUE is the color of deep water and sky. Call it the color of heaven in a different cosmology than the one jet planes fly through. How did blue, beautiful blue, become associated with sex and pain?

Blue movies. Marlene Dietrich, made herself famous in Fritz Lang's *The Blue Angel*, luring the suddenly befuddled professor from his stodgy life. Which of them do you identify with?

Out of the blue of sky without shade, out of slavery, its history of black labor for plantations. To pick cotton was to wear bracelets of thorns, to bleed until there was no more blood, until there was only music, the blues, pouring out of their veins.

Blue as in holding the note too long. Breathless. Jazz. Fuck. Jazz. Words which mean the same but are not of equal value. The difference qualitative and not quantitative.

"Don't fuck with me, man!" "Jazz me, Baby, jazz me."

Blue eyes. Rita's eyes were slate blue, the universal color all infants share before the iris individuates. Nikos' eyes were dark, deep, almost black. Mocha. Coffee with chocolate. Such a rich and bitter brew. Addictive. Pierre's eyes were hazel, light filtered through green wood in a forest.

In spite of herself, by birth, by genes, by their pigmentation, Rita's eyes were aligned with the Nazi doctor quizzing Primo Levi at Auschwitz. In such eyes Primo saw method. He saw clinical detachment. He saw himself, reflected from those azure orbs as from a distorting mirror.

To reflect not to respond. To be objective where sensitive (not subjective) is its true antonym, its antithesis.

Language is not objective. Language affects how things are seen. Not like putting on another pair of glasses, like putting on another pair of eyes. Language is organic, the alphabet of the chromosomes. The heart a diphthong with the deepest tone. The Nazis have tainted scientific objectivity. The world needs the arts. The world gets gas ovens. The ovens work objectively, burning evenly according to body mass. The naked bodies condemned by the laboratory. Impersonal. Asexual. Sifting through the bones you look to the size of the skull and pelvis to sort male from female.

Rita wanted to identify with her Italian half, her dark-eyed inner self. She dribbled a little more cream into her coffee, wondering at the morbidity of her own thoughts, facile as they might seem, the weight of the questions trivialized by the setting, under the Campari awning of her favorite café.

The place was filling up. Rita sat waiting for her friends to show up for dinner. She should have asked for milk instead of cream, but she didn't want to bother the waitress again, who had just swung by with a tray loaded with drinks. Squinting, Rita marveled instead at the brightness of the day and waited agreeably for Margo and Alice. She could not have done this with any degree of comfort or confidence had she been waiting for a man.

The blueness of the sky was worth meditating on,

worth perhaps converting to an earlier world view to appreciate fully. Cerulean blue, that shade still had something of heaven, at least in the beauty of its name. Maybe she could believe in it after all. The other day she had felt strangely touched by a prayer card which had arrived through the mail slot of her door along with a Woolworth's flyer. The prayer of Saint Francis of Assisi. Above the text, a naive drawing of the monk sweet-talking the animals. Did he speak to them in Italian or in their own dialects of chirps and growls and yelps?

Rita sat in the outdoor café on Bloor listening to the city's language, to the horns of traffic, to sirens, to orders for more beer. She was a little early for her dinner rendezvous because she had left the office during the afternoon coffee break to shop for a new pair of sandals. The shoes she had been wearing, espadrilles, were from last season and had finally worn out. Or rather were looking so conspicuously ragged that she realized, sitting at her desk that morning, the little toe beginning to peek through the dark blue canvas, that she would have to give in and buy a new pair. Utilitarian footwear was always harder to replace; the others, the dress-up shoes, were in constant and plentiful supply, attractively displayed in the windows, and subject to the whims of impulse buying. The Clarks and down-unders were always hidden somewhere at the back of the store.

It was hard to find anything comfortable enough. Rita liked to walk. But women's shoes were designed for display, not circumambulation. High heels shorten the calf muscles, show off a more desirable contour.

It wouldn't kill you, of course, to walk in them if the boyfriend were right around the corner, about to pick you up in his red Corvette. Otherwise, forget it, she thought. Or rather she would have liked to have forgotten it. However, she was not immune to fashion. She was a woman. It was only *human* to need to be sexually attractive.

And to feel sexually attractive she had endured the rigors of initiation into high heels in secondary school. After all wasn't that why they called school after puberty "high"? Boys had equally arduous rites of passage like playing football, sweating in all that heavy gear, tackling and wrestling with each other — and all to get a date with a girl? It was part of the sex game. You might be as self-conscious and as intelligent as you like, but the game plays on. You're in or you're out.

As if to confirm all this, Rita watched the crowds hurrying home along the street, women with their bouncing, off-balance gait, juggling bags and parcels, men and their miraculously free stride, their arms pumping, making good time along the crowded sidewalk. That was what "penis envy" was all about. Men kept their hands free in order to hold the precious member to urinate. Men could direct that stream anywhere, make their mark on the world, and play with themselves at the same time, which accounted for their autoerotic and technological superiority. Rita determined then and there to buy clothes with good pockets, get a really compact wallet, and see if she could do it. Live without a purse.

She would have to confer with Margo and Alice, she thought. It was relaxing just sitting there and free associating, free to gripe some might call it, knowing it was Friday and time was again open for her, at least for a couple of days, free from the tightly scheduled slots of the work week. Canned time. Now something more natural was available to her, fresh from the tree.

She dribbled a little more cream into her coffee, a slight

extravagance. Later she intended to run off anything rich that she ate that night. Early the next morning she would take a long jog. The three friends routinely met for dinner, every Friday, followed by a movie or drinks at their respective residences. Three women from the post-priest culture, weary of therapy and wary of marriage counselors, trying to meet each others' spiritual and emotional needs. "Support," they called it.

Alice and Margo arrived at the same time. They had been working together for the last few months on a film about aging. Margo was producing it and had hired Alice to edit. There had been times in the past, golden times, when all three women had worked together on the same film, a time when Rita used to write and direct her own productions, when she had ideas, the courage to push for them, and the friends to share it all with. But, she, Rita, had sold out. She felt that keenly again as she watched the women arrive together, talking excitedly.

Rita's skin prickled with the heat. Then she felt a sudden chill, perspiration which had formed around her neck and shoulders rolling in surprising drops down the hollow between her breasts. Perhaps her friends had guts, but they also had husbands. Margo had been married for over twenty years and Alice was about to marry the man, a lawyer, she had been living with for the last three.

Rita smiled broadly in welcome, unconsciously shaking her head at the same time at herself, trying to whisk away that envy, not liking it in herself. Tell it to the bank, she thought.

The women hugged and kissed enthusiastically. Rita found their warmth and vitality infectious. Margo plopped herself down in a seat that was directly in the sun. With a broad and theatrical gesture, she removed the scarf wrapped, turban style, around her head and shook out her long, black hair, hair which was oriental in the dark density of its pigmentation. Margo loved the sun, but she was too impatient to sunbathe, "busy" she called it, so she made sure she got as much of those 'medicinal' rays as she could on her daily rounds, driving in her white convertible Volkswagen beetle with the top down, dressed in short pants and skimpy halter tops. It was impossible not to notice her. A dark Anita Ekberg. One man sitting at a table opposite to them was openly leering.

Margo was close to six feet tall and made Alice, sitting next to her, look like a child in comparison. Alice with her honey blonde good looks thought of herself as mousey and withdrew accordingly, shoulders always caving forward as if to protect her relatively flat chest, her posture in sharp contrast to Margo's squared shoulders, Margo who flourished her body like a loaded gun she had every intention of using.

"What are you drinking? Looks like coffee? I could use a drink with a little more kick to it."

"Sure, if you'd like to stay here to eat, that is? They have Upper Canada ale on tap but the mainstay of the menu is macrobiotic. So my guess is that you want me to pay up and pick a place with real food. But it'll have to be both good food and not greasy. Chinese is out. I've O.D.'d on Szechwan," said Rita.

Margo kept her chair well back from the table, out at an angle to give her plenty of leg room, crossing her long shapely legs as if unaware of the male notice she attracted, absorbed in her own pleasure in them.

"Well, what about Italian, eh?" Margo pulled out a pack of extra mild cigarettes and paused in her speech to light one. "Or does the 'obvious' still escape you. Some pasta and bottles of chilled white wine. With a gallon of acqua minerale to make spritzers and wash all the food down. Yummmmm."

"If it's Italian you want, I'll choose. I know a really nice little place on College, just south of here. Pricey, but really exquisite."

"Sounds great to me, Rit. We're in the money. We've signed up with a distributor who guarantees action for our film. You've got to outgrow this health food stuff." Margo looked at the menu on the board and wrinkled her nose in distaste as she read aloud from the dessert listing, "Tofu carob cheesecake. Don't you know that Adelle Davis died of cancer? My theory is that you need a certain level of these preservatives and additives in your diet to develop a tolerance to their toxicity. Like taking minute doses of arsenic until it can't hurt you anymore. Why pay $1.29 a pound for 'organic' carrots, maybe grown down wind from the nuclear plant? Even polar bears have dioxins in their fat. It all adds up to death by poisoning. Why pay more?"

Guilty about having held up a table for just one coffee, Rita left twice the cost of her drink as a tip for the waitress. There was a queue of people waiting to be seated at a table who smiled to see them go. The women made their way to Margo's car which was parked on the other side of the street. Margo led the way across the road, weaving through traffic, stopping it mostly. A woman right out of *La Dolce Vita* striding across the avenue, transforming Bloor street into a Roman via.

It was only a few minutes drive to the Italian place. Alice sat primly up front with Margo who had donned her tinted aviator specs for driving. Rita sat in back with her legs along the seat. To say stretched out would have been an exaggeration. She wondered what it was that drew big people to small cars. Overconfidence? She herself would have appreciated more steel between herself and a possible collision.

They made good time in spite of traffic. It was quite early for continental diners, so they had no trouble getting a table at the restaurant. They chose to sit in the patio section of the enclosed inner courtyard which was studded with large potted palms. The plants formed a natural awning for the patrons. When the waiter came they ordered white wine and mineral water right off. He returned shortly with a bottle of the house wine, chilled in a bucket of ice. He promptly uncorked the wine. It made a popping sound as the cork was released. The cool wine in the heat breathed visibly from the neck of the bottle. When the waiter prepared to offer them the ritual of tasting and approving the vintage, Margo shooed him away. She had decided to take over and pour their drinks herself. For Rita, she mixed a spritzer, very light on the wine with a squeeze from one of the fresh lemon wedges placed as garnishes in small dishes at all the tables. For Alice, Margo made a regular cooler, half and half, while she filled her own glass with the golden liquid, adding a splash of mineral water at the end as if an afterthought.

"Now to begin." Margo settled into her seat as into an easy chair for a good read. "You've heard all about our film driving down here and now we want to hear all about you! What have you been up to this week? I called Monday afternoon, no luck. Tuesday, ditto. Etc. Etc. What do you do at that job? You're never at your desk."

"What do I do? Fuck my boss, that's what I do."

"I see. We've spent twenty hours a day working on a film this last week and you've spent it in bed." Margo chuckled drily, then thought again and frowned. "You don't mean Bilodeau do you? Have you been sleeping with that jerk again?!" Margo knew Pierre; in fact, she had turned down the opportunity to know him better, in the biblical sense. "Rita, you know that guy is a lech and a patronizing macho asshole to boot! Whenever I'm forced to have any dealings with him, I'm ready to kill. You know how much I hate pseudo-liberal men, Jimmy Stewart on the outside, Kirk Douglas on the inside."

Unlike her friend, Rita kept her mouth shut. She let Margo bitch about Pierre without commenting. Some time ago Rita had decided that to survive within the system required a low profile and keeping your head screwed on tight. Rita simmered. Rita fumed. And Rita always avoided confrontation. The catch-22 for her was that she was female in a male bureaucracy, there was no winning. She knew it. She also knew that she had made a major mistake by getting involved with Pierre.

"I can't seem to help myself. You know I tried to stop seeing him, even though I had broken it off with Barry and have been sitting on my hands so to speak for the last couple of weeks. Pierre's wife is pregnant. The baby's due around Christmas, I think."

"That's what I like about you, Rita: your commitment to solidarity, to sisterhood." Margo adopted a more formal language to sharpen the thrust of her irony. "Sisterhood means that you can always count, at such trying times, on the other woman to take over those conjugal duties which become onerous when your belly's sticking out by two feet." This was a polished and often repeated phrase. When Margo had been pregnant with her second son she had suspected Bo of having an affair with a female cop, his partner for a while. Margo became so suspicious and bitter that Bo was forced to transfer to another division, although the only reason he gave was that he was sick of druggies.

"Give me a break, will you! I'm not exactly trying to bust up the marriage. And I didn't start it up again myself. He called me in. How about the men taking a little responsibility for what happens? Or is your sisterhood against that too?" Rita was feeling guilty so she was getting very angry. Margo — who understood this — started to smile in a knowing way which Rita found even harder to tolerate.

"He called and you jumped! I think you can do better than that." Margo started to sing in a mock operatic fashion: "I'm just a girl who can't say no," and "When I'm not near the boy that I love, I love the boy that I'm near-rrrrrrrrr."

At that point Rita turned to Alice for help. Margo had a tendency to dominate the conversation, not out of lack of generosity. If she had not been carried away by her chastising of Rita in this case or some argument she was particularly committed to (and what wasn't she particularly committed to?) she was always generous, always trying to draw others in. This was usually absolutely necessary for Alice, who was deferential and self-effacing to a fault. Alice had been too well trained by the nuns, a small and obscure sect in an order of Grey Sisters who could have taught the Jesuits a trick or two. Men invariably thought of her as a lady. Some dismissed her as such, while others recognizing a dying breed, cherished her, found they could easily resurrect their chivalry for the petite blonde. What rusty vestiges of it they had left that was uncontaminated by irony that is. Otherwise the risk was too great, to be found cavalier or worse, old-fashioned. A man could relax with a woman like Alice without having to test the ground like a mine field before every phrase or action. He could relax and find the companionship of a warm and intelligent person, in fact — what may still be most men's ideal woman — a good listener.

Responding to the pleading in Rita's eyes, Alice rose to her defense. "Quit that, Margo. Leave her alone! Can't you see that Rita's having a really bad time of it? You've been married for more than half your life, ever since university — and that string of guys you dated when we were living on campus! You've never been alone. Neither of us knows what we might do in Rita's shoes."

Hearing Alice defend her gave Rita's guilt the edge over her anger, making her feel more ashamed than anything else. "Margo's right. I'm behaving badly and I know what I'm doing and I continue to do it anyway. A new low, morally, for me." Then trying to lighten the tone and get away from her "sins", Rita confessed, "*Mea culpa, mea culpa*," tapping her chest lightly in mock contrition. "But I absolutely refuse to fast for it. Let's eat. Call the waiter over, whoever catches his eye first, and let's order. I skipped lunch. I'm starving."

Margo stood up slightly in her seat, or rather made the motion to stand up, and easily caught his attention. Quite hungry at this point they all ordered full course specials. Rita chose a side dish of pasta along with her entrée. It was her father's cooking that had taught Rita to love pasta. Her mother was a meat and potatoes chef. But Sundays, her father would cook pasta alla primavera, with vegetables he had grown and picked himself from their garden, incomparable. Then he would serve *ossobuco*, a veal stew, or chicken with rosemary, her favorite, not alla romana in a tomato sauce, but simmered in white wine and butter and deep golden olive oil. That night she ordered chicken and fusilli with a creamy sauce made with broccoli. Margo ordered lasagna and a Caesar salad, and Alice ordered some gnocchi and a veal dish, *saltimbocca*, meaning literally to jump into your mouth.

"It's that good according to the gastronomical legend," Rita commented as she translated the names of the dishes for her friends. Because of her father's passion for food, she had learned the Italian words for various dishes and vegetables before the English ones. He would always tell her everything he knew about the recipes he prepared, their regions and origins, any customs associated with their enjoyment. In that way he tried to preserve some of their Italian heritage for her. A sensualist about food, Rita found her taste and appetite shaped by her father's. And although there was no question in her mind that her father loved her mother, she was sure he stayed so thin because he hated her cooking. But Sunday was the only day he was allowed to enter the domain of his wife's kitchen.

The friends drank more wine, then devoured the bread. It was good, peasant bread, with a thick dark crust and a substantial, though air-filled, body. The women ate several pieces each, until it was all consumed and Margo, holding the empty basket upside down, signaled to the waiter with a broad smile for more. Margo justified all indulgence in food as a "healthy appetite." She liked the idea of being slimmer, but could never bear the sacrifice of so much pleasure. Because she had no trouble attracting men and her husband had no complaints (about her figure), there was nothing to trade off. Anyway if it came right down to it, she would have a hard time choosing sex over food or vice versa, each had its own and not entirely unrelated, she felt, rewards. Margo continued slathering the bread with butter.

"I've done it again," said Alice, who had stopped eating. She was absent-mindedly breaking a slice into tiny pieces, as if she intended to feed birds. "My eyes are always bigger than my stomach. I'm stuffed on the bread and wish I hadn't ordered such a big dinner. This heat and the wine on top of my period is making me feel real queasy. Excuse me but I'm going to have to go to the ladies' room and check the damage. Would one of you please ask the waiter if they could change my entrée for an appetizer? If it's not too late?"

"Do you want one of us to go with you?" Rita asked, touching her arm.

"No, thanks, that's okay, Rita. But if you could just take care of changing my order. It'll be a big relief not to have to think of facing a lot of food."

"Fat chance my period would ever effect my appetite!" Margo laughed after Alice left the table. "So how do you do it now, Rita?" Margo stuffed another piece of bread and butter into her mouth, paused briefly to chew, then continued. "How do you keep that weight you lost off? I can lose weight too, you know I can. In the last five years alone I've lost and gained a hundred pounds, twenty up and down each year."

Rita, unlike Margo, was more than a big eater, she was a compulsive one, looking to food for more than pleasure. There was something that was ravenous in Rita, a hole, a gaping hole, at the center of herself. It was an abyss where a woman should have been. To try to plug it up with chocolate was laughable, but she had tried. In fact Rita had been chubby from trying until a few years ago. Now she was lean. She maintained her weight loss by running with a permanently installed inner censor around food.

"I haven't been able to change my obsessive behavior, my compulsive eating, so I just redirected it. Whenever I find myself getting hungry too much, I cut back radically on my meals. I find I can never satisfy my appetite. I can only thwart it."

"Ah, but living without cake and wine is no paradise.

I won't do it! I have to have paradise right now. Slice up the angel food cake, heaven. No, I won't do it! Not by words alone does woman live! There's nothing more comforting, there's nothing cozier than a good meal like this with friends. Al fresco."

"I'm surprised to hear you getting romantic about food, Margo. You wouldn't stand for any kind of sentimentality in your work. You'd cut that scene so fast it would make Hitchcock's shower scene in *Psycho* look slow. Am I right? But you believe in an afterlife of chocolate mousse cake! I gave up on the idea of comfort after Nikos left. Nothing comforts me anymore. I lost that inner appetite and now the outer one is easier to control. Nothing comforts me. Well, maybe sex, but then . . . I'm not married. That might also help explain what the hell Pierre is to me, it's not comfort I find with him. It's something else. Something like distraction, but that sounds too flaky. I guess I can't explain it entirely. Even to myself. Maybe I'm self-destructive. That sounds plausible. Maybe I'm a nymphomaniac."

Rita was caught at the climax in her self-searching confession by the waiter who arrived with their dinners. He was placing each dish on the table with the slow and studied indifference of someone listening intently to every word.

"I guess it's too late to ask for an appetizer instead of the entrée for our friend, huh?" Rita was relieved to be interrupted.

"Rather. As you can see, all your dinners are served."

Just then, walking rather stiffly, Alice returned to the table. The sight of the steaming food made her grimace. She sat down and nudged her plate away from her.

"Are you alright?" Rita touched her arm again.

"No, but I will be. In a few days that is." Alice whispered to Rita to get rid of the waiter who was offering to get the "ladies" more wine. The "ladies" declined and then

Alice felt free to speak again. "The curse is early this cycle. What awful timing. Paul and I were going to go on a trip to the Catskills this weekend. Tomorrow morning. Now he won't want to go. When we're staying in a motel, he can't get far enough away from the bleeding woman on the rag. He hasn't forgotten our first trip together and there was real passion then, you know, the relationship was new and we were blind to everything. We woke up covered in blood. The sheets, even the pillow cases, were smeared with blood. The bed looked like the site of a axe murder. Paul was afraid of what the chambermaid would think so he left a big tip, a wad of money. I can still see it, those green American bills on the bloody sheets. It made the whole thing look much worse than it was. But who can argue with Paul?"

"Nikos never minded that, but I did. I have a lot of pain with my period, but luckily not so much blood loss because I'm constantly borderline anemic. Although the pain kills me, it's a tidy execution."

"I'm glad I don't know what either of you is talking about. I never feel a damn thing. A couple of tampons later and it's all over with. But more interesting than this talk of menses is your sexual behavior, Rita. What did you call it? Nymphomania?"

"Alice wasn't here for that part of our conversation. I was hoping we could drop it. You know me, I was just talking off the top of my head. I'm always blowing up everything I do *wrong* way out of proportion."

"But this interests me too much to let go of the subject," Margo insisted. "Nymphomania? That's a clinical term, but what does it really mean? Or more importantly, what do *you* mean by it? Do you mean you're insatiable? Do you mean you're constantly stimulated?" Margo waited for a reply, head tilted to the side inquisitively, as if asking her to describe flu symptoms.

"None of those things. I just mean that I'm compulsive and not discriminating enough in my choice of partners. That I use sex like a drug, like alcohol, to obliterate my consciousness, my loneliness if you will. My aloneness. With the threat of AIDS all around though, the act is now more like driving a fast car, following in the tire treads of a couple of existentialist heroes of mine, Albert Camus and James Dean, around the bend and smack dab into a tree. That's the only kind of suicide I understand. I feel like a sex junkie sometimes, promiscuous when it is no longer fashionable, promiscuous when it's downright dangerous. In the sixties, in the age of Aquarius and free love, I was an uptight middle-American virgin, if you know what I mean." Rita paused and started vigorously cutting up her chicken, a plump white breast. Flecks of rosemary, looking like pine needles in the sauce, clung to its skin. She skewered a piece with her fork, lifted it half way to her mouth, and paused.

Alice looked at the piece of chicken on Rita's fork and then looked quickly away. She had pushed her chair away from the table and it was clear that her legs didn't quite touch the ground. She seemed to be addressing her dangling shoes as she spoke: "Sometimes I think you're your own worst enemy, Rita. Pro-mis-cu-ous? I don't know what nymphomania really means, although I've heard of it, but I think I do know what promiscuous means and it seems to me that that's not you. If you were, I doubt you'd be hanging out with the girls on Friday nights."

"Let me explain what I think it means, Alice, I think it means indulging, yes, indulging is the right word, in casual and irregular sex. That's a definition that sure fits the bill for what I do with Pierre. When a decent guy comes along like Barry I don't know what to do with him. I let him go."

Alice interrupts: "Rita, you're too hard on yourself. Barry wasn't right for you. He's much too conventional. You felt stultified dating him. I hardly think you could have lived with him."

"Yeh, I can't believe you're still beating up on yourself for dumping that deadbeat," Margo added in agreement.

"Well, it was easy. I could tell that it wasn't love. No anxiety, no nervous palpitations, no . . . excitement! For in love I have to feel as if I'm in the grip of something that's bigger than myself."

"But do you have to be comatose? Brain dead? You must forget more than yourself when you jump into the sack with Pierre," Margo snapped in disgust, then added more thoughtfully, "What you have, Rita, is not a case of promiscuity, but fin de twentieth siècle polygamy, a form of monogamy that's actually consecutive polygamy. Does the fact that Liz Taylor is romantic enough to marry all her lovers reduce the number of her liaisons any? Alice is right. You'd be cruising the single bars, better known as meat markets, if you were a real slut — forget that Freudian shit, now there's a monosyllable with impact — and we know you're strictly vegetarian — if you ask me, it's Pierre who's the slut!"

"Bars! You both know that's not my scene, although they are full of men and the natural place to go, I suppose, if a single girl wants to meet some. But I wouldn't know what to say to them, you know, the kind of men you see in beer commercials. Sure those guys have cute butts in spite of the calories in the brew and all of them seem to be looking at the girls, but it's clear to me that they really prefer each other's . . . company."

"Don't we also a lot of the time? I mean to be fair to real men and not beer commercials."

"Alice, we can always count on you to sacrifice satire for good sense," Rita shrugged and smiled, "but it's easier to blame them when I'm not examining myself, my own behavior, you know."

"It's not all your fault, Rita. Till death do us part has lasted two years max for me and with one guy — remember the Dutch writer I met at the film festival, it lasted only two weeks. Until I met Paul that is. Margo here has been the exception for a generation I'd say. Her marriage is built on rock . . ."

". . . and roll. What about their fights, Alice?"

"That's our secret for a successful marriage. We yell and scream. We don't build up resentments. You're the one with a problem, Rita, and it's simple. It's jerks. You meet too many jerks who turn you into the dumb bunny who loves too much."

"No, Marg, Nikos was not a jerk. The problem was me. The problem was, is, in the way I love men I guess. I think I'm just trying to get away from myself or something in myself or not in myself. Oh hell, I wish I knew what I was talking about. I can't possibly really love Pierre, can I? So what am I doing?"

Both Rita's friends shook their heads in dismay.

"What bothers me most is that I'm acting against my better judgment and even my finer instincts. I don't know how it happens but I become strangely passive. I feel as if I'm in a trance when I'm with a man. I no longer know what I want or what I think. They have to want and think for me. I guess that's not classical nymphomania or sex addiction or whatever's the latest psychobabble term, is it? I don't even need to be aroused myself. I just need to be led."

"Laid. You just need to get laid."

125

12 *The Journal*

MAGNOLIA, the deep musk and sweet scent of a flower which simulates the odor of a woman's sex. Its blooms are startlingly white with an aureole of pink. Their oversize heads weigh down these diminutive trees, such a fragrant burden in the thick air of southern Ontario summer.

Few of the plants here are full grown trees. They appear to be new growth, like the nouveau riche in metropolitan suburbs. The flowers flourish with their beauty like small white flags. They are like the descendants of a second wave of settlement to Canada from the States, loyal to an old glamor.

You wake again to that scent of magnolia talc on female genitalia, as if you are still a boy, still sleeping with your aunt. Aunt Lucy, Our Lady of Nightmares. When did they begin and when had it become your responsibility to protect her from them? You remember Aunt Lucy, don't you? You remember her large overripe body, how it was mottled blue, like a melon going to mould. You were afraid to touch her, afraid your fingers might poke through to the other side, sink into softness, sink into sticky liquid juices and seed.

The stink of magnolia talc she used after her bath was overpowering, the talc she had shipped to her from Mark's & Spencer's, an anglophile affectation she preserved along with her black puddings and plum cakes. And under that scented talc was another odor, always conjured by the perfume emitted by such flowers: the smell of lilies as they begin to decay, both pungent and sweet, as if their vegetable sex too were composed of flesh, a flesh blown by flies, a flesh with its monthly letting of blood.

Such vapors are exuded by dying things, the green that foams in ponds. Salt stings the nose with its piercing odor, the salt that has failed to preserve the meat.

The labia trembles like a large underwater plant about to devour a trout.

Your arm would go numb under one of Aunt Lucy's enormous breasts. Sour, the smell of old milk from waxed cartons was her other smell. The first night she wore a frayed elastic contraption around her waist to hold up the sanitary pad. The night she pulled off her nightgown!

"It's too hot! Mickey! Oh, Mickey!" she called. "Remember to drink your milk. Your mother's milk. Remember your mother, Mickey, your mother."

You remembered nothing. She pushed her breast into your mouth and you obeyed. You sucked the vacancy from her larded breasts, white and riddled blue with veins, like the complex map of a foreign country in which you are lost. For which you are lost. You sucked that vacancy into yourself, the vacancy of women, your own new organ of blown glass, pure, yet malleable. A new life spilled from your loins. Where Mickey the boy had once been, Michael, the man, escaped like the poor bastard who, to finish something, hurls himself through the sealed window of an office tower.

Shattering with the glass is your woman's organ, the

organ that resonates within, from that diluvian, that inter-uterine time, before your male gender emerged. This is true to biological time. This is experienced as the ringing of bells, a ringing to be heard only by saints or hermaphrodites.

Your limbs felt leaden from sleep, sleep in a hot room, darkened by shades. Your room. Lily already up. Your face on her side of the sheets which she has stained with menstrual blood.

Aunt Lucy would die soon. She has been dying in the terminal ward of the Princess Margaret hospital for two months. Cancer has wasted her body. Her body has become skeletal. Only the smell, the familiar rotting smell hasn't changed, but has intensified, like desire for a lover you feel most sharply in her absence.

Aunt Lucy would soon die. You have avoided seeing her since marrying Lily. Lily has willingly and mysteri-ously assumed that duty for you. Aunt Lucy in hospital, her body reduced, a bag of old rags cast off for Goodwill, a bag which has already been rifled by the truly poor who live in the streets. You saw Lucy once in her private room at the hospital. What you saw was startling. You saw different features emerging from her face, a face which had with fat defied such definition for most of her life. A face more disturbing than even the face of those night visits to which you were led like a sleep walker. Mickey. Mickey killed a long time ago. The face of her brother, Mickey.

Yes, your legs feel leaden, ten pounds heavier, as if your body were retaining too much fluid. Your body feels like furniture transported to a rented and empty house, left in crates, wrapped in sheets, and shrouded in the dust of former tenants.

It must be a brilliant day outside because you feel blinded, like a man emerging from a cave into sunlight, squinting, or like a man stepping away from a powerful film, the images clinging to his eyes in sticky cobwebs he can't brush away. Whatever it was you wanted to see of the day, tugging at the drawstrings of the blind, hearing the snap of the roll as it flies up, you find instead a summer street where an adolescent body (boy or girl, your eyes can't focus sharply enough to distinguish) pulls a nearly empty wagon of daily papers. A small dog runs back and forth around the blue-jeaned legs, barking. That is not your body.

Your body is a body whose tickets and keys and money are in other hands. This is your body. A wooden puppet in the hands of a ventriloquist. This is your body. You can watch the show. You can watch yourself being manipulated but you are not afraid of what you might be made to say or do.

Mother, you called her Mother. No. Mickey called her Mother. It was Mickey.

You go to the bathroom. The mirror assaults you with the face of a blonde woman, her gagged mouth and bruised neck. You squat down and pull from out of the cupboard below the sink some Windex and paper towels. You spray the glass and wipe her face away. You begin to see that other face. Not the one you were born with, but the one that evolved. The fine lines around the eyes are the signs of an old age you were given prematurely, as a small child. Your startling platinum hair. You have the whiteness of an albino, but your eyes are blue. Today your skin has its own bluish cast. Nothing of pink and aerated flesh about it. But the blue of bruises. Bruises on some blonde girl's neck.

It was the deeper darkness of thunderstorms that made Aunt Lucy afraid, that made her call you into her room. It was not she, but you, who walked down the hall, ravaged by the blue flash of lightning, its sudden illumination offering you vision without sight. Blindly to the end of the hall, blindly to open her door, blindly to creep to her bed, blindly to touch the coolness of brass at the foot, the wonderful coolness of the metal you stroked. Waiting. Its coolness, for which you were grateful, was as unexpected and as welcome as the rough dryness of a snake's reptilian scales.

The woman cowered on her bed breathing heavily, puffing, rasping like a toad in a swamp. The bedding was in chaos, damp with her fear. Her lust. In between those musty sheets you lost the liberating freshness of the storm, its keen blade cutting into the heat and lethargy accumulated by the long, hot August day. The violence of the thunderstorm made you almost glad to be awake, to be alive after car crashes. As if from some highrise window you were watching gasoline tanks explode. They light up the sky above a stretch of highway. You view the victims and sip your tea. You walk away unscathed.

But in her bed you were immolated. The heat of her body, the heat of another body in bed. Her fear and her need for you were something you did not understand. What did it have to do with electromagnetic displays at night in the heavens?

On Victoria Day she would watch the burning schoolhouse and laugh. Together you would use up a package of sparklers, engraving things in the dark, important things you can no longer remember. Things you were unable to speak. Smoldering. Wordless.

Your daily routine feels like a subdivision built over a graveyard. The sunlight pours into the bathroom through opaque and stained glass. The window is open a crack to allow that breeze which sweeps in from over the ravine, with its fragrance of grasses, to enter the room. You smell the weeds that bloom there thickly, weeds that in naive mouths are pronounced as flowers. They are transformed through such innocence in the same way as a shaft of sunlight makes particles of dust, auriferous. Sunbeams.

You watch a seed clock drift through the window and settle on the blue Royal Velvet bath mat like a parachute that has abandoned its diver.

You showered before bed but this morning you need to shave. You got your exercise last night. Your fingers are stiff. You flex them for a few minutes, like a child in front of a toy he mustn't touch. He may only look. His hands open and close, open and close.

You shave your face, your neck. The face that you see sometimes is that of nobody you recognize. You are his barber. Who was your father that he should have to die again now through a woman's body? Who was your father? Your mother? You had too many. You had more than one. Too many mothers. Aunt Lucy. Lily. Your children's mother. Your former teacher. A teacher is a father. You marry her and she becomes your mother. She forgets her teaching. You are disappointed. You can't tell her that you wanted no more mothers in your life. That you hungered for a father.

It's later than usual when you go downstairs. The children are eating breakfast in the solarium. Lily is standing in the kitchen, sipping a cup of coffee, her back leaning against the counter. She has not joined the children for breakfast. There is no place set for her. She turns to speak to you. She opens her mouth and then shuts it again, like a fish out of its element, trying to breathe. She puts down her cup of coffee on the counter and approaches you. Her body seems to be moving towards you in slow motion as if dragging itself through shoulder depth water. She puts her arms around you, lays her head against your chest trying to comfort herself for what she has to tell you, as if saying it alone will make it effectively more real. As it must.

"Darling, I'm sorry, but your Aunt Lucy . . . they called from the hospital. I didn't dare wake you. They called earlier. They said she died. Michael, she's dead."

"Dead." You pronounce the word in an exploratory way like a chef tasting a dish he has prepared for others. One he does not particularly like. For someone he despises.

There is little doubt but that you knew this all along. You feel something like freedom to hear the parents who have been dying for thirty-eight years pronounced finally and irretrievably dead. A deep sigh, a shudder escapes from your body. It is something like what you have read in ancient texts described as the involuntary release of the soul.

It was no accident that pushed Aunt Lucy towards her mound of earth, but a long and lingering illness. Now you are your own man. That woman who came to look like your father, who spoke in his accent, his voice so dimly remembered, however altered in pitch, in frequency, is dead. And what, and who must follow?

13

Lily

LILY was driving the taupe colored BMW which was equipped, on Michael's insistence, with extra-heavy rubber bumpers. For a woman with a poor grasp of spatial relations it was extra protection against the hazards of parallel parking. All women, according to Michael, suffered from impaired right brain function.

Lily liked the car because of what she thought of as its unobtrusiveness. The vehicle was solidly built and low to the ground. But the autobody was not her body, she couldn't drive through a parking lot the way a cat can squeeze into and out of a cupboard.

With the glass rolled down and his elbow poking out the window, Michael sat silently next to her. A powerful draft blew his hair about, the wind like a woman in an ad for Aqua Velva, aroused by a whiff of cheap cologne, her fingers everywhere.

The children sat in the back, Tom behind his father, unconsciously mimicking him. The boy's arm was not long enough for him to rest it comfortably on the window ledge, so his elbow was pointing up as if propped in an awkward sling. The pose was his father's pose, but his coloring, dark hair and dark eyes, were his mother's. Against the opposite window sat Sophie whispering to her doll. The girl had her father's Viking blondness.

Tom seemed to ignore his sister completely, but was actually listening without letting on, his eyes darting sidelong glances. He held his head rather stiffly, tense from concentrating on not betraying any interest, but unable to contain a sniff of disdain at Sophie's ignorance of the gravity of the day. Sophie was just like any girl, still talking to her dollies.

Lily also listened to Sophie's whispers as to the cries for help of children buried in a mudslide, as to her own inner cries. Sophie was explaining to her Barbie that Aunt Lucy had died: "Like Gabriel." Gabriel was the wonderful tabby Lily had as a pet before she met Michael. Returning home late one night, a new moon subtracting light, Michael hadn't noticed the poor cat in the driveway. Gabriel had become slow and stupid with age. The cat should have been asleep, safe in his box with its hand embroidered quilt made by Aunt Lucy.

The irony of it was that Gabriel loved Michael. They excelled in being feline and beautiful and aloof together. So it must have been with regret that Michael pulled their pet, badly mauled, out from beneath the wheels, and silently broke its neck. It must have been with regret, although Michael never expressed any. Still, he helped the children give old puss a proper burial in the backyard. Michael had even purchased a rose colored granite stone carved in the shape of a cat to mark Gabriel's grave.

That had happened in the spring. It haunted Sophie. Death began to define itself for her under the lilacs where the cadaver of her pet fertilized the roots. She imagined his bones would emerge through the furred darkness: death baring its teeth. "Will the lilacs smell of cat? Will their purple buds become fuzzy like pussy willow?" Sophie would ask.

Lily had conducted the service. Sophie had whispered the only prayer she knew besides grace: ". . . Should I die before I wake". Tom had jeered at Sophie for making such a fuss about an old cat. He threw a stone into the shallow grave they had dug, Gabriel resting wrapped in an old comforter like a baby curled in sleep. "It's just a silly old cat." Tom jeered. "They use dozens just like him in experiments every day."

Lily often thanked God that her second child was a girl because it did not make it appear so conclusive that there was something wrong with her, Lily, when her daughter shared so easily in her sentiments. While Tom — Tom was another species. Male, his love dissipated in jerking arms, in irregular and unruly behavior, homely as his cow lick. Were all men and boys like that, she wondered? Lily had no male friends and she did not understand her husband. How could she judge? Even her father was a mystery to her. He had been an engineer working in South America, scouting for veins of rare metal. He had traveled and worked in dangerous, difficult, and unknown territory. How could a woman and a child, a daughter follow? Her mother who had wanted to go with him resented being excluded from his "adventures". But when he disappeared into the jungles of Brazil, all his caution for them seemed justified.

"I hope the funeral won't upset the children too much. I'm afraid it might be traumatic for them. Michael, it's not too late to turn back and call a sitter. Why don't we? It *feels* like a mistake to me."

Michael seemed to be thinking seriously for a moment about what she said or to be coming back from a great distance. He frowned in concentration, creating a furrow, an exclamation point between his brows. "Tom can handle it. I've spoken to him already, and Sophie is too young to understand anyway. There's nothing 'traumatic' in the service itself. It will be simple and mercifully brief if my instructions to the minister are respected. And I'm sure Reverend Sisley will comply. Aunt Lucy was tithed for life and even unto death. He should be satisfied."

As far as Michael was concerned the discussion was over. When Lily turned to look at him briefly he had already gone back deeply into his own thoughts. Grief? Was it grief? He lit a cigarette. She heard him inhale before she smelled the smoke from the tobacco. He flicked his ash into the tray on the dashboard. His smoking made her feel uneasy, anxious, as with the crescendo music, the escalating beat of the sound track of a thriller, for hearts pumping to capacity, fuelled by adrenaline. She knew that the man beside her, father of her children, was a stranger. She expected there must be an end soon to that obscure drama which was their life together. With no explanations. He never talked to her! Even if he didn't love her anymore, even if he had contempt for her, she wanted him to tell her plainly. She continued silently to agonize about his indifference. She thought that she wanted to be told in plain, unaccented, flat English, through which vowels drop and form as, on an oiled surface, do water globules, round and full and transparent. Then she could not fail to read him correctly. That way she would not fail to distinguish her wishes, her fears, from the reality of his feelings.

But they were driving to the funeral of the only parent Michael had really known. How could she ask him then, with the children listening? How would she even formulate the question that could encompass all the answers she needed? He had a right to his silence. A right to be withdrawn. That day. But did he have a right to his solitude?

Did she not also feel his pain?

Unable to ask the larger question, Lily asked about the simple act that was puzzling her: "When did you start smoking, Michael?"

"I've always smoked," he replied, and then in apparent and complete contradiction, "I don't smoke at all. As far as you and the family are concerned. It's a small vice. I like to keep it to myself."

"But of course, Michael." Lily rushed into an apology, distressed at what might appear a lack of sensitivity on her part. Wasn't she equally self-absorbed, absorbed in what he must be thinking or not thinking of her? "I wasn't criticizing you. But I am very surprised. Surely it's not like you! And I've never known! How could I not know? You never smell of tobacco . . ."

"Perhaps you forget that I shower regularly," and in a stinging tone he added, "Look at the bright side Lily, you don't have to clean up my ashtrays." This silenced Lily quite effectively. And he didn't relent in the least, knowing she was hurt, the wounded bird look in her eyes, enlarged and puzzled by pain, the fall of a young bird who has barely known flight.

He was glad to be able to sit back and smoke while Lily navigated the car through the heavy traffic on Eglinton to the expressway exit. She was competent. He could relax, assured that she would not allow her personal distress to interfere with her concentration on the road and jeopardize the lives of her family. But he was disappointed in his wife much in the same way as a man who thinks he has purchased something rare, a relic in Rome, comes home to find it is counterfeit and can be had more cheaply at the Woolworth's in the Latin quarter of his own home town. Lily's thoughts revolved around recipes and cleansers, managing the household, the children and their lessons. She had stopped thinking, she was no longer a professor but a maid and a chauffeur. She was a good chauffeur.

Such was the nature of his disappointment. He did not believe in female fears. Women liked to disguise those fears, their dependency, as self-sacrifice. He could not believe that it was sacrifice for her child that kept a woman at home, away from the demands of a profession. Their real motivation was far from noble. Women simply did not like to drive home in the dark. Women easily abandoned all ambition for security. In caring for children they tried to stay children. To avoid responsibility for their own lives. That was what women called *love*.

They were driving northeast on the expressway to Pickering. Aunt Lucy had continued to live in Markham township in her house. It used to be the 'country', acres of farm land all around. The open fields offered a sense of space. His aunt had hated the very idea of a condominium. Lily had tried to talk her into moving into town, to be closer to them and the children. "All that housing in a row, people packed like tinned herring." Lucy joked that she would prefer to wait until she died to be pickled.

At the funeral parlor Lily had cried, slow silent tears cascading down her face, spotting her blue silk blouse. She had always found Aunt Lucy endearing, a fuzzy, chatty, cheerful old maid in Laura Ashley oversized floral print dresses. Huge on her in the end. But when she was alive and well she used to squeeze her plump body into the flowery frocks. She also sported scented handkerchiefs and wore floppy straw hats in summer. Lucy liked pretty things. Perhaps she thought she could transform herself in that way.

A walrus in petits fleurs. That was how Michael remembered her. As a walrus. As a sea cow. That image was transmitted by an act of will over the unbidden image he was trying to block, the puppet in the box. In the end, when her body was wasted by bone cancer, the many folds of fabric of her dress draped as they were designed to do.

Lucy, the remains of Lucy, wore unfamiliar and lurid pinkish red lipstick, her eyelids were dusted in wedgwood blue. And there was an odor, but that odor was familiar, a scent, the scent that used to emanate from her, from her clothes permeated with a favorite talc. The powerful perfume of magnolia and something else assaulted Michael. That something else was barely disguised: fumes of the embalming fluids. He remembered too well the talc she smothered herself in, to keep her cooler in summer, to absorb the moisture, the excess perspiration of the overweight woman. It formed a sickly sweet paste in the crevices of her body.

Summer is a good time to die. The dead need not queue, waiting for the ground to unfreeze, for the earth to relax into soft loam. The job of the gravedigger is easy then. Warm and alive, the soil teems with grubs and insects, and the living, active, burrowing roots of plants and trees. The coolness below would be inviting after the fever of her last days, the coolness of a cellar we don't think of as the end for us, but as the aging of good things. Like wine or the storing of a harvest. Apricot preserves. The moulds that ripen our flesh like good strong cheese. To the head propped on a pink satin pillow Michael said: "You always liked to be comfortable!" He was shocked to hear his own voice, to have spoken aloud. In public. It made him feel uneasy. To have spoken so baldly to whatever might remain in the room, whatever essence of Lucy. Undead. A man of science, he was more superstitious than respectful of his aunt, of what thoughts she might now be free to read. He did not want to encourage visitations. He had been visited all his life. He knew ghosts. So he wanted to bow out with the mutual respect of diplomats at a banquet, freeing themselves from a wooden exchange. To move on to the dance and the drinks.

Lily had been watching him more closely, with greater concern, since he had spoken aloud. She darted around him, touching his elbows lightly, the small rapid movements of sparrows from branch to branch. Michael stood stiffly by the coffin. Only his hands were animated, deep in conversation with the invisible. He had not cried but his distress was apparent to Lily. And Lily felt relieved to see him suffer. She felt she could be in sympathy with his grief and so understand him better, suffer with him. She felt more like his wife at that moment than she had in years, since the birth of Sophia, when he stood beside her at the hospital bed, doing the deep breathing with her to help her control the pain of labor and the birth, which was like a sunrise they had waited all night to view together.

She inched closer to him, standing silently beside him, wanting him to feel her support without interrupting this last rite, his conversation with the dead. When he turned to leave, she had taken his hand and they had walked back to the car that way, holding hands. He had let her do it. She had held his hand. His hand hung loosely in hers as if it were resting in a much larger and plumper hand than her own.

When they arrived at the church that morning for the funeral, they saw a half dozen cars parked along the side road, the loyalty of the few friends in a spinster's life. The church was a simple building, constructed around the turn of the century, a rectangular box-shape with an elegant steeple which housed a bell, a real bell, that had to be rung manually to make its beautiful baritone resound. There were windows evenly spaced along the sides of the north and south facing walls. Outside, those walls were reinforced with new aluminum siding and painted white. That was Lucy's church. She had baked for it, prayed in it, and played bingo in the basement once a week ever since any of the parishioners could remember. For charity. Always contributing heavily to bazaars with new old clothing and knick-knacks she took a fancy to and then didn't know what to do with, and costume jewelry of which she was enormously fond for little more than a season.

Lucy had known the Reverend Sisley very well, both having aged with the parish. Michael remembered his frequent visits for afternoon tea. Especially when his wife had been ill. Michael would be sent out to play or driven to a movie and picked up three hours later and then dropped off on the way home by the priest. Poor Aunt Lucy, a love life of boys and priests and now the sweet kiss of earth dropped from a spade. He might have been better able to laugh or sympathize had he not been a victim of it.

Inside the church, the light shone through the stained-glass figure of the archangel wielding his sword in a cerulean heaven. It made Michael's own pale hair seem blue and other-worldly. His head was bent, striking an attitude of prayer or avoidance. They all listened to the minister's eulogy for Lucy Skelton, the late and generous Lucy Skelton, who would be missed, her generosity would be sorely missed, although it was a generosity they would continue to enjoy because of her will. Lucy's final gift was a tithe on all that Michael would inherit.

In the end Lucy was rich enough and thin enough, everything that a woman might want to be. Within the polished wooden casket with its plain cross inset in ivory on the lid, Aunt Lucy would be buried with the exquisite cheekbones Michael had never seen in her real life. Cheekbones bequeathed to the afterlife. To cultures of moulds.

If it was scandalous that her heir and former ward for whom she had been everything! a mother! had hardly visited her through her illness, let the Reverend cast his sidelong glances, his judgments. The unselfish Lucy who never complained of neglect. Because she had no right to! They had not spoken frankly or looked directly into each other's eyes, to see that carnal knowledge they had of one another since Mickey was fourteen, since the Reverend had gone back to a recovered wife.

The service was over and Michael joined the pall bearers. He helped carry the left side of the coffin, the left side where the fluttery heart of the old maid had once been beating. The coffin felt incredibly light to him, as if it were made of popsicle sticks glued together, the kind of box he had used as a child to bury a pet frog, while it was still alive, as an experiment. He had wanted to dig the amphibian up again and study its skeletal remains.

Yes, the casket was light, but it was Michael's legs which were incredibly heavy. His feet felt swollen and blunt, as if he were balanced on two club feet, his knees rusted and rigid, the tin man left out in the rain. Michael had no heart. He wanted no hearts. They were all like emptied boxes of chocolates, the kind sold on Valentine's day, the candy invariably stale. The heart-shaped boxes were ornate, meretricious, reminiscent in their construction of the satin lining in Lucy's plush casket.

Michael swayed under the lightest of burdens as if he alone bore the weight of that burden. Old Mr. Clarence Northwood nodding his head at him in encouragement was satisfied now, judging him to be a man, a man who did not display his feelings, as a man should not, but who felt the loss of his aunt deeply nonetheless. The wives did not understand. That was understood. They judged manliness to be coldness, perhaps the calculation of an heir too busy bookkeeping to care.

Lucy was to be buried in the churchyard. This was a privilege their family had been awarded as special benefactors of the church. The yard was crowded with old graves of historical interest, and Lucy had liked to walk among them, in fact had often taken him as a boy to visit his family, to read their headstones. Now Lucy's stone was to read something sentimental from Shelley that the Reverend had chosen for her. The stone was Sisley's gift, the parish's gift. To honor and remember her there had been a special collection made among the congregation for money to purchase it. But the bulk of the cost came out of Sisley's own pocket, the inner vest pocket by the heart: "Why dost thou pass away and leave our state?\ This dim vast vale of tears, vacant and desolate?" from the "Hymn to Intellectual Beauty."

By the open grave they all took turns sprinkling ashes on the coffin. Sophia burst into tears, rubbing the ashes she had gathered in her fist around her eyes. Lily lead her away to clean her sooty face, to try to console her. They walked down the new asphalt path leading to the rectory to wash up, Sophia's sobs and the click click of Lily's black pumps. Michael listened to the weeping and the sound of retreating footsteps, the female wails, the heels.

Tom slapped the ashes on the coffin like turtle wax, as if he were polishing the car, and then he brushed his hands clean on the back of his gray dress flannels, lifting the back flap of his navy blazer so that the dirt wouldn't show. Michael observed it all but didn't say anything to his son. He was withholding to the end his own gesture. He wanted to be the last to greet Lucy on earth. The first to damn her to hell.

Lily was touching his arm: "Darling, it's time to go. Are you all right?"

"Fine. I'm . . . fine?" he muttered as if he did not understand what the word meant, "fine" sounding like a cipher in a foreign phrase-book. In his mouth he had the sour aftertaste from drinking milk.

"Shall we go to the reception the Sisley's have so kindly arranged? We should go to it Michael because it was really our place to hold it for her friends. They've been most gracious to make all the arrangements."

"And well they should. Lucy paid them handsomely to do so. In advance." He paused, dropped the acid tone, and said very quietly, "You go if you like. I can't. I won't. Please call a cab for me. I'll wait here for it."

Lily went into the rectory to make their excuses. Nervous and apologetic as she was, she did not offend. Mrs. Sisley cupped her hands around Lily's hands and patted the fist they formed as you would a child's. And the Reverend blessed her. Then Lily had to pull Tom away from the dessert table and pick up Sophie from the couch in the library where she had fallen asleep. When Lily returned, having taken the children back to the car, she found Michael standing exactly where she had left him, immobile as any of the statuary that decorated the tombs. She led him away like a sleepwalker, as if careful not to wake him.

Back at the car, the children were waiting quietly. Tom was hunched over a book, reading, and Sophie was singing softly to herself under her breath: "London bridge is falling down . . . my fair lady O-o-o-o-o-o."

Lily drove again. She was exhausted, preoccupied, and

trying very hard to concentrate on the road when Sophia broke into a horrible wailing cry. "My dolly, my dolly, what have you done to her?"

"What's the matter? Tom, what's happened?"

"I haven't the foggiest notion what she's squawking about, Mother."

"Look, Mommy, look." Sophia removed her seat belt and poked her head between the bucket seats to show Lily her Barbie doll, "All her clothes are off. And her head's gone!"

"Tom! Where is Barbie's head?" affecting her sternest voice. "Give it back at once!"

"I don't have it."

"Well, where is it then?" The boy didn't answer. He grimaced after Lily had turned her head round briefly to give him a meaningful look, but he pulled the doll's head from his pocket anyway and silently gave it to Sophie. Seeing the doll's head renewed Sophie's whimpers.

"Darling I'll fix it, ummmmmmm, her, as soon as we get home. Or I'll get you a new one. So don't worry."

"I don't want a new one! I want her! Is she dead, Mommy?"

Lily sighed deeply. "Darling, things that can be fixed are not dead. Please sit back and do up your seat belt. It's dangerous. We can't be so easily fixed. And if I can't repair Barbie, I'm sure your Daddy can."

Sophie brightened with hope. If her Daddy would do it, she was sure her doll would be healed. "Daddy would you fix her at the Hospital? Would you, Daddy, would you pleeeeeeassssse!"

"Yes Sophie, but only if you'll stop that sniffling. Give me the doll." Michael took the Barbie in one hand and the head in another, looking at one part and then the other, as if he were unsure of how they might be connected. The torso was made of smooth rubberized plastic. Large featureless mounds representing breasts were sculpted on the chest. The belly was flat with clearly defined muscular lines as if the torso were indeed supporting a uterus. The buttocks were also sculpted with a copyright mark and the date 1966 engraved in the small of the back. *Philippines* was written where the tail bone would be. He pushed the head back onto the knob of the neck with a twisting motion.

The doll had blue eyes and matching eyeshadow, pink cheeks, pink lips, clear white and even teeth smiling from the permanently parted lips. The hair was long, a pale, shimmering silver blonde. He had placed the head on backwards so he adjusted it. It made a small squeaking sound as he turned the head forward. The legs were long with seams down the front and back. The bare feet were arched, so the doll could not stand without support. She balanced precariously on her toes as if wearing invisible high heels. At the bottom of her feet were holes, one on each foot, as if stiletto heels might sprout out of them. The legs were attached on a rotating socket on the hips, very high on the hips, as if made for deeply, cut-to-the-waist body stockings. They could rotate almost full circle, perform amazing contortions.

"Did you fix her Daddy? Did you fix her?"

Michael stopped his examination of the doll, as serious and as studied as a professional examination of a patient, and looked back at his daughter over the top rim of his eyeglasses. He straightened the doll's limbs and handed her over to Sophie. "She's fine. If you can find her clothes, you can dress her again."

"Oh, thank you Daddy! Your the *bestest* Daddy in the whole world! I'll cover her with my lace handkerchief for now and then if Tom won't tell me where he put her peaches 'n cream dress I'll feed his G.I. Joe to the big dog next door."

Lily felt she had to put a stop to *that*. Her voice was sharp. "I'm surprised at you, Sophie. Getting destructive is no way to settle your problems with your brother." Then she pointedly directed the rest of her remarks to her son, "If Tom wants to wear her dress, next time he'll have to ask for permission first. To *borrow* it."

Tom squealed with outrage, "Take the stupid old thing!" He pulled the doll's dress from the crack behind his seat and threw it at Sophie. It was so light, a bit of pastel fluff, thin synthetic silk and tulle, that it seemed to float towards Sophie, an empty suit, no survivor, moving through deep space.

14

Rita

I T was a perfect day with a hot, lemon yellow sun and cool wind. It was a day for drinking black steaming mugs of coffee and eating gelati. Bitter and sweet. Fire and ice. Rita sat with Alice and Margo in Alice's living room. It was a day too good to waste the way they were wasting it: looking over patterns for china and silver. Paul, Alice's live-in companion and now 'fiance', had bowed out of this particular decision-making process. He had cornered Bo, Margo's husband, as soon as the couple had arrived and abducted him to the lake to windsurf.

"What a rat. Running out on you like that, Alice! It's his responsibility to take care of this wedding shit. It's his mother's idea, isn't it? You should let him get married without you!" Margo bitched for Alice. Margo was irritated because she hadn't seen Bo all week. Margo had hoped to drop in on Alice, offer her expert advice on cutting through the bullshit in the nuptial preparations, and then slip away home where she had a pitcher of martinis and two cocktail glasses chilling in the fridge. An afternoon of love as during those blissful and lazy days that memory alone, alas, was re-running for her in golden sepia tones. She thought it would make them both feel better about each other. Golden, as in sensuous, sun-bronzed skin, not golden as in senior citizen. Bo had been working nights and she had been at the studio day and night producing her latest film. More than twenty years of marriage, but still she needed something from him on a regular basis. Margo was the kind of woman who never had a headache.

Alice's reaction to Paul's refusal to do his share in the wedding preparations was simply to become mildly depressed. She was glad to have her friends there to humor her, especially Margo, whom Alice could count on and allow to be angry and contemptuous of Paul for her, to express the frustration, the anger, she would never allow herself to vent.

Paul and Bo had met through their women and had become close friends. Their bonding was convenient for Paul and vital for Bo who found himself isolated because of his job with the police department and his "strident" wife. Bo often needed to be reassured of the logic, at least on his part, of his arguments with Margo. During the worst of their disputes, he would stay out all night, camping on their couch. Bo would get up with Paul, who woke with the sun, to have breakfast together while Alice continued to sleep. This gave Bo the time he needed to hash over with Paul the details of his latest argument with Margo. It was important for him to know what another man thought. Otherwise he might begin to believe he was crazy or stupid, that he had to be dead wrong every time.

"Why am I doing this?" Alice moaned as if she did not know the answer. "She must think I belong to the yacht club or something. It's not practical, silver. I'm going to have to keep polishing that stuff. Or at least for her visits. I know Paul won't do it. He says we can just keep the 'shit' closed up in its box, drag it out when his mother comes over for visits. And that's turning into almost every weekend. She lives in London, Ontario, not alas, London, England, where her standards are set. It seems like a waste. Real silver. My stainless steel cutlery doesn't match but it's good enough for me. It's a lot of money spent on stuff I don't want."

"Alice, why don't we just pin the patterns to the wall and throw darts."

"But, Rita, you don't understand!" Alice declared. "I'd already picked a pattern. I chose something called Homestead, the cutlery with looped handles and Blue Willow pattern for the china. But mother-in-law-to-be decided that they didn't go together, plus she didn't think that they would be appropriate for our lifestyle and social calling. 'Choose again,' she orders!"

"Phew! You're marrying into that! I know what I'd do. I'd tell her to set her table where the sun never shines."

"Come on now Marg, Alice couldn't tell off her cat let alone her mother-in-law!" Rita took the catalogue from Alice and peered intently over the patterns.

"How about this one, 'patrician', it's relatively plain, it has some small detail work, but seems inoffensive enough. And dammit if it doesn't have a snooty enough name. It's probably more along the lines of what your mother-in-law may have in mind."

"I guess so." Alice said weakly, then added more warmly, "Thank you, Rita. I'm really sorry to bother you with this at all. If someone had said to us ten years ago — or even six months ago — that we would be spending weeks trying to decide on china and silverware, I would have said you're crazy. Why does wanting children and getting married have to change everything so much? And Paul's mother, who has been ignoring my existence, hoping that I'll just go away at some point, has to phone me every day with some detail or other, as if she were the mother of the bride and not the groom. The wedding's strictly for them, you know. She's reserved a country inn outside of London. The guest list consists of their family, and you girls for me, but mostly their family, which I suppose I am marrying into."

Controlling her ennui over Alice's in-law problems, Rita suggested they move into the garden. Margo asked for another drink, to which Alice replied: "Sure, Marg, help yourself."

Rita laughed as she exclaimed, "She usually does!"

"It's a good thing you're laughing, Rit. Otherwise I wouldn't know that was supposed to be funny." And then she asked, "Are there any lawn chairs out there or should we grab some on the way out?"

"You'll have to drag them out from the back porch. I thought it was going to rain last night so I took them all in."

While Margo was poking in the fridge to see if she could find anything good to eat as well, Rita and Alice dragged out a few lawn chairs and set them up. The garden was big and beautiful with a shade maple to one side, near the house, and a vegetable plot in a sunny back corner. The tomatoes were ripening, looking bright and plump among the lanky and trailing green beans, the young zucchini. The romaine patch was overgrown, curly topped leaves, turning to purple.

Margo came out with a large tumbler of iced tea. She dragged a chair into full sun and sat back, stretching out, crossing her legs at the knee. She was wearing short shorts. When she walked, the cheeks of her buttocks hung out generously. Such shorts had been fashionable and daring the year before, now they just looked daring.

"You don't go walking around in those things do you, Margo?" Rita asked.

"What do you mean, walking around? Of course I do!"

"Well, they're rather revealing aren't they? Summer is hoot and holler time enough isn't it, without provoking it?"

"Provoking, eh?" Margo was visibly irritated. It was most annoying to have this kind of comment coming from another woman, and a friend at that. The kind of comment she expected only from the worst of men. A parable would be necessary to enlighten her friend's point of view, so she launched into one of her sermons on the lawn chair: "Well, you know the first time I saw somebody in these shorts, I was driving the car east along Bloor Street. I remember it was a Saturday morning, the twins were sitting in the back, this was quite a few years ago, they were still just boys, reading comics and squabbling in the back, not the students of political science and philosophy at McGill they are now. Anyway, back to our story, the heavy traffic was not office bound, but The Bay bound. And this cyclist, much more nimble in the traffic than us in our family wagon, was speeding ahead. The cyclist was peddling like a racer, body bent, almost hugging the frame of the bike, if you get the picture. From the back view, the buttocks looked higher than her head. And those legs, so graceful, so slim, were pumping overtime to move the bike. Let me tell you, I was jealous. It even crossed my mind that I should run her down when I saw that Bo's eyes had darkened and narrowed with what he likes to call 'appreciation'. Then we were alongside the cyclist. I wanted to get a look at her face. I was hoping she was a real dog up front. Boy did I feel foolish. The cyclist was a man with a day's growth of beard! I wanted to get behind him again so I could have another look. Made me wonder what had made me think the cyclist was a woman. Was it his slim shapeliness? Was it the fact that the body was on display? Boy, he was beautiful though, he was a dancer on that bike."

"An interesting anecdote and it proves my point, although in your story the danger comes from a jealous wife!" Rita laughed.

"Cut it out. I'm serious. I'm trying to make a point. And it didn't happen that afternoon. My point is something that might have happened and is a kind of philosophical projection from that incident." Margo looked into her glass, drained it, and turned to Alice. "Have you got anything real to eat?"

"I've got some hamburger. I thought we'd make a barbecue and all have dinner together when the guys get back. I was going to suggest that. They should be here soon. And they can play the backyard chefs. They like that."

"I think that that's a delicious idea, but I was thinking more in the short term. Immediate gratification. Got any nibbles?"

"Gee, Marg, I'm sorry. Paul wiped out the chips last night watching *Saturday Night Live!* I've got some animal crackers and that's about it."

"Forget the cookies. We need them like a hole in the head. I want to know what point you're trying to make with that story, Marg."

Just then they all heard the car. Paul was parking in the garage at the back of the house, the entrance through the lane. The men were red faced, sunburned, from the intensity of the light on the water. Energized by their outing, they seemed younger than when they had left a few hours before. The men entered the scene like a squall.

Paul was slight in build, with a thin beard with bald

patches. He was certainly no longer a boy, yet he acted like a boy affecting the manners of a man. The deeper tones of his voice resonated in a rehearsed manner, echoing with the hollow timber of the broadcaster. In contrast, Bo was a rangy, large-boned man, who was unconsciously masculine through sheer size. He had a large dark moustache and bushy brows that grew together in a single dark arc bridging his eyes. His voice was raspy. It made everything he said sound whispered, secret, intimate, as if directed to your ear alone. It was sexy, although he didn't need that in his line of work. He wasn't on television; he was a detective with the Metro Force. But that voice made people inclined to think he might be on the other side of the law. At times he found their mistake useful.

Paul made much of his own windsurfing abilities. He bragged about having to help Bo pull himself out of the water twice. Bo took it all in good humor. He was generous in nature and secure in his manliness, not macho. He was inclined to indulge Paul because he needed Paul to help him think things through all the time, the women-things about Margo which baffled him because he hadn't graduated from university, he thought.

Both men went into the house to get bottles of cold beer and then they came back out again carrying their chairs under one arm and a bottle by the crook of its neck in the free hand. Margo was complaining about the seats. "These plastic weaves always leave welts on your bare skin. They stick. You shamelessly continue to betray your class, Paul, working for legal aid and shopping at Honest Ed's."

"Don't blame Paul. Keeping these chairs is my idea. It's not his fault. As you know I've had them for years, from leaner times. Maybe I should replace them, but I get attached to things. I feel that I'm losing more than an object

if I throw something away. I feel that I'm losing all the after-
noons that you've lounged in these chairs bitching about
them, for instance."

Here Rita found an opportunity to bring the conversation back to their earlier discussion: "A couple more
inches of material on those shorts, Marg, might help!"

"What's bugging you anyway, Rita? You got something against female buns or what? If I were a man would
you still be complaining?" For the benefit of the men, she
retold her story. "Do you remember, Bo?"

Appalled at being described as leering at another man,
Bo denied it. Margo ignored his denial and continued with
her argument: "Suppose it had been another street. Suppose
it were residential say, and late at night, or say, even Bloor
street, but nobody around, like three a.m. on a Sunday
night, and I forced him over and had my way with him; or
say you, Rita and Alice (since Bo doesn't remember a thing
anyway), were with me, and we forced this guy off the road
and raped him. So he reports it to the police. What are they
going to ask him? Lieutenant Bo Civic Force, for instance,
are you going to ask him what he was wearing at the time?"

"That's not only a hypothetical question, it's an absurd
one. I've never had a report from a man of being raped by
women or a woman. Technically I don't think it's possible. Another man, that's another matter. What do you think
Paul? Ever had a client ask advice about whether to report
or press charges for rape — male clients that is, female
rapists?"

Paul sniggered, "No. But there's that case in the States:
the beauty queen who chained the young Mormon to her bed
for a week. That would be pure fantasy for me and the guy
wanted to have her jailed!"

"What I want to know is: do you ask women who

report rape what they were wearing or don't you?"

Bo gave a resigned sigh. "Yes, we ask them what they were wearing, where they were and why, where they've just been, anything that might be pertinent to the crime or might have precipitated it in any way. But most men can't be raped, not by women at least, because they have to be willing, they have to perform. That should be obvious!" Turning to Paul, he said, "I'd like to know how that Mormon got chained to her bed in the first place."

"Dunno. I think the story's apocryphal. Something to do with the reaction of the American press to feminism. On the rampage they think."

"Yeah, you can't even trust a beauty queen these days to smile and spread her legs!" Rita grinned in mock Miss America fashion, showing off her immaculately white and beautifully even teeth.

"Bo, you're wrong. Men can be raped. I bet I could do it. If I wanted to, that is. Men have to get turned on, maybe, I'll give you that, but they don't have to be willing! Isn't it just possible that three women could turn a man on, in a way he doesn't really like or want? Arousal during rape is a red herring that has been getting male rapists off in the courts. It doesn't change what they've done, how they've hurt. It's still a crime. It's a humiliating experience. You're used and then you're trashed. What's more it's even more humiliating to report it to the police. That a man would be as much a victim as a woman in such circumstances I have no doubt. What makes it rape is that the act is forced. Against a person's will. We all know what happens if you get turned on during a rape and you're a woman, legally that is. Does she begin to feel responsible for what she didn't want? Is it no longer a crime then? And frankly, chances are, the way things happen in mediaville, television land, and Hollywood films, with their mixing of sex and violence — that Molotov cocktail — you're more likely to get turned on during a rape than on a weekend holiday with your boyfriend!"

Bo was angry and discomfited. He hated having to take the stand in Margo's court for the whole of the Metro force, for The Police everywhere and anywhere in the world, their billy sticks wagging, mostly in their pants according to her. Bo hated to have to stand in for that primitive, violent race called Men. To take the rap for every man. He was getting tired of it, almost too tired to defend himself any more.

"That's outrageous. And you know it! What's your real beef in this?"

"My beef, as you call it, is veal. That women are encouraged to be, expected to be — and then dismissed and ignored if we're not — sexually attractive. We're valued that way almost exclusively. Then we're cross-examined if we succeed in being 'ravishing'. Sexual appeal suddenly becomes sexual lure, sexual come-on. Hey, it means we're asking for it. When some man decides he's going to take a woman like it or not. Men can be attractive and not worry that it might justify an assault."

"Okayokayokayokay. We're onto that again. Well I agree with you. And attitudes are changing. The law will catch up eventually."

"But will men catch up!" Rita broke into the discussion, "And by men, I mean rapists. I wasn't blaming you for how you looked in your shorts, Marg. I wasn't siding with *Them*. I just don't want it to happen to you or me. Call it discretion, discreet dress. What it really is, is camouflage in a guerrilla war."

"Well, I don't agree. I could be wearing a halter top or a string bikini or a track suit and it would amount to the same thing. It could happen anyway. The outfit isn't the trigger. The only difference between the victim in a bikini and the victim in a nun's habit lies not in how the rapist treats her — you can't change that easily, not with those sickos — the difference lies in how the law treats her."

"You make it sound like the police are the problem. Tell it to the woman raped in High Park one afternoon last summer. She wandered around, bloody and in shock, all the concerned citizens passing her by. Till the police came along. She might have a different point of view on that."

"And then she might not! But I'm not blaming the police. I'm just pointing out that their line of questioning reflects the very things about this society that makes rape not only possible, but as I see it, probable." She looked at Bo directly, saw his distress, and modified her tone. "Without men like you on the force — Oh, listen to that word, no less, The Force — Bo, it would be *Most* probable. But it really pisses me off. Twenty years of feminist debate and liberal talk and the rape victim still has to prove that she is *Innocent* before her attacker can be proved guilty. What kind of justice is that? The rapist doesn't have to prove that he's innocent, he's innocent until proven guilty, he has his human rights and all the benefits of our judicial system. Something's wrong here. In a recent trial — did you hear about this one? — a judge came right out and said that a rape was less serious, not a major offense, because one of the rapists had been her boyfriend. The guy brought a bunch of goons along. It was a gang rape, but it wasn't serious!"

"She might have been better off just charging them with assault."

"That's right, Rita." In his capacity as legal counselor, Paul pronounced, "It used to be worse, before the rape shield law, all a woman's sexual behavior could be brought into court. And now it's on the table again, questioned, as you know. I think they should reclassify rape, change it to assault. We're getting action along those lines. It would make it easier to prove that a crime has been committed. There's so much old morality, Victorian sexual attitudes, associated with the word rape that it obscures the whole matter."

"Yes, Paul, you're with me on this one. To change history, you have to change the language, the legal lingo. But our laws and judges come right out of that Victorian mindset, when sex was thought to be something that happened, if regrettably, only between consenting married couples. In the dark. In their nightgowns and long johns. For purposes of procreation."

Margo pulled herself out of the lawnchair, unsticking her legs, gave the back of her thighs a brush as if she could rub away the red welts. She went over to Bo and put her arms around his neck, cooing in his ear. He placed his arms around her waist and she sat on his lap. Two giants. Rita wondered if the chair would hold up. Margo could forget an argument as quickly as she could start one. "Are we going to barbecue or are we going to go home? What do you want to do, Bo? Let me warn you that the meat at home might as well be on the hoof. It's in the deep freezer."

"I have plenty of hamburger for us all. Some chili dogs as well, made of tofu, for Rita here. We can put them on the grill. Sweet corn, salad fresh from the garden. I was hoping you could all stay. Paul will set up the barbecue, that's his job. I'll prepare the patties. Rita, you're in charge of salad. Bo is the chef, and Margo, you can set up the picnic table and keep the drinks going."

"Sounds great. I'm going to get another drink for myself right now. Something my grandmother wouldn't *imbibe*. Anybody else want one?"

So they all busied themselves around the preparation

of food and drinks. Five adults, no children around, five adults in their middle years, but feeling very young, basking in sun and companionship. Although Rita, Paul, and Alice had yet to leave their 'youth' for the responsibility of family, Margo and Bo had earned a second one when their two sons left home to study at university in Montreal. Over twenty years ago, the couple had met at a protest march, Bo, the cop, Margo, the political protester, burning her bra on campus. The passion of such conflicts still fueled their relationship.

Paul was having trouble negotiating the barbecue. Bo decided to help him. "Get us both a drink, will ya? Tell Margo to make mine stiff! The way she knows best!" he chuckled.

When Paul and Margo returned from the kitchen together, they were both tippling from their rum and cokes. Margo handed Bo a big glass. Bo stood expectantly, spatula in hand, as the meat broiled, spitting and sizzling as the fat dripped into the fire. Bo probed the biggest patty, the one he had marked off as his own, every few seconds, afraid of over-cooking it. The others seemed to like their meat 'burned', so he didn't worry about theirs. His burger was beginning to stick a little. He tried to help the spatula out with his finger and accidentally touched the grill. Lightly, but enough to scorch his skin. He sucked his finger silently for a moment without complaint. The finger blistered, the skin rising like a pocket of fat in the broiling meat.

"Are you wounded in the line of duty?" Margo joked.

"Thanks a lot. It's pot shots at the cops today, all day, I suppose. Especially your husband." He stuck the edge of the spatula into his burger. It bled red in the middle and he lifted it off and set it to the far side of the grill, away from the flames, where it would stay warm but not continue to cook too much. Using the spatula to conduct his speaking, Bo wagged it vigorously to get the group's attention: "I hope that you'll never have to wish that there were more of us on duty. I know one woman who must. She was raped in her own apartment last week. She doesn't know how he got in either. Picked the lock. Easy as ABC, I could have done it myself with a credit card."

"What happened? Did she recognize the guy? See him?" asked Rita, who felt the most at risk of the women there.

"Actually, it's quite a grisly story. One I'm telling you because quite frankly I'm worried, but we're not going public with it just yet, so keep this all under your hats. Her neck was so badly bruised, it's a miracle she's still alive. He tried to strangle the poor kid. But it's a strange case, and not the only one like it that we've had recently. The girl said that she was starting to black out and the next thing she remembers is that he's nursing her, getting her to drink a little water, take a few pills, checking her pulse. Real professional. Apparently he was going to kill her and then something happened, something like conscience maybe, anyway he relented. Can you figure it?"

Bo paused, spatula raised, going over the details of the case silently in his mind, then he continued. "That girl never saw his face. He wore a stocking over his head, pulled tight, flattening his features. The guy had no reason to kill her outside of getting his jollies that way. He must've known that she wouldn't be able to identify him. Anyway, as I said, keep this under your hat. Margo, you're my wife, you know everything I do. And Paul, you're a lawyer, you know what confidentiality's about. There are several recent unsolved cases like this one. We've got our man. His modus operandi, that is. We only need to find out who he is!"

"You think it's one man? How many cases are there?" asked Rita.

"Quite a few, four reported, so there might be twice that many. It's hard to say. No dead, no bodies to stack, thank god. John Harrison spotted the M.O. and started keeping track of those cases together, trying to find any links, you know, among the victims. All the women were single, living alone, and basically residing in this west-central radius of three or four miles of Toronto the Good becoming Toronto the Dangerous. None of the women knew each other. None of them saw his face. We know that the guy wears pantyhose over his head, knotted in the back in a pony tail. The basic build fits. None of them thought they knew him in any way or recognized his voice. Somehow he finds out about these women. First he rapes them. The sex is over in less than two minutes from what I gather. Then he tries to kill them, all in different ways. And that takes a while, that seems to take much longer. It seems to be some kind of a vicious game. He stabbed one girl, missed her heart by a fraction of an inch. We think he knew exactly what he was doing. He must know anatomy. But he didn't let her bleed to death. No, he doctored her up. It's easy to guess that he's had some sort of medical training. Pretty damned sophisticated too I might add. He could be a nurse or a paramedic. But my guess is he's a doctor. Not only does he have access to supplies, pills, he's had some surgical experience as well I would say."

Margo jumped into the monologue at this point. It didn't take her long to formulate some questions. Bo sometimes accused her of taking even less time to draw conclusions. "Did you check the victims' doctors? Whatever you do you should double check the gynacologists. If a doctor's a real misogynist, most often they seem to specialize in that.

Because just think of the opportunities for loathing and torture!"

"Yeah. Harrison's already done that. Came up with zilch. That's why he's asked me to help him with the case. He's been working overtime. The wife claims she doesn't recognize him when he comes home from work. She sets the dog on him. The animal who cheerfully licks his face. At least the creature's got some sense even if she doesn't! Anyway, we're keeping all of this hush, hush, till we figure out what's really going on. We don't want to alert the guy that maybe we're on to him. We don't want copycats either, trying to cash in on a free ride, or getting caught and taking the rap while the 'real' psycho, by that I mean the more inventive one, gets away."

"Did any of the women die?" Margo asked.

"No. In fact, I don't think your average psychopath could pull it off successfully. But I wouldn't bet on it and it sure don't stop them from trying. The severe shock these women are in is bad enough. I saw and talked to the most recent victim. I don't want bodies, dead bodies, on our hands. There's a level on which I find sex crime incomprehensible. I don't know what to compare it to."

"I do," said Rita. "It's like Jonathan Hawkins in Bram Stoker's *Dracula*, turned into a geek, eating flies, rodents, trying to swallow as many lives as possible."

"Yeah! There are some cannibals among them, that's for sure! I can see an element of that. But to snuff a life for a sex thrill is like killing somebody for the small change they have in their pocket," said Bo.

"Get off the pot! You don't know what you're talking about there. It's primal stuff. It's not a transaction!" Margo responded heatedly.

Bo looked at her and shook his head. "Marg, I don't

mean to underplay the seriousness of the crime at all. I'm sorry, believe me." Then noticing that his burger had darkened enough to be considered cooked, he said: "Give me a break! I'm supposed to be cooking and my burger is burnt!"

15
The Journal

WHEN she turned off the tap, the silence which ensued seemed deadly. It felt surreal as the silence of the wilderness where somehow a waterfall has been shut off. A torrent dammed. A stillness where no bird sings, where no insect announces its singular, needling presence, a stillness where some feline crouches, ready to pounce.

The woman bent over to test the water temperature of her bath, running her hand back and forth, back and forth, an idle paddle where a current does all the work of transporting the canoe. Drifting downstream.

I was watching her through the crack of the half-open door, her body caught in a bar of incandescent light, like an insect preserved in amber. The bedroom itself, where I crouched, was dark except for a small reading lamp that had been switched on by the bed. It had the romance of a room lit as if by a single candle. If I should place a bottle of white wine to chill in a bucket of ice, I might be mistaken for a lover, not an intruder.

She dipped her foot into the bath and pulled it out quickly again, running more water from the tap. The tub was steaming, eerily, like a lake in the woods in the morning after a frost. In the fall. The way we imagine the waters of prehistoric times were cloudy with evolving life. Choking with sea monsters.

Her long, lightly rippled, copper hair, was burnished light, like a sunset reflected on a dark lake. It parted naturally around the nape of her neck into two thick ropes, as if she had worn braids all her life.

A large black mole signaled the beginning of her left buttock. A dimple, one above each cheek, gave a soft yet sculptural effect. As she squeezed and released the gluteus muscles, she rotated her hips, first to the right, then to the left. Then she stretched her whole body, balanced on her toes, reaching with her arms, as if pulling some imaginary rope. She was dragging an anchor from the ceiling.

The red-headed woman was darkly tanned to the bikini line of her hips. The center of her beautiful back was defined by a bra line. It made her seem more obscenely naked, a brown girl in a dazzling white bikini of flesh. I wanted her to turn around and show me her breasts, exposed as if by a bra in which the cups have been cut out.

After testing the water again, she turned off the tap. Bracing herself along the sides she eased herself into the tub. She sighed deeply as she lay back and shut her eyes. Her hair was bright sea algae. Her hair was a red tide.

My fingers were checking my face for the nylon, like a blind man for the features of a stranger. The coarse bristles of my summer rapid-growth beard poked through the sheer weave of the hose. It felt itchy; I would need to shave again before I could sleep.

Some things are set up. Some things decide themselves. I would walk into that bathroom removing first all of my clothing. All except for what most appropriately might belong to her, the nylon stocking, my mask.

The white trillium of my sex was erect. The white trillium with its purple center, richly veined, would lead the way like a divining rod. To water. To the spirit.

16

Lily

LYING in a bath filled with very hot water, oiled and perfumed, was for Lily more than a luxury. The steam, the texture of the water altered by the bath oil, were almost enough to propel her into that sense of existing in another dimension, the planet before genesis and those nagging burdens of sex and food. Lily soaked in the tub, her dark curls drowning at the nape of her neck, her head resting on an inflated bath pillow. She watched her body, white and swollen, enlarged and blurred by the fluid lens of the bath water. She watched her finger tips gradually pucker and blanch. This session, alone and out of time, though not outside of routine, was as essential as those little blue pills she had to swallow to sleep.

The baths were barely enough for survival. Survival of the senses. The skin is the most expansive of the organs of sex.

But she had to have the pills to supplement, to relax fully. As two bright blue bodies dissolved in her stomach, her thighs melted too. They were buoyant, glistening mounds above the water level, which she observed idly as she lay back, arms resting along the sides of the very large and antique bath tub. The tub was set on a raised platform. It felt like a stage. The antique porcelain surface of the tub was more radiant than her skin, she thought.

Supported on carved, bronze paws, the tub was a fabulous creature from some mythological realm. Its spout was in the shape of a griffin's mouth through which steaming water continued to flow, just a trickle to keep her bath very hot. The pipes sang and her anxieties diffused. She often nursed a fantasy in which she waved a vaguely poached hand as the tub became animated and flew away with her through the skylight. Somewhere.

Could she get the bath hot enough, she mused? It would have to be boiling. She remembered a story she had read in the newspaper about a couple in a hot tub somewhere in California who hadn't noticed the intensifying heat as they drifted into unconsciousness. Their bodies were found curled in the fetal position, two lovers, in the end as indifferent to one another as are any organisms laid out for a meal. For a repast. Pink as shrimp bobbing in a clear and aromatic broth.

She wouldn't be afraid, she thought, to fly away forever. She would be elated. She could see the dark shadow of her tub crossing the full and harvest moon.

Lily bent to turn on the tap more fully. Boiling hot water poured out of the bronze griffin's mouth, its gaping beak. The gargoyle's eyes watched her floating legs. Those white, bobbing thighs seemed only vaguely connected to her, as if they were two kites for which she had forgotten she held the strings. Her legs were barely longer than the legs of her daughter, and certainly shorter than her son's, who seemed, at this point in his development, all legs. Lily's limbs were the exact length of her twelve-year-old self, at which point she had stopped growing. These child legs on a grown woman's body made Lily want to laugh.

Her legs were fatter than they had been and dimpled now, but not very different from those of the adolescent girl who had loathed the changes in her body. Lily had panicked at the emissions that had dyed the waters in the toilet bright red.

The sexual metamorphosis had been disturbing. The shock from the new growth of pubic hair had made her body feel alien to herself, as if she had suddenly sprouted feathers. She had shaved her vagina because she found the hair coarse and ugly. But the itching from the re-growth had been much worse.

Black blood with its smell of decaying fish. Like the sand dollars the children had found on a trip to the ocean. The shells were brown, coated as if with fur, slit on their undersides. The children forgot about their collection, left them in the trunk of the car for a few days. But Lily would never forget the stench. She imagined the gangrene of amputated limbs to smell and linger in the air that way, the same inviolate odor. Those sand dollars had to be properly treated to be saved. That brainless muscle, its body, its being, exhumed. Dried to the color of chalk or bone, with the texture of fired, unglazed clay, the shells could then serve to ornament your home, find a niche among the knick-knacks.

Lily thought of her children asleep. She had dutifully tucked them both into their beds, the boy reluctantly submitting, the girl licking her hand with a kiss like a kitten with no roughness in its tongue. Michael had been closeted in his study, the room eerily dark except for the hot glow of his desk lamp casting a red aura around his pale face. She had knocked and opened his door to wish him a good night. He had looked up from the pages of a periodical, peering over the rims of his glasses at her or rather in her general direction as if not understanding something. He had cleared his throat and she had closed the door and climbed the stairs to run for the refuge of her bath.

To be possessed by a house or a household, which was lonelier? Lily had no friends. She had had to sacrifice them all for Michael who did not believe in friends. And her colleagues had not approved of faculty women marrying younger men, a former student no less; she had jeopardized her chances for a tenured position.

Her family had been no help at all. She had known in advance what her mother would say. Her mother lived by aphorisms, a less kind mind would say clichés, what the woman substituted for thought, what she believed to be wisdom. Something like, "You've made your bed; now you must lie in it." Her mother had refused to even try to influence Lily about her marriage to Michael, although she never warmed to him. She called Michael Skelton an "odd duck" when she probably meant "cold fish." Lily's lover, Lily's husband-to-be.

What did other women do in her situation, Lily wondered? Was there a manual she could consult for the would-be wayward wife? Her literary models ended disastrously: Anna Karenina, Madame Bovary. But for examples from contemporary life should she look to day-time soap-operas? Should she ask Oprah what to do?

Did Michael ever pick up women in bars? Lily dismissed the idea right away, not because of his love or loyalty towards her, but because she couldn't imagine what he would find to say to them. She giggled at the thought and then was startled by the sound of her own laughter. It sounded foreign, like a western jingle played on a sitar. No, she couldn't imagine Michael making chit chat with some strange woman. What could he do? Offer to check their breasts for lumps? But patients — how many patients would be drawn to him? Those women would see him at his best as the brilliant healer. They would trust him and then they would depend on him, which was next to love, if not love itself.

17
Rita

THE setting sun bruised the sky to violet. As the light turned blue the air seemed to thicken and slow Rita's jogging pace along the beaten earth path of the ravine. Her legs felt weighted down, as if she were wading through water.

The slopes of the ravine were fragrant with wild grasses and blossoms. She ran to the lub-dub of her own heart beat, to its crescendo, not to the banality of rock variations played on a Walkman. She was dismayed by joggers equipped with their canned music, as remote from the natural world as astronauts moving through the atmosphere of another planet. They were all deaf to bird calls, deaf to the melodious scales robins sing to each other in the evening, deaf to the intense pitch of cicadas singing in the high heat. At least for the most part, these philistines kept the jingles that moved their hips to themselves. When she heard "Candy Man" leaking from one woman's unit, Rita, with a sprinting action, passed her as quickly as she could.

That evening Rita had pushed herself to the limits of her endurance, pushed herself into the bloodbath of light that was the red and setting sun. Then in the dusk she had walked slowly home, cooled as if by the silvery lamplight. The waistband of her running shorts felt wet and cold against her hot skin, her T-shirt clung to her breasts and shoulders.

The house was dark. She bent over to pull a key out of a zipped pocket in her running shoe. As she turned the key she thought about the worst part of living alone: coming home to a dark place. By the lighted dial of the digital clock in her stereo system she had to make her way to the switch on the floor lamp in the living room. The green illuminated numbers were flashing. She would have to reset the time. Luckily Rita had not come home while the power was still off because she could never remember where she kept her emergency candles. Anyway, she suspected she had used them up for a dinner. A small sacrifice for romance?

Rita pulled off her damp T-shirt. Her shorts were also dark with dampness at the crotch and at the back where the perspiration had run freely from along her spine. She switched on the light to the stairs and made her way up to the bedroom. Her legs felt leaden and tight, especially her thighs. While she ran a bath for herself with some lilac scented bubbling salts, she did some more stretching, concentrating on her quadriceps and hamstrings.

The bath would help her relax those muscles. She had pushed herself hard and felt the reticence of her body, the protesting around the joints. The body had to be pushed to its limits to get beyond those limits. It was difficult to associate the pain involved with "growing pains". Such pain had a purpose, a benefit, but did it have an end? Perhaps there was just one end she could imagine. The obvious one.

Exercise experts and enthusiasts glorified the many benefits of sports. For the narcissist, body tone and retarding the aging process. It stopped for nothing; not even for the revised faces emerging from beneath the hands of the

Brazilian plastic surgeon. For the addictive personality and the depressed, the runner's high. That was what Rita wanted, escape and weight control. She had never loved her body enough before. In her twenties she would have envied her current figure. Now all she envied was the Rita who used to sleep in until noon and wake only to make love with Nikos.

One hand gripping the top of the stair railing for balance, she pulled her calf a little farther back to increase the stretch in her quadriceps. Through the open bathroom door she could see a mound of bubbles rising from the tub. She released her leg and ran in to shut off the tap.

The door bell rang the moment she dropped her shorts to the floor so that she had to pull them right back up again. It seemed part of a single and continuous action. She cursed at the timing. She felt very damp and sticky and chilled. She did not want to look in the mirror before she answered the door. She had some idea of what she looked like just then and she knew it wasn't good. Her hair was matted around her brow line and straggling at the back of her neck. She hoped it would be Margo calling on her and not Barry or Pierre.

The doorbell rang again. A very long ring and then an impatient short one. Rita pulled on her top, draped a towel around her shoulders for warmth, and ran down the stairs bare foot, yelling as the doorbell rang again, "I'm coming!" She jumped the last two steps, landing lightly on the balls of her feet, and sprinted to the door, pulling it open wide.

A tall, squarely-built male figure stepped out of the darkness. There seemed to be something predatory in his stance, a man lurking about the house, a man who has just stepped back from spying at her window. Rita's reflex was to slam the door in his face, but he stepped inside before she could react. With relief she saw that it was someone familiar, Bo, dressed in his blue wranglers and a gray sweat shirt. Because of his neatly cropped gray hair and very black moustache he certainly looked like a cop. Although he had always been a big man, Bo's promotion meant that most of his time was now spent at a desk which accounted for a weight gain of twenty-five pounds. The clothing that used to fit him so naturally looked constricting.

"Glad you're home. I'd just about given up and was leaving."

"Sorry to make you wait. I was upstairs running a bath." She looked down at herself. "Excuse how I look. I just got back from a long jog in the ravine." She gestured in a off-hand way to her pink shorts with matching top, some white netting at the midriff, in a shiny satin-like material which had become opaque with dark wet spots. She knew the outfit was pretty when it was fresh. "Come in. Sit down. You want a beer or something?" She loved Bo and felt herself relax with him as with her women friends. She trusted him. She thought that men like him should be cloned so that all women might be happy. Margo was lucky.

"Sure," he said stepping into the living room and looking around very thoughtfully. Then he turned to her and asked: "How do you run in this heat? You've got stamina, kid."

"It's not so bad in the evening. No direct sun and lovely breezes in the ravine. The vegetation is positively lush. You can smell the chlorophyll. There's more oxygen in the air. I swear you can smell it."

Bo followed her into the kitchen where she went to get the beer. She opened the fridge and pulled out two lites. She turned around and accidentally walked right into Bo's arms because he had trailed too closely behind her.

Rita laughed, "What are you doing? Shadowing me?"
He laughed too.

"Listen, you're out of luck," she said, "all I've got is lite beer. Would you rather have some liquor? I've got some Gordon's."

"Nah. Give me the lite. Tastes like piss, but Marg has been giving me the business about the spare tire." He despondently poked the generous bulge hanging over his belt. "I notice you've been keeping pretty trim. You look good. You wear a lot of pink, huh?"

Rita could imagine how she looked at the moment and she was sure that it was not *good*. "Yeh. I wear pink to disarm my enemies."

Bo looked bewildered at that and said, "Maybe. In that artsy-fartsy business you're in. Not the world I know. Not out there, not out on the street, kid, where they're looking for victims. What can happen when they look at those shorts ain't rosy. Yeh, those shorts just might be a neon flag."

"Now that sounds like me preaching to Marg the other day. Am I getting back some of my own good advice?" she smiled broadly, with ironic tolerance.

"You're getting more than advice." He pulled a small package out of his pocket. It was a gift wrapped in the colored comics from the weekend paper. "I was going to give it to you for your birthday and then I thought that your birthday's a long way off and I'd feel pretty foolish saving this deadbolt if anything happened to you in the meantime."

"Thanks, Bo, I . . ." Rita very impulsively gave him a great hug and quick kiss on the cheek. Then, suddenly feeling a little awkward, Rita turned to rummage around in a drawer for the bottle opener. Her hands were searching, but she couldn't find it among the spatulas and whisks.

"Forget it, Rit!" Bo said as he removed the cap with his teeth.

"Good goddess, Bo. You didn't have to do that. Here's the stupid opener."

Then she added, throwing one shoulder back, hand on hips, rotating that shoulder, in an imitation of the exaggerated come-on of Mae West: "There's a little macho in the best of you boys."

"Yeh! It disillusions your girlfriends!" Bo smiled wryly on one side of his face.

"That's right, Bo," Rita continued, laughing through her nose, "but I'm not criticizing you! I'm only teasing. You know me. We've got similar contradictions in us, men and women both. Clint Eastwood turns me on. I want to marry him and make him my care bear, if you know what I mean. I want to be the blonde bombshell you respect and promote into *positions* of uh" — she paused for comic effect, so that the double entendre could be fully savored — "of uh, responsibility."

Bo gave his rapid fire laugh, then took a long drink from his beer bottle.

"I don't suppose you really wanted a glass for that, did you?" Rita laughed.

"Nope, thanks. This is just fine."

"Well, it's too gassy for me straight from the bottle," Rita said as she pulled a mug out of the cupboard with GIRLS JUST WANT TO HAVE FUN written in bold red caps.

After downing the beer rather quickly, Bo burped and asked Rita if she had any tools.

"Yes I have tools, a complete set. You name it, I've got it. Screwdrivers, hammers, metal files, wrenches. I even have an electric drill my father gave me for Christmas a couple of years ago. I used to watch him fix things around the house. I guess I picked up a lot subliminally. I find I can handle most of the small repair jobs around here. I'm not intimidated by mechanical work. I had a roommate in college who literally couldn't change a light bulb. She'd panic when one burned out and wait for me to get home. The last time I saw her, she had her own place, a TV with some rabbit ears sitting on top. They weren't connected but she couldn't figure out why the reception didn't improve no matter how she pulled and arranged those shiny and apparently insensitive antennae. Anyway she was the bad example that made me glad I grew up to be Ms. Fixxit."

"You're something else, Rita. Margo with all her bluster and twice your size is more like your former roommate. She waits for me to do everything. Unpaid housework I call it. And unappreciated too. But this is one job I'm going to save *you*. Think of it as part of the gift, to make up for the lack of proper wrapping paper and card."

"Sure, Bo, thanks. But this is still a pretty safe neighborhood, isn't it? Or is there something I should know about?"

Bo hesitated, not wanting to scare her, but then thinking perhaps she needed a little scaring. Better scared than dead for this woman, he thought. His wife Margo was cocky and that was okay, that worked as a kind of protection, but Rita had this air of vulnerability, in spite of her smarts, which worried him.

"Let's not waste time. Get the tools," he said simply. "I'll tell you all about it as I work."

When Rita came back up from the basement with a bright red tin tool box, she found Bo at the front door, fanning it back and forth, testing the hinges, checking the wood. He opened the tool box, rubbed his hands together and set to work, talking to Rita without looking at her, his body concentrating on the task at hand.

"This won't take me five minutes. I've put in a few of these locks before, both at the house and our cottage. How about some music to whistle to as I work?"

"Sure. Great idea." Rita hit the play button for the record she had been listening to earlier that evening, a medley of jazz vocalists — "mere alcohol doesn't thrill me at all" — witty Cole Porter lyrics, Dinah Washington's clear, vibrant alto getting no kick from champagne.

Bo shook his head sadly as he inserted each screw, concentrating in the effort to be accurate. Then he tested the door. He put the tools away and brushed his hands off on the back pockets of his jeans. He was pensive, a frown line dividing the eyebrow that grew straight across, in a single sweep, over his dark eyes. "Remember those rapes I told you about at the barbecue? The rapes John Harrison is investigating?" he asked, joining Rita on the couch.

"Yes. It gave me the creeps. The guy's obviously a psychopath!"

"Methodical. Intelligent. The worst kind. Not like those hell-bent bikers! Yeh, the bikers' behavior is pretty crazy. Totally wild. Apparently those guys are acting out very primitive and undisguised emotions. These psych seminars I get sent to really help me with my job. Confuse things you know, so that you don't know who's the good guy and who's the bad guy anymore. But that kind of destructiveness is not evil in my book. That's a tornado, if you know what I mean. The damage they cause is a kind of accident. Because if they're unconscious, then they can't be fully responsible, can they? Mind you I book them if I catch them and throw them into jail. I throw them into jail and I feel safe once they're in there. They don't frighten me until they're out again. But when a criminal is obviously using his head, when you can see the logic operating in what he does, whatever his motive might be — money or sex thrills — it's never worth the human life he destroys to get it. I see that as a real failure in our society. That shakes me up. I need to believe in the system to be a cop. I need to believe in human intelligence, a higher order of things, not just in bigger and better self-service franchises. I don't want to be in any way working for that guy, if you know what I mean."

"You're trying to catch him, aren't you? What do you mean working for him? You know, it seems we spend a lot of time and energy explaining why two young thugs bludgeon an old lady to death with a baseball bat because of their unhappy childhoods. And it doesn't change anything. We don't put our money where our mouth is. More of our tax dollar goes to build better jails, create professional killers in the army, than for daycare."

"I guess so. You know it's easy to bust small time crooks or kids pushing drugs on the street, some chick with a dime of heroin who's peddling her ass. They don't understand the system so it steamrolls them. But your white-collar criminal gets away with murder because he built the system and so the system believes in him. For me it's a big problem. There's got to be a way of making judgments that's not corrupt. When the big time drug pushers — importers may be the truer name, more like corporations — never get caught, I know there's something wrong. It makes me wonder about my job. So I prefer homicide. I have a better chance of arresting the right man."

"Listen Bo, this discussion is making me thirstier and you more despondent. Maybe you'd prefer a real drink now?"

"Sure. Come to think of it, make it one of your gimlets. But easy on the lime cordial. I'd like an extra splash of
soda and lots of ice."

"But I thought you loved my gimlets! You always rave
about them!" Rita was ready to pout over the one thing
she made that she prided herself on. She never cooked.

"I do, I do!" he exclaimed. "I just need a light-on-
the-calories version of it. No offense intended against your
world-famous recipe."

Rita laughed heartily at this. It was an explanation
that she couldn't argue with. They moved back into the
kitchen and sat around drinking at the little table in the
breakfast nook.

"This mystery, this case, it's bothering me. It won't
let up. I worry at it all day long, night too, like some tooth-
less hound at an old bone. What I think I understand about
crime is probably a product of my Catholic upbringing.
That's your background too, so you know what I believe
about wrong-doing and sin. Remember how we were taught
that it's not a sin unless you know it is and go ahead and
do it anyway?"

"It's not a sin, it's a tornado! You're quite a convincing speaker. How else could I continue to listen to such
crap. You missed your calling. You should have been a
preacher or a judge."

"Okayokayokay, so I didn't go to college but let me tell
you I have to make my way along with the graduates in
psychology and criminology. After I interviewed that girl,
the one I told you about last weekend, raped in her own bed,
and I was trying, I'm still trying, to understand what happened to her, well sometimes it makes me question it all.
Harrison asked me to join in the investigation. Strictly it's
not homicide, but it stinks like it."

"So what have you found out? You were going to tell me."

"She lives on Chestnut. The victim. You know where that is? It's practically in your own backyard!"

A prickle of fear ran down Rita's spine. That evening she had walked along Chestnut on her way back to the house. Her mouth felt suddenly very dry so it was hard to speak. "Did you know that last Sunday?" She bit her lip.

"No, I didn't know a thing about it then. I just talked to the girl on Friday. Harrison had talked to her before that, but he doesn't know you, so the street didn't mean anything special to him. And —" Bo paused as he looked at his empty glass, then interjected, "I guess I really slugged that one back." He showed Rita the empty glass. "I have to have another one. More Gordon's this time though."

In order to deflect the tenderness and the attraction she felt for him, Rita pretended to be annoyed with Bo. "I was wondering why it took you a full week to run over with that lock. Some friend you are!" But she smiled and added, "Just kidding! You know me, Ms. Kidder."

She walked over to him, touched his cheek gently, took away his empty glass, and went to the counter to mix more drinks.

Bo followed and continued to explain himself. "I talked to her on Friday. I went shopping on Saturday. I drove by your place. You were out. I'm here again today and I've installed the lock for you. Now I expect you to use it. That I can't do for you. Look through the spy hole before you open the door at night or anytime for that matter. This guy is working your neighborhood!"

"I guess I really should be scared, huh?"

"I think you should be careful. Use the lock. This whole case is going to break to the papers soon. I don't

183

think we can keep it under wraps much longer, nor should we. We're no closer to catching the guy, yet rapes like this are happening at a rate such as this city has never seen before. If he were a real killer, it would be like having Jack the Ripper in our midst, but one who isn't slumming for the most part, one who seems mostly to prefer women like you."

"How cheering it is to know that you're wanted!" Bo's intensity was making Rita nervous. She handed him his drink.

"You're wanted alright, Rita. Never doubt that." Bo pronounced this very softly, as he brought the glass to his lips, just before taking a sip from it. Rita wasn't sure if she heard it right.

"What's Margo up to tonight?" Rita asked belatedly, peeking up from the depths of the drink she was pretending to contemplate.

"I don't know." Bo had quarreled with his wife and wanted to feign indifference. He squared his shoulders to prove it. "And quite frankly I don't give a damn," he said too hotly for it to be true. "I haven't seen her today. We had another fight yesterday and she threw me out. Some weekend I'm having. So I slept at Paul and Alice's last night. I'm fed up. I've had it up to here," he said, his hand under his chin, pushing it up to demonstrate the limit of his tolerance. "She has to fight every battle she has with the outside world, with capital M-E-N, with ME. These late-blooming feminists are the worst. I met her fresh out of high school, a preppy undergraduate, one summer and whammo, we tie the noose. She was going to university because that's where the boys were. But those hippies weren't too keen on matrimony. Then I saved her the trouble of completing her education. When she was rewriting her story I became the obstacle."

"Sometimes Margo takes it out on the wrong people, her friends, whoever's in the line of fire. But you have to admit she has guts. She's not like this guy I once dated, very political, you know the type, flirting with the communist party. He raged all through dinner that he had been served white toast when he had ordered whole wheat. He raged at *me* throughout that whole dinner, but went tweet, tweet, tweet, whenever the waitress came around and when she asked how we had enjoyed our meal he smiled for the first time that evening. It's easy — and a moral imperative of sorts I suppose — when the proletariat are not your relatives, or girl friend, for that matter. God, and to think I went out with that guy for the whole of my first year in college." She took a sip of her drink. "I've never been so liberated that I haven't tolerated assholes."

Bo complained bitterly: "Margo always takes it out on the wrong people. The wrong man. Me." He lightly rocked his drink from side to side, making the ice cubes clink. Then he put the glass down and began to pace restlessly. "Listen, Rita. Do you mind if I smoke? I hate to do this to you, to someone who's managed to quit, but I need one badly." He threw up his arms as if in defeat.

"Go ahead. I haven't buried my ashtrays." She went to the windowsill and brought back one of those anonymous round tin ashtrays you see in cheap restaurants and cafeterias. It had two cigarettes half smoked and stubbed out in it.

Bo lit up one of his Matinée Lights, not commenting on the butts, but surreptitiously examining them.

Rita didn't even try to resist smoking. She took the package from Bo's hands and pulled one out. He lit it for her without comment. She bent too close to the match and felt the phosphorous searing her sinuses.

Smiling whimsically, Bo said, "I suppose I should feel guilty, except that I can see this ashtray has already had some action. You've had some company there."

"Oh, I haven't really stopped smoking entirely, you know, but I've cut down a lot. Really I have. Do you think I could run and smoke like a trooper at the same time? My trick is not to buy them anymore. I figure that bumming smokes from friends will inhibit me. Shame me, you know. But I seem to be shameless at times. I have to admit that I've even been mooching them from my secretary. Still I've cut down to maybe a pack a week. Not bad, eh?"

Rita slid open the patio door and created a draft. "Getting a little stuffy in here with our smoking isn't it?" The breeze carried in the perfume of mock orange from the garden. As if their fragrance rendered them incandescent, the bushes glowed faintly white. Nikos had planted those bushes. Their scent was loyal to him and disturbing for Rita. From nowhere, perhaps because of the lingering scent of the mock orange, more powerful in the summer heat than the smoldering tobacco, and the muted strains of music coming from the living room — "Everytime We Say Goodbye . . . what in the world am I supposed to do" she felt a slight shiver — "How strange the change from major to minor" — and the tranquil sadness which follows when moved by music or sex.

Then Rita sucked on her cigarette with the anxious look of a baby getting no milk, just a lot of air. She suddenly felt very tired, relieved not to have to talk for a few minutes. She shrugged her shoulders trying to loosen up, to free them of the invisible weights that seemed to be balanced on them, bell-shaped brass weights with 50 kg. engraved in Roman numerals. The more clearly she visualized them, the heavier they became.

"You get a lot of stiffness in your neck, don't you? Desk jobs do it to you. Let's move back into the living room. If you stretch out, I'll give you a massage."

The living room was only dimly lit. Rita put on the soundtrack to *Last Tango in Paris* because she loved Gato Barbieri's sax, the parody of Latin dance rhythms in the score. Then she switched on another lamp, an old brass one with an octagonal shade and thick ivory satin with gold tassels. It looked as if it belonged in a boudoir. The lamp seemed designed only to keep light dim for intimacy. So Rita switched on the spot light she usually used to read by as well. "We need more light. We don't want to nod off in mid-sentence after our drinks, do we?"

In the center of the room was a thick Indian carpet in muted shades of turquoise and pink. Rita dropped to the floor and stretched out on the rug, cushioning her face with her hands. Bo knelt closely beside her and started kneading her very tense neck and shoulder muscles, unknitting them slowly and methodically, applying pressure at various points with his thumbs. The massage made Rita cry out with something between pleasure and pain. Bo continued to massage, deeply, hypnotically. They no longer spoke. Bo worked his fingers along the spine down to the small of her back. Then he moved to kneel astride her body and sat down on her buttocks. She could hear his deep and regular breathing louder than her own. His weight was warmth, his weight was seductive force, but the stiffening of his penis broke the spell. Rita could not afford sexual intimacy with her best friend's husband, not morally or emotionally. She looked up for guidance from the digital display of the stereo: 11:15 p.m. was not etched in stone. Time was catching up with them.

"It's late, Bo," she gasped, squirming out from between

his legs. And he didn't try to stop her. He moved aside immediately. He didn't speak but his eyes were searching hers, her mouth, for some sign connected to what was happening between them, but she avoided his eyes. She made herself busy with picking up the glasses, denying the intimacy through chatter.

"I hate to throw you out, but if you don't go back home you'll have to think about crashing somewhere and I'm sure Alice and Paul will want to know one way or the other soon. Are they expecting you?" she asked, flitting nervously about the room, straightening pillows, moving ornaments, the frames of family portraits.

Bo got up slowly and a little stiffly from his knees. "Yeh, I'd better shove off. Paul has an early morning court date tomorrow, so I think I might as well try and go home and face the music."

18

Lily

ILY woke to darkness. On the nightstand, the illuminated numerals of the digital clock radio flashed from 5:03 to 5:04. She pulled herself wearily out of bed. Her legs felt leaden. The sheer blue silk of her new negligee from the Dreame Shoppe clung to her thighs. She felt cold. The lingerie was a useless yard of fabric. She had been hoping that it would make her feel pretty.

Lily pulled aside the curtain to look out. The moon was still bright, the moon that forced a swelling in her blood. That moon was gibbous, waning from full, its left side losing definition. Face of long suffering, pale face singing, features stilled in the bass note of a requiem mass.

Seated on the edge of the bed Lily looked down at her thighs and legs in the moonlight. Her thighs seemed wider than they were long, the clinging material dimpled with her flesh. She wanted the angular thighs of models, models in ads for Calvin Klein jeans. Those ads made her ache strangely with more than sexual desire. She felt a yearning more powerful than the response she imagined a male might have: to possess, to penetrate. She felt a yearning to annihilate herself. To be that other.

A woman obsessed by an unrequited love. A woman hopelessly in love with her husband. It felt more quaint than ironic. Irony would allow her to feel superior to it. No, she was a fool. A middle-aged fool, that's what she was. A woman who did not know she was a matron, a woman demeaned by adolescent cravings. She longed for the leveling out, the change in glands which released wisdom instead of estrogen into the bloodstream.

She turned to look at Michael, who was a bulky form under the bedding. His broad back was turned against her. His breathing was regular, deep, and hypnotic. She listened. Could she enter his dreams, the way he entered all her waking thoughts?

Absorbed by her concerns about her husband she had no thought for herself, for what she was, for what she might become. Her thoughts were only for vacancy, for what she was not.

Near the clock was the phone and by the phone was a glass of water. She filled the water glass every night, even though she never woke from thirst or nightmare to drink from it. Little air bubbles rose along the sides of the glass.

It was still dark and perhaps that was enough to account for her sadness. It felt like a winter morning. She was awake too early. What she felt was a simple sadness, a seasonal disorder. It was the melancholy induced by the autumn equinox. Each day would offer less and less light, each morning would offer up a deeper darkness.

She tried slipping her feet into her slippers, left neatly beside her bed. They were tireless servants standing at attention, anticipating her need. The slippers felt tight. Her feet must be swollen. She was eating too much again. She couldn't walk past Bon Ton, the pastry shop, without experiencing such a weakness in her knees that it forced her to stop and purchase half a dozen chocolate eclairs. Then dizziness forced her to stop again and sit on a bench in the park where she ate them all. The rich white cream would squeeze out the sides as she bit into each cake. Lily got rid of the evidence of the box in the trash bin, but later she found traces of the cream on a sleeve of her navy wool jacket. So she scrubbed the evidence off with an old toothbrush and some liquid detergent and then sent it to the dry cleaners. No one would ever know about it.

She pressed her guilty, greedy, abdomen which felt tender and sore and was perfectly oblong as a football. She wanted to kick it.

The air was beginning to thin, turning gray and blue. It was getting progressively lighter outside, but the house, the bedroom clung to its own darkness. Some child walked along the street pulling a shopping buggy filled with newspapers. The child seemed to be moving in slow motion. It was a young girl or a very thin boy with long hair, falling to the shoulders. Lily could not even be sure of the gender of the child who delivered the paper because the Skeltons paid for the morning news through the mail and the service remained anonymous.

The child turned up her walk, folding a paper very tightly, rolling it, pulling an elastic band over it. Those were the dark blue bands Lily pulled off while brewing coffee. From closer up, Lily imagined then that she could discern the beginnings of breasts on the child, a puckering in the middle of a snug fitting T-shirt. The child was so thin, her body bent like a bow about to be shot.

The brass mouth of the mail slot snapped open. The paper made a soft thud as it hit the marble tiles of the entrance. Lily could hear these small sounds amplified by the stillness of the sleeping household, and because she expected what sound would be made and her mind filled in the tones, as a child connecting numbered dots completes a crude picture of a bell in an activity book. Lily imagined the routine of the newspaper girl as if she were observing herself, as if she were thirteen again, without hips, without cellulite, as if close observation were a kind of love and not the kind of marriage that canceled her out.

19 Rita

IN the dimness of the back aisle of the locker room at the Y the naked ribs glowed. For her workout Margo had pulled on a T-shirt, black with two fluorescent views, front and back, of a skeleton. Margo's back pack was propped against the bench next to Rita, and her street clothes were thrown into a heap on the floor. Margo kicked the clothes into a locker. The black sweat pants she wore were quite frayed at the ankles and a rather large hole yawned at the inner thigh. Around her forehead she wore a black sweat band with white skulls in a smiling ring.

Rita adjusted her tights at the thigh where they had puckered, wiggling as she tugged them up through the French cut at the hips of her leotard. Margo was watching her, envying her narrow waist. Then she caught a sidelong view of herself in the mirror at the end of the hall, a long glass with dressing room lights bordering all around it. Margo made a face at herself. Although Rita was always insisting that Margo was "Felliniesque" and that she should make a pilgrimage to Rome and introduce herself to the master, Margo really looked like a character out of a Bergman film, a personification of death, minus the hooded cowl.

And Margo wasn't impressed by Fellini. *La Strada, Amarcord*, those flicks were so much "fucking opera" to her. Like zabaglione, nice maybe, spirited, but basically froth, whipped egg yolks and sugar, basically just a dessert. While the gothic world of Bergman was something to reckon with. Not, of course, the red gold beauty of Liv Ullman, but the gray porridge features of Max Von Sydow. In black and white.

Like tainted fish, sex was always a little dubious in Bergman films. So dinner is served in the boudoir. Trout. Given a choice between the seafood and the husband, it is clear that the wife would rather poke the fish. Later she inserts her broken wine glass into her vagina and smears her lips with her bloodied fingers. Like applying lipstick in the dark. This makes the woman smile for the first time on the screen.

But frigid denial was better than the way Fellini's cameras made fun of women. Simpletons and hookers, enormous breasts and hips, no, the kind of hips you can only call haunches, enough to satisfy a gang of school-boys, all at once.

"What's on your mind, Margo?"

She said nothing for a moment. "Don't you know it's not fashionable to dress like a gym bunny anymore?"

"Is that right? What? Did you read that in Vogue?"

Both women went through the motions of the aerobics class without talking. Margo had introduced Rita to the club. Before that Rita had been fat, puffing after a couple of flights of stairs, not able to run a block to catch a bus. And like most recent converts, she was extremely zealous about her workouts. What surprised her most about sports was that it did not lead her away from her inner life, her intel-lectual life, as she had always expected that it would, the muscle-head effect evident among male jocks, those with some sort of sophisticated microcircuitry in their heads only for statistics like baseball scores. But what Rita had discovered, to her surprise, was that physical activity, in the form of continuous, rhythmic motion, often led her more deeply into herself.

The women didn't speak again until after their showers. Rita was blowing her hair dry, running her fingers through its thickness and tossing her head so her curls wouldn't flatten out. Drying her hair that way gave it an uncombed, unkempt look she cultivated. Margo was already dressed. Rita sat wrapped in only a towel, the towels provided by the gym which were really too small. She had it tucked in at her breasts, but the terry cloth was not long enough. It ended short of her sex, which was more combed and controlled in its narrow — as if designed for bikinis — triangle than the hair on Rita's head.

"Let's pick up a bottle of bourbon on the way to your place Rit," Margo said pulling up one leg on the bench beside Rita and resting her elbow on her knee as she bent over and peered intently at herself in the mirror.

"Sure. My place is good," Rita smiled as she ran her fingers through her hair and continued to blow it dry. "I get tired of the attention you attract in cafés."

"Yeh? Well part of me could use that attention right now, but another part, a very vital part, wouldn't know what to do with it." Margo spoke dejectedly. She seemed uncharacteristically vulnerable.

"Are you still fighting with Bo?"

"No," she said tightening her lips, "we're not fighting, we're through."

"Marg, you've been married and fighting for twenty years! Ever since I've known you, each fight has been the last fight. So excuse me if I don't get all broken up about this." Rita shook her head partially to emphasize her disbelief and partially to facilitate her hair drying. "Marg, I think you simply don't know how to argue with a man. That's why you have to throw poor Bo out every time you have a disagreement."

Margo's eyes were dark and glittering. "Poor Bo, eh? Well I didn't throw your poor Bo out. He left."

"So what? I don't understand. You don't mean to tell me that after twenty years of marriage this is the first time he's walked out on his own?"

"This is the first time that I've watched him walk out. Watched his back, the way he squared his shoulders and picked up his bag, without looking back, as if he had already left or was in some airport. The only thing he has in mind is his flight out, the little sexual thrill he'll feel at lift off when the plane vibrates with the light on its wings and all over . . . I kept trying to talk to him, but my face, my words, might as well have been signals from a TV late at night, after the station's stopped broadcasting, after you've fallen asleep, you know, scrambled. Snow."

"I'm sure you're wrong, Marg. Bo is still nuts about you. You just make him a little crazy some time, that's all." Rita tried to state this with absolute confidence, but a hint of doubt entered her voice, doubt that she knew what Bo was feeling at all and she stopped talking rather too abruptly.

Margo picked up on Rita's hesitation right away. When you're prepared to believe the worst, you hear the slightest inflection that might confirm that belief.

"You're not telling me something! I can smell it. I smell a rat. So give me the facts, ma'am. Just the facts. Don't you dare try to protect me! Do you think I can be hurt by a man? Do you think I'd let a rattlesnake of a man hurt me?" she demanded.

"There's nothing to tell. You'll have to ask the man."

"If snakes could talk, Rita! Don't play games with me. You know I won't stand for it. You've seen him, haven't you? I want to know! I want to know everything." Margo was irritated, but she bit her lip and changed her tone. "I'd tell you, Rita. You know that. If you were dying of cancer I'd tell you."

"Cheerful, aren't we?" Rita said keeping her face perfectly deadpan, inscrutable. "Listen, Marg. You're out to lunch. I *saw* Bo, alright. Last Sunday. He came over to my place and installed a dead bolt for me. He mentioned the fight. I thought it would have all blown over by now."

"How cute. He installs a lock for my friend and for me he leaves the front door wide open, as if he were expecting me to run after him or something."

Having finished applying her makeup, Rita moved over to her locker and quickly dressed. "You know Marg, *I* would have. *I* would have run after him and *begged* him to come back."

The women walked out into the parking lot at the back of the building where Margo had left her car. Margo had forgotten to pull the top down. It was raining lightly so the seats were damp. She found an old rag in the glove compartment and started to mop up the dampness, swearing through tight lips to herself, "What the fuck good is a convertible beetle when it rains every other fucking day in this town."

"We can just make the liquor store if we hurry."

Luckily Spadina was clear, with very few vehicles on the dusky avenue. The street lamps were spilling gold light, which served to illuminate the texture of the rain, that otherwise denser sheet of darkness, like a gray mission blanket with some yellow stripes along the borders. Margo flicked on the interior car light and proceeded to put on some mascara, peering into the rearview mirror as she drove.

"Are you crazy, Marg? You want to get us killed or something?"

"Nah! I just forgot to dress to do it. To men that is. To kill men. What a fantasy life I have. This eye stuff was in a sample kit they gave me when I bought some hypoallergenic shampoo at the Clinique counter. I wonder if it really makes any difference." She peered into the rearview mirror and batted her dark lashes at herself. She wasn't checking the traffic. Switching off the overhead light, she threw the mascara wand into the crumpled Simpson's bag beside her.

"Fuck! I should have changed my clothes. We should have decided to go out! Who's going to see us slugging back Jack Daniels in your kitchen?"

"We can see each other! That was the idea, remember? I'd like to try to talk some sense into you!"

"I'm just DC, not AC, Rit, if you know what I mean. I'll bet Bo isn't wasting any time."

They stopped in front of the liquor store. Rita offered to stay in the car while Margo went in to buy a bottle. She said she'd keep an eye out for cops — they were illegally parked — but what Rita really wanted was a few moments to think. She was tempted to get out of the car and walk home, except that she decided that wouldn't help her friend. But in order not to commit what would amount to suicide, Rita slid over into the driver's seat. Though she didn't have much experience driving stick shift, she was sure it would be safer than letting Margo stay at the wheel. Her inexperience was safer than Margo's anger and despair.

Soon Margo came out of the store with a brown paper bag. She was wringing the neck of the bottle, twisting the paper bag around it as if she were strangling it. When she saw Rita behind the wheel of her car, she merely raised an eyebrow and got into the passenger side.

"That was fast."

"Home, James," Margo ordered. She placed the bottle between her legs and folded her arms under her breasts. She crossed her legs at the ankles and settled back, determined to be perfectly comfortable.

After a halting start, Rita managed to get the car to run smoothly. In a few minutes they were parking in front of her house. At the door Rita had to rummage through her handbag for the key. Margo stood quietly beside her, the bottle of bourbon secured under her arm. As they stepped into the house Margo turned and gave a sidelong look at the new lock, that glaring clue that she did not know how to interpret.

It made Bo present in Margo's suspicions and in Rita's memory. Rita pictured again his broad brown hands expertly, thoughtfully, handling the tools, his head bent over the task, humming to himself a few bars interspersed with a few remembered lines, his looking up at her as she re-entered the room, as she made her own inconsequential music, the chopsticks expertly played by ice and glass of their drinks. Rita remembered his smile and the warmth of his hands massaging her shoulders and she sighed.

But what Margo saw in the lock was betrayal. What she felt was sharp resentment. "Nice guy! Real worried about his wife's friends," she said sardonically, looking very pointedly at Rita. Rita's face was pleading, innocent, full of affection and regret, her eyes crinkled with sorrow. It was a face one could trust if faces were to be trusted. It was definitely Bo who was not to be trusted, Margo decided.

While Rita switched on several lights all over the house to make things more cheerful, Margo, curiously, as if for the first time, looked around the house and up the dark stairs. Rita put a record on the stereo. Benson. A soft and easy jazz voice which just might make her friend nostalgic for a man like Bo, nostalgic instead of angry.

Margo continued surveying the house, picking up a pillow on the couch in the living room then dropping it, opening closet doors where she stared too long at Rita's black wool coat hanging in its plastic wrap from the cleaners, stored away since the spring, a ski jacket carelessly tossed on the floor, a red leather jacket with padded shoulders hanging on a hook, its shoulders permanently squared. All small. All incredibly narrow and belonging to a woman. She closed the door and looked around the place some more, randomly, distractedly, while Rita went into the kitchen to pour drinks.

"How do you do it?" she asked Rita as she accepted a bourbon.

"How do I do what?" Rita answered just before she tossed back half of her drink, choking on it.

"You know. Live all alone in this big house."

"Hell. It's my house. And besides liking my own space, it also happens to have a lot of good memories."

"Oh. So it's a haunted house. That explains it. That's exactly what would give me the creeps and drive me out." She slugged back the rest of her drink and said very quietly, "I'd find it real depressing. I'm putting ours up for sale. A real estate office called last night and I said go ahead and list it."

This was going too far, too fast, and Rita was shocked. She couldn't understand what was happening to her friend. "But did you talk to Bo? Did he agree to this?"

"No," Margo replied, at first in a very small voice, and then with growing volume and heat she continued, "No. I didn't talk to him. But I got a call from his attorney. I spoke to the lawyer. It seems Bo wants to make it legal.

This separation. You know he likes things defined. The jerk. The bastard. The wimp. Didn't have the fucking nerve or the fucking decency for that matter to call me himself." Then after trying to take a drink again from her now empty glass, she continued: "Never marry a cop, Rita, they believe in the law more than they believe in their own fucking homes!"

"Gee, I'm sorry Marg. I had no idea it had gone that far. And frankly I'm quite surprised at Bo, not calling you himself, that's not like him . . . He's not a coward." She paused for a moment, sipped her drink, looked at the ice dissolving from precise squares to soft liquid curves, and then frowned.

"Not a coward, eh? A lot you know about Bo! Guess who had to tell the boys we were splitting up?"

"Did you call Joshua and Jonah to tell them?"

"Well, ya, somebody had to. Can't exactly leave it until they come home for Christmas to find the house sold and their things in storage."

"It's all happening too fast! I think you should talk to Bo before things go any further. He may have tried to reach you. His lawyer may be an eager beaver, you know the type. Remember their livelihood depends on bad will between you. He may have beaten Bo to it."

"Yeh. Beaten Bo to the punch. I wish I had!"

"Call him, Marg! Talk to him for god's sake. You can't just let a twenty-year-marriage go down the drain! I know *I* wouldn't. I'd fight for it!"

"Oh, yeh?" Margo scoffed. "Just like you grabbed the legs of your Adonis as he was going down the ramp for Air Greece? It was ciao, ciao, to marriage then, and hello to office romance."

"That's not fair," Rita protested. "There's no comparison. Ours was a short marriage of convenience, you know that. Besides do you know when he asked me to stay with him? The magnanimous gesture, eh? Two fucking minutes before boarding! I couldn't believe it. I cried and cried. Marg, as much as I loved that man, as much as I had been dying to hear those very words, I couldn't! I wouldn't give up my life, my culture, my career, for an afterthought, no more than an afterthought!" Rita's eyes were spilling over with tears. "I was crazy about him! You know that!" Rita let out a deep breath, slapped her thighs definitively and sat down beside Margo on the couch. "But I made the right decision. It was a half-hearted proposal, asking me when he knew damned well I couldn't go with him. And I can't, I *won't* live on half a heart. Ever!"

"Well there's nothing ambiguous about Bo's consulting a lawyer, is there? I'm not going to talk to him. He can talk to my lawyer!"

"I think you'll be making a big mistake Marg, if you do that. Don't play the game. I think you've pushed him too far this time. For all the times you've asked him to leave, I think he probably needs, at least for one time, to hear you ask him to come home."

"He can rot waiting for me to ask him. He can bloody well rot!"

"Well, he won't rot. He's an attractive man, you know. Warm. He's got a lot to give. You can throw away a good marriage to hurt him, but it won't destroy him. You're just cutting off your nose to spite your face." Rita slapped her hand across her mouth to shut herself up.

"Well it won't destroy me either. I'm not exactly a dog, you know. I can see he's buttered you up very nicely with his nice-guy-with-the-lock routine. Sabotaging my friends. The fucking jerk!"

The stereo was replaying Benson's version of "This

Masquerade." Rita decided to mix more drinks and hope that Margo would cool off while she was in the kitchen. Rita called out over her shoulder as she was leaving the room, "Please, no doubts about who your friends are, eh?"

And Margo shouted after her, "Have you ever regretted it? I mean have you ever thought you might have made a mistake not following Nikos to Greece?"

Rita backed into the room at the question. "Hey. Give me your empty, will ya, I forgot it." Laughing ironically, she added, "My answer won't help you. It's an answer not designed to reassure, but true. Sure I regret it, every day of my life I regret it, but my regret doesn't in any way change the way I would behave if I could go back in time to that airport. I'd wave him off again."

"Yeh? Well after the sayonara you should have sold this place. Cleared the decks. That's what I'm going to do. No haunted houses for me. No *housing* regrets. Frankly this place gives me the spooks tonight. I don't know why I've never noticed it before. It's as if something were bottled up here. Those gothic awnings. This isn't a home. It's a church! A fucking cathedral where one little nun services a faith that is long gone."

"Thanks a lot. You know I'm no nun. Give me a break. Do you really think I'm that pathetic? Would you hang out with me if I were? You need that other drink," she said eyeing the empty glasses still in her hands. "And so do I."

"Make mine a double this time," Margo ordered, sprawling in the rattan easy chair and browsing among Rita's books there.

Rita wasn't doing a bad job on the liquor herself. A good drunk to purge the system, to let you know the next day how miserable you really feel, could be sobering in the end. Wasn't it ironic how one had to get drunk to get

sober, she thought, that the pain of a hangover was prefer-
able, a good distraction, from the anguish that eventually
must be felt, the anguish that would very quietly and
patiently wait for her on the other side of all those drinks,
like a child waiting for her mother to pick her up after her
music lesson, a mother who is late, a child who has never
before experienced being abandoned.

Margo waited for Rita to come back with a fresh drink
for her, playing the guest for all it was worth. She kept
looking around the house restlessly, as if it were a puzzle,
as if the details of furnishings and decor would, perceived
in the correct order, yield a solution, a Rubik's cube har-
mony of colors falling in place.

"If I have to, I can go it alone," sticking out her chin
a lot, as she said this to Rita who handed her another drink
without comment. "I'd rather be alone than compromise,"
Margo continued.

"Alone? Yeh. Join the crowd."

"Hardie, harr, harr. You missed out on your real career
as a stand up comedian."

Rita reminded Margo of what she had, as recently as
a few weeks ago, been lamenting: "I thought you had given
it up, the dream of the golden age couple riding their lazy-
boys into the sunset of late-night TV, where nobody has to
face their own death ever. Not alone. Certainly not awake."

The scenario worked, reassured Margo somewhat,
both with its bleakness and with its triviality. She was no
longer part of such a bare-faced lie, Rita could see that.
Margo would gladly abandon such numbing comfort for
something real, something to give new meaning to her life.

"Of course the other side of that vision of connubial
bliss seems equally unattractive: withering in some institution or depending on Meals on Wheels, if you can't afford

the institution. You, at least, Marg, have produced a family, children who'll help foot the bill even if just to get rid of you."

"And you have that job with a pension plan."

"Aha. You begin to understand my clinging to that 'boring' job. Not boring really. But I am burnt out. And for all I know our generation will bankrupt the government pension pay-outs anyway. They'll be sending us out into the snow. Not very cheering, though it beats, to my mind, ending up a bag lady in downtown Toronto, sleeping over the sewers for warmth in winter."

"Maybe you should keep this house after all," Margo said thoughtfully, looking around the room from another angle, like a prospective buyer, with a sense of potential ownership coloring her view. "We could all move in and start a co-op retirement home. Interview and hire our own nurses if necessary, but do as much as we can ourselves to stay vital, if not young." In a life that was solidly conventional, Margo was very good at coming up with creative schemes. She had a talent for organizing her own needs into a collective endeavor.

"That's a little premature, isn't it? I don't think we have to set up a home right now do we?" Rita laughed. "Are we going to get plastered tonight or what? Any more booze for you?" she asked, saluting Margo with her empty glass. "As you can see, I'm more than ready myself."

"Sure. I want to get poisoned."

"Just relax there Marg. I'll weave back in a second."

Rita was by then drunk enough to think what the hell anyway to anything — to love, to sex on the sly, or to exercise, what was the real difference? Work without pay or pay without work, take your choice, fill in the blank. A lifetime. That half-hour script with commercial breaks that's

over before you know what it's about. Instantly forget-
table.

When Rita returned with more drinks, she found
Margo sitting on the floor looking through her records,
tossing the ones she wanted to listen to like frisbees onto the
couch.

"Good shot. You pay for any that miss."

"Have you got anything more recent than the Stones
age? This is the kind of stuff my mother listens to!"

"Yeh?" Rita said, not taking offense, laughing with
good humor, "My mother too. But a little bleached, for
her Tommy Dorsey comes before Louis Armstrong in the
alphabet." Rita settled herself into a seat and proceeded to
tell Margo what to do with her life, something she would not
have ventured to try sober. "But to get back to what you're
going to do about Bo. First of all you're not going anywhere tonight, plastered. Your sober driving earlier this
evening would be enough to straighten me out right now. No
suicide missions home, please. Got it? You sleep here on
the couch. So remember you're staying all night and just
make yourself comfortable. Check out the facilities for our
home twenty-five years down the road. Remember you're
not wasting any time here, even if you are mostly wasted. If
I were sober, I'd say call him right now, or should I say if you
were sober, Marg. Call before it's too late and there's too
much pride burning all those flimsy popsicle stick bridges
built by the heart. Maybe even if it's just for selfish reasons, I'm going to talk some sense into you. I like Bo and
seem more worried about losing him than you are."

"I was going to make some sort of cute comment along
those lines myself," Margo interjected, "but you seem to
have beaten me to it. Is it all that bad? Being free? Seeing
whomever you goddam want, when you want it!"

"Some men," Rita replied, "men I call my friends mind you, tell me that they've had it with women of our generation. This is a twist on middle-aged executives who leave their wives for younger women because we're mostly *not* married to these guys. They say we're more interesting, perhaps, but we're definitely more trouble than we're worth. They're getting even by dating much younger women. *Postfeminist* women. These men don't have to put up with our confusion about roles, with our bullshit. *So there*, they say. One guy asked me to imagine a shop like Tim Horton's, the day-old donuts packaged and on the back shelf, on sale for twice the price of the fresh ones. Which would you choose, he asked me?"

"Well, two can play at that game you know. There's this kid we just hired fresh out of film school as a gofer. Hey, he gets my coffee and he gets my donuts. I send him out for the little bits, what you get after they punch out the holes I guess, a whole bag full of those, and I eat them all. I don't bother to count how many are in the bag. This hunk, a double for the young Elvis, with a sexy, southern drawl, follows me around like a puppy. And hey, why not I say, I've got experience as well as good looks. I'm active, I'm dynamic. Don't let those jerks you call your male friends sell any of us short," Margo said cocking her head at Rita defiantly, as if Rita were the problem for a whole generation of women and it could be decided in their dialogue that evening.

"But Margo, you wouldn't settle for that, for a kid, would you? What has he got to offer you besides a young body? For me, it's the brain that's the sexiest organ."

"The brain has hardly been Bo's department," Margo scoffed. "My taste has always run to beef."

20
Lily

THROUGH the open doors of their bedrooms, Lily could hear the breathing of her sleeping children: Sophie's little sighs and the snorting sounds Tom made as he turned restlessly in bed. What were they dreaming about? Lily thought she could hear their heartbeats, thought she could hear the drumming of their hearts as she imagined the lub dub dub, as if that beating were part and an echo of her own. In the bathroom Lily imagined all this as she stood, wrapped in a towel, staring into the mirror of the medicine cabinet. The glass was obscured by the steam from her hot bath. Lily bent down to pull the Windex out of the cupboard below the wash basin and sprayed the glass, wiping it clear with a paper towel. She had to scrub where flecks of food from flossing their teeth had congealed. Then the glass sparkled, then the glass was lovely and clear. But the face within its surface, the face trapped in its depth, was not, she thought. It was not a face that she wanted to know herself.

When she opened the medicine cabinet, the pale visage, mercifully, disappeared. On the top shelf of the cabinet were the prescription drugs, the ones that had to be kept out of the reach of children. They were safety sealed so that even she had a hard time opening them. It was necessary to align the caps very precisely and then to press down in order to snap them open. She pulled out one of the containers, the one with the little blue pills. Her dream pills. The cabinet door she left open so as not to see that face, that face like a white balloon kicking around the house, forgotten remnant of some festivity. She noticed the balloon shrinking daily, pale and ever more wizened, woolly with grime.

Lily shook the little container of pills. It played like a rattle. She shook it again. It was the little music her life would make for her. It was not a melody, but a ditty.

Sleep, *sweet balm of hurt minds*. What would it mean to be Lady Macbeth and not to be filled to the *toe top with direst cruelty*? To give suck and to stop there, to never pull the babe from your nipple?

That night she aligned the cap expertly. It unsnapped easily. She heard the click of release as if the sound were magnified by a microphone. Every sound on that floor seemed intensified, but in the study below, downstairs, there was a hush deep enough to suck up even the knocking of her own heart.

One before retiring, prescribes Dr. Skelton. Lily reread the instructions. Then she stared at the insignia, the crest of the hospital pharmacy in the corner of the label. In her hand she held the doctor's recipe for rest. Rest without peace, that's what she knew each night, rest without refreshment. Rest without recreation.

She poured a handful of the drug into her palm. She closed her hand into a fist and gritted her teeth. She was clutching very hard, so hard that she felt her nails cut into her palms. One by one she noted the contents of her medicine cabinet: dental floss, toothpaste, three tubes, three different shades of pink lipstick, all marked samples and not for sale, an emery board, pearl nail polish, a bottle of Oil of Olay. The middle shelf was Michael's: it had his razor, the old fashioned kind, a straight blade and a leather strap, a brush, and a pot of shaving cream. The top shelf contained the iodine and a small bottle of calamine lotion as well as the prescription drugs.

She was not counting sheep, she was not trying to sleep, she was Scheherazade, buying time with the small tale in each pill, the small tale of little worth and less entertainment so she might be reprieved for one more night.

Lily opened her hand. Her palm was stained blue. Her hand was perspiring heavily and so was her face, beads of moisture ran down her cheeks, dropping off her nose. In a sudden action, surprising herself, she threw the pills down the sink. She had to shake some of them off her hand. They clung to her skin. She had to pull them off one by one. The drain swallowed the pills.

She recapped the container, placed it carefully back up on the shelf with the others. She took nothing to help her sleep. All night in bed she visualized the drain, that deep furred darkness into which her dreams had disappeared.

21
Rita

WITHIN the halo of lamplight Rita studied the cover of a new novel about the brittle state of contemporary romance called *Miss Behavior*. The photo on the back showed the young, smiling and pretty face of the author. The toothy smile was a disguise for cynicism, Rita knew, for she had read all her books. With a thumbnail she slit open the plastic film enveloping the volume. Because its spine was stiff with newness, the novel resisted reading.

An hour and a half and several chapters into the book and Rita thought that there was no escape quite like satire, the recreation of laughter. "Ha!" she barked, recognizing most of the characters in the novel. Then she laughed at herself, to herself, feeling sane, feeling wise, feeling in control, the various levels of critical internal voices neutralized, or more accurately, harmonizing with the chorus of voices from the novel. With such a book in hand, she could not feel lonely.

The evening was cool enough for her to light a fire. The hearth crackled with warmth; the flames made party noises, chattering and crowding the room with shadows. Sunday morning had been idled away browsing in bookstores after which Rita enjoyed a light meal, a late brunch at a popular little restaurant which served mimosa, a cocktail of champagne and orange juice, with your eggs. She felt satisfied enough to make do with an apple and a cup of coffee for supper. The apple, half-eaten, was rusting on the butler nearby.

As she looked up from her book, intellectually engaged and relishing her solitude, as she looked up from mid-sentence and frowned slightly, her eyes fell on the telephone just before it rang. She was startled by the ringing. The coincidence made the call seem ominous, so she let it ring several times before answering it.

She clapped the book shut, dropped her legs from the half-lotus position, and walked across the room to the phone. At the sound of the deep tones of Pierre's voice she felt that familiar constriction in her throat.

"Come over tonight. I want you. Take a cab. I'll pay." Then because she didn't immediately respond, addressing the silence over the wire he added "*S'il vous plaît,* Rita. *J'ai besoin de toi.*"

"Come over? Where?" Rita repeated, not understanding what he wanted.

"Yes. Come over. To my place. I'm alone. Take a cab. I'll pay." There was an urgency in his voice that he would not explain.

She had "What's up" half-formed in her mouth, as if she had to chew the words a little before she could speak them. Her pleasant solitude was spoiled and yet she did not want to not see Pierre.

Sensing her hesitation, Pierre continued in a rush, "Rita, you must come! *Je suis desolé. J'ai besoin de toi, mon âme, mon propre âme!* Or I must go out into the night and forever lose myself! You can change that. So you must."

Pierre was not the same man in French that he was

in English. Rita wished she knew more French. She liked it when his French idiom intruded into his English speech. Which indeed represented the true voice of the man? Which of the two voices might speak love to her? She did not want to obey the English, but she gave in to the passion in his French.

"I'll come. I need to change though. You call the cab for me. I'll be ready in fifteen minutes."

Rita looked at the book lying face down on the chair in the spotlight of the reading lamp. She felt a twinge of regret. But she was no longer in the mood to laugh at the feelings her need would not allow her to deny. Love at Pierre's convenience. "And where," she wondered out loud, "is his wife tonight?"

Walking over to the hall mirror to examine herself, she turned her head slowly to the left and then to the right. She was looking for the slackness of middle age around the jaw. Her eyes were bright and assertive, as if she could argue with the reflected image. Rita had inherited the mirror from her maternal grandmother; she loved its carved dark wood frame.

Although the clothes she wore were comfortable, Rita chose to change her sweat shirt for something sexy, a black silk jersey which made her body appear fluid with motion. As she changed her top, she wondered if she should shower again as well. Pierre was always so meticulous, his white linen shirts, his suits. But what did he wear at home, she wondered? She only saw him dressed for business or at premieres attired formally in evening wear. Where no other man dared to go, Pierre wore a tuxedo and tails with such naturalness that he made his colleagues seem uncouth, like farmers selling wilted produce from trucks, turnips tucked awkwardly under their arms.

But Pierre's clothes were for public view. They were
costume. Up close you didn't notice his clothes. You felt
his presence. His eyes were dark and his gaze was elliptical.
Looking where? The fool hopes at herself. The fool, she
is a fool. It was himself he was watching, his power over
women and certain susceptible men.

Rita wanted to solve this riddle of a man and learn to
fit into him. She wanted to be so natural in his arms that he
couldn't deny what must be plain. That they belonged
together. That was more important than being in love. Such
naturalness could go on forever.

Her doorbell rang and she hadn't washed. The decision had been made for her by the driver of the black and
yellow cab at the door. "Taxi, miss?" The cabbie was
surely too young to call her that, a wispy beard straining to
get a hold on his face, the bristles so sparse and fine the
effect was little more than a blurring of his features.

"Yes. Sorry, I'll be right out. Give me just a minute
will ya?" Rita ran back upstairs and into the bathroom
where she inserted her diaphragm. Then she packed for
overnight by throwing a toothbrush, an afro pick for her
hair, and a tube of spermicidal jelly into a back pack. She
pulled her wallet out of her purse to see how much money
she had left. Five dollars wouldn't get her a third of the
way to the Beaches where Pierre lived, so he had better
pay. That would be embarrassing, she thought. To have to
run in to ask him for the fare. To avoid the potential for
humiliation, the dependency, however momentary, to
which she might be subjected, she wondered if she should
simply give the driver the five and say thanks, but I've
changed my mind. She continued to wonder even as she
grabbed a jacket and ran out to the cab.

Pierre was waiting on the lawn as her cab pulled up in

front of his house. From his soft leather wallet he drew a twenty dollar bill and shoved the money at the driver through the open window of the cab, waving away the change due with his other hand. Then he made his way briskly around to the other side of the car to open the door for Rita. She stepped out of the cab and moved towards him. But looking at the neighboring windows that were beginning to glow in the twilight, he backed away from her. Then in a firm but casual fashion, Pierre put his hand on her shoulder and led her through the front door he had left ajar.

Once inside Pierre picked her up awkwardly, heaving her over his shoulder as if she were a rolled rug. What may have been intended as an act both primitive and passionate on Pierre's part felt like parody or farce to Rita. Was she too fat or was Pierre not fit enough to perform?

Rocking with the action of his gait, Rita perceived the scene as through the eye of an unstable and moving camera. She had no time to focus in detail on the home, but nevertheless she was impressed by the hue of antiques and the jewel colors of Persian rugs. The light in the house was not bright, but a golden light reflected from the rich wood. Everything in the house had the air of being preserved, embalmed.

As Pierre carried her up the staircase, she turned her head to try to look at his face but only saw into the dark vortex of his ear. At the motion he paused very briefly to bite her shoulder. His passion had a peculiar violence which was unfamiliar, his teeth sinking too deeply into her shoulder, breaking and bruising the skin. It made her cry out.

"Pierre. Stop it! What is this King Kong number you're pulling, anyway?"

He took her to a bedroom where he pushed the door

open with one elbow, without releasing his hold of the body, Rita's body. He kicked the door shut behind them and dumped her onto the bed.

"Shut up, shut up. I'm tired of your jokes. I'm tired of your talk. Your endless talking. Rita, shut up and let me make love to you."

She kicked off her pumps and he pulled off her slacks in one long motion. He tugged them off her ankles, where they clung, then threw the pants onto the floor. They looked like the discarded and darkened peel of fruit. Her panties were inside out. Rita could see that they were lightly stained with blood and guessed that she must have ovulated. Had her diaphragm slipped, she wondered? She needed to stop Pierre in order to check it, but she lost her breath when he pulled her jersey up over her head where it caught, rolled around her neck and covered her face. Rita tried to get it off but Pierre pinned down her arms. He threw the entire weight of his body on top of her so that she couldn't move. If she had not known Pierre so well, if she had not loved him, she might have been frightened. Instead she felt bewildered.

"Pierre! For god's sake, get this thing off my head! I can't breathe!" She felt crushed, unaccustomed as she was to his full weight bearing down on her. He held her wrists above her head with one hand, with the other he tore off her bra. She felt her breasts separate, pulled to the right and left by gravity. He had not removed his clothing. The bulky cotton knit of his sweater, the stiff canvas of his jeans were scratching her skin. She heard the swift friction of his zipper. He had raised his body slightly to pull it open with the free hand. He pushed her legs roughly apart and thrust himself inside her. Rita's scream was muffled by the jersey.

Her cry seemed to be coming from another room, no

place where she lived. All her consciousness had slipped down to her sex, to the piercing pain of his entrance. Her mind, her personality had been effectively erased. He beat against her, hard surf against a soft sand shoal and her body dissolved in pain and then in something like pleasure as her body lubricated. Her body wanted to save her with pleasure. Save and enslave.

Pierre continued, seemingly interminably, fucking her, wanting to bury her, to bury himself in her. Rita felt as if she were being ripped up to her navel. She was suffocating under his weight and the knit of the jersey covering her face. Everything seemed to be choking her. The rhythms of his body faster and harder. He was a prize fighter sinking his gloved fist into a punching bag.

Then he released her wrists and grabbed instead her shoulder for more leverage, thrusting himself deeper. Her pain was searing. She grasped for the brass of the head-board, icy to the touch, trying to find strength enough to pull herself away from him. Guttural noises, prelanguage, were escaping from between Pierre's clenched teeth. He began punching the bed very hard to the rhythm of his thrusting body. And then he screamed, a scream which started low and deep from his throat until it reached a pitch which was almost female. A scream pulled out of his throat like a long silk sash from a magician's sleeve. Then he collapsed. His weight became dead weight. His penis slipped out of its own accord as his erection withered.

Stunned, Rita released her hold on the headboard and pulled the jersey off her head. She watched Pierre — incredulous, she watched the man. His mouth was open, his teeth bared against the soft skin of her chest. His dark hair was damp against her neck. She turned her head and could see in the reflection of the mirror of the wardrobe a man fully dressed lying on top of a half-naked woman. The scene was pornographic. What Pierre had just done to her had nothing to do with making love. Perhaps it would be impossible to ever make love with anyone again. Least of all with Pierre. Any illusions she had cherished about what she might mean to him, about love with him, about loving him, had just been annihilated. The man had needed her that night in some way that had nothing to do with the woman she was. He had used her. But worse, she had allowed herself to be used. What had she herself been looking for?

Rita was hurting very badly but she was not frightened. She had never been frightened in spite of the ferocity of his attack. She seemed to recognize in the violence of his love-making a force which perhaps was driving her as well — impersonal, destructive, a force she had instantly recognized and respected even as it made Kobe steak of her sex. She tried to push his body off her, lifting his shoulders a few inches with the back of her palms and easing herself out from under him at the same time. He stirred, groaned, then rolled over and sat up on the edge of the bed, his head bent down, his back to her. He reached into his pocket and pulled out his cigarette case. He turned slightly and offered her one first, avoiding her eyes.

"Ever the gentleman, eh Pierre?" Rita said bitterly, but she accepted the cigarette anyway. After putting two in his mouth, he snapped the silver case shut. Its click had the sound of finality. Then he lit both cigarettes using a heavy ceramic lighter which he took from the night table beside the bed. He popped the burning pacifier into Rita's mouth.

Pierre inhaled deeply from his cigarette and blew smoke out in clouds, watching himself through its billowing haze in the wardrobe mirror. Rita coughed and sputtered as she inhaled. Her body was seized suddenly with tremors. So she pulled the duvet up to her chin for warmth. She smoked and watched, with mild curiosity, the hand with which she held the cigarette as it shook. Pierre did not speak to her until he finished smoking his cigarette, until he ground the butt emphatically into an ashtray. Then also noticing her trembling hand, he took her half-smoked cigarette from her fingers and snuffed it out for her.

With his index finger he tenderly traced the outline of her cheek and jaw. He shook his head as if to himself and said, "I'm sorry Rita. I'm crazy tonight. Just crazy!"

Rita looked at him, not understanding, waiting for him to continue. Pulling her arms under the covers, she sunk deeper into the duvet. She turned her head away from his caressing hand. He stopped trying to touch her face, clasped his hands in his lap, and spoke to his own reflection in the mirror.

"Kathleen is in the hospital. The baby is lost. Blood in the water. Bloody blood. My child a clot she passed like urine."

"Your wife had a miscarriage? Is she in danger?" Rita seized on this anxiously.

"No," he spoke softly, barely above a whisper. "No. She did not have a miscarriage. She had an abortion." Then he laughed ironically. His laughter frightened Rita more than the sexual assault. He spat on the good wool rug; he spat again on the scene in the wardrobe mirror. "She dared to forge my signature, my consent to the procedures. The sow. And that dyke she has for a doctor! I blame her for believing Kathleen, for encouraging her! Along with the abortion she performed a tubal ligation." He smiled, his lips stretched with hatred. "She thinks she has fixed my wagon with this. She thinks I suppose that this marriage can go on with itself."

"But I don't understand! How could she terminate the pregnancy at this point?" Rita shook her head in disbelief. It was not legal, let alone ethical, to abort a foetus which might be viable. "You knew the sex from an ultrasound and had named him —"

"*Pierre, le petit Pierre, c'est moi. Elle voudrait touer moi.* She is a murderess."

"I'm sorry."

"Yes. You should be sorry. Because it is your fault. It is always you women's fault."

"My fault! What did I have to do with it?!" Rita could not find the courage for outrage. To her dismay she felt vaguely guilty, something in her believing his words, his judgment. "What do you mean? I don't even know your wife!"

"Ah! But she knows you. She knows what you were to me." He laughed again, emphasizing the past tense. "The little secretaries. They did not bother her at all. She said that she found it all sadly so predictable. But it did not make her sad. When she guessed. It was for her evidence of her own superiority. But you. You are a different kettle of fish, my sweet. You are like her, but you have made a life for yourself. Yet you enjoy her husband too. That, she said, she could never forgive."

Rita looked around the room, stunned, feeling the full weight of her complicity in the events. She was in the woman's house, if not in her very bed. Rita wanted to leave immediately. Wrapping herself in the duvet, she searched the room for her pants. She dressed herself using the duvet as a kind of tent. Pierre was not paying any attention. He lit another cigarette and continued to blow smoke at his reflection in the mirror. Moving to the door, Rita found a useless rag, what had been her bra. Wanting to recover every trace of herself she stuffed the torn lace into her pocket.

"I'm leaving," she announced. "I'm going home."

Pierre simply continued to smoke. He cocked his head, exhaled and said with a slight shrug, "Suit yourself." He did not accompany her to the door. She found her way out into the night alone, not very clear of her direction but heading towards traffic lights she could make out several blocks away. Luckily had enough change for the streetcar. A young law student getting off that line at the corner near where she was boarding had been raped and killed the year before. Someone had spray-painted in red the figure of a woman's body which alerted Rita to the potential danger. From the outside. Rita shivered involuntarily, then squared her shoulders as she marched to the nearest stop, as vigilant as she had been trusting earlier that evening.

22
Lily

LILY lay in bed in the dark and listened. She didn't sleep — or maybe she was dreaming that she was awake all night. On the edge of things. She faked sleep. Or sleep faked her.

Nothing in her routine was visibly altered. As usual she spent a good long hour soaking in a hot bath after which, dressed only in her bathrobe with a towel wrapped around her head, she tapped on Michael's door to wish him goodnight.

Michael too seemed to never change, never to need to change. He was as abrupt as ever. That night he cleared his throat and ordered, "Shut the door," as she turned to go up the stairs to their bedroom.

"Ssssorry," she said thickly, as if from a drugged drowsiness.

So she turned to close the door but just stayed there, standing at the entrance to his study, one foot in the door, one slippered foot, a woman suspended between intention and action, as if she were too weak, as if her blood were too thin to complete the gesture. Was she numb or just dumb? Was she afraid? It was not shameful to be afraid in danger. It was shameful to be afraid to talk to her husband directly about what she was feeling, to be afraid where there was no threat, but only this refinement of too much gentility, or too little, only this paralysis of her will. She longed for a violence of sorts. To wake her up. To wake them both up.

But she just stood there looking at Michael.

He got up from his desk, dragging his seat back, almost knocking it over in his impatience. His legs seemed to get tangled in the chair. He couldn't get to the door fast enough. He couldn't lock away her face quickly enough. It persisted. It rippled in front of him like his own reflection in muddy water. He kicked the chair.

"Can't you see that I'm working? Dammit, Lily, get to bed."

And while he was making his way across the room to the door, she shut it in his face. She slammed it shut, then stumbled backwards with a sharp little intake of breath, as if she had been slapped. Was this the woman who pulled the door shut so softly each night, was this the woman who closed it by turning the handle and releasing the knob so gently that not even the catching, that not even the click of the lock could be heard? No, this was the new woman who dared to feel the slap.

Michael stood in front of the shut door listening for her steps retreating up the stairs. Listening for her to be gone. The window of his study was open and he could hear the wind in the trees. Or was it the trailing of her robe against the nap of the rug? He couldn't be sure, he couldn't distinguish such involuntary, rustling sounds, but he didn't open the door to check, to see if she had gone up to bed. He stood perfectly still, letting his mind empty itself, until he felt himself swaying, his body moving as involuntarily as trees in the wind, as the branches and leaves of a barbed and flowering bush, filling up with darkness, behind which something, someone else, lurks.

23 Rita

COMPLEMENTING her dark mood Rita dressed in black for the wedding. But only that meat dress she had seen at the National Art Gallery — the concept of a woman artist — could come close to matching her feelings of self-loathing. If we believe in image, that we are what we wear, then let us dress in sirloin, not satin. If I ever wear pink again, it will be veal, Rita thought.

Rita was the black bride, the shadow for her friend, Alice, who smiled from the head table in a traditional white wedding gown. Although Alice wore no veil, her head was crowned with baby's breath. If anyone has nothing to hide, it's Alice, thought Rita, but I, I'm the ink blot on that immaculate page of someone else's marriage, the contract that's in impeccable parchment waiting for the quill pens behind the altar. Rita had scrawled her own signature in ballpoint a few years back.

It felt ironic that Alice and Paul had chosen the anniversary of her marriage to Nikos to wed. Eight years had passed and her friends must have forgotten the significance of that date; they thought it was important because it was Labor Day weekend. Even Margo seemed to have forgotten her big sacrifice for that day: an hour of shooting time from her film to serve as her best woman. And Achilles, a comrade of Nikos, showed up for the groom. Achilles had surprised her with a small bouquet of roses which she had pinned to her jean-jacket. Nikos also wore denim with his only white shirt and a tie he had to borrow from Bo.

The whole service lasted about ten minutes. Rita remembered that she did not feel any different, did not feel married afterwards. She had been told and half-believed that marriage was to love as donuts are to a diet, a homely form of sabotage. If she didn't feel any different, she certainly felt hungry. They all did and went for some souvlaki on the Danforth. At the Byzantium the meat was underdone, which may have been the most remarkable thing about that day. The lamb bled on her plate. The sight of the blood made her feel queasy. She just left the chunks of skewered meat on the dish, the untouched meat staining the rice pink. All she could do was wave a fly away determined to enjoy the feast she so shamefully neglected.

"Have some salad then," Achilles coaxed. "Eat or you will become just skin and bones. No good for this man or any man." Achilles chuckled, poking Nikos in the ribs and winking slyly at her. He ordered more wine, filled Nikos' glass to the brim, then the glasses of the others. He raised his own for a toast:

"Strength to the bridegroom. And fertility for the bride. May you make many babies!"

"A toast for the bride and groom! Paul and Alice and to their living happily-ever-after!" Bo the best man was calling for everyone's attention, raising his champagne glass high. Everyone in the room raised their glasses with him. Startled out of her reverie, Rita lifted the champagne glass with a sudden jerk that sent the liquid spilling a little over one side, sprinkling her dress with the libation. Her fingers felt sticky. She was more than a little drunk, but she felt that she had the right to be. After all such occasions were more than a little sad. Not for the party celebrating, one certainly hoped, but for many of the friends gathered there, familiar with the minefields around all such crossroads in life. Wrong directions recalled. Right for some. Just damned wrong for herself. She was projecting. There was no need to be anxious for Alice. Alice always knew what she was doing and did it in her own quiet but assured way.

Rita looked at Bo, master of ceremonies for his best friend Paul. Bo was wearing a tuxedo which was a little too tight. He moved as if he were being restrained by a straight jacket. Margo was on the other side of the head table. She was still his partner, at least for this wedding, but she managed to ignore Bo for the entire banquet. Margo looked as awkward in her satin gown as Bo did in his tux. They still shared a kind of style — or rather discomfort with it. It really was a pity, for they were made for each other, Rita thought. They looked so much alike in their awkwardness they could have been brother and sister.

Rita picked up another glass of champagne from the tray being passed around by one of the waiters. The wedding reception was made up from a Geritol crowd, so she found herself with no one she knew or wanted to know. She decided to develop a deeper acquaintance with the champagne. Besides it was the real thing, French and good. Not too sweet, although it went down as easily as cream soda.

The bubbly was dangerous stuff. The wedding made her feel maudlin. Marriage. All the arguments against it, all the need for that kind of bond, love glue, crazy glue. Support through thick and thin, ahhhhhh! to even have the intention!

Bo approached Rita. "Ya wanna dance, kid?"

"Why not, ssshure," she slurred. She threw one arm around him and dipped in an exaggerated tango pose.

"Hell, no, Rita. That's not the way you do it to this kind of music. You just shake your bootie. You just stand there and shake it." He placed her a couple of inches away from him. But she seemed in danger of toppling over and he relented. He put his arms around her and smiled into her hair. "Okay, so we'll do a slow one to 'Grapevine.' I've got so much explaining to do to that other half of the table that it doesn't really matter anymore what I do. It's too late. I'm free as a bird. And that's just the way I want it." Bo was resting his chin on her head and talking into her curls. In a remote corner of the dance floor they were doing a slow two-step that had nothing to do with the Motown rhythms being played.

"When I was a kid, I never had the nerve to ask a favorite girl for the slow dances. Buckle polishers, we used to call those numbers," he continued. "See this!" He lifted one foot and shook it. "Size thirteen! And with my build, I played football then, the biggest guy on the team. Well they're not easy to maneuver on a dancefloor, these clod-hoppers. I wanted to get real close, you know, feel her breasts against my chest, nuzzle my leg in between her knees to lead her back and around. I rehearsed it in my head a thousand times and with a broom. But my feet wouldn't go for it. Every time I tried to get close I'd end up stepping all over her high heels! And those things are so brittle they snap like match sticks! Believe me I know from experience."

"You don't mean from wearing them though, do you?" Rita laughed openly and Bo laughed with her.

The music was changing. A lot of people left the dance floor to sit at the tables that were lit up with little shaded

lamps. The building was designed in wings for greater intimacy in dining. All the tables were set in alcoves of the
room, while the central space had been cleared for dancing. The party was small. The place could accommodate a
lot more people and not feel crowded. By day and all
through the summer it was a country inn.

Some windows had been opened and Bo and Rita
were close enough to feel the night air, cool, damp, and
fragrant. It cut the smell of the tobacco smoke. Rita and Bo
kept on dancing to the next number, "Midnight Train to
Georgia." It didn't matter what was being played, they
did their two-step to the rhythm of their conversation.
Their dance was mostly just shifting their weight from one
foot to the other with their hips swaying slightly.

"What's with you and Margo? Is it really over?"

"Do I need to tell you? Don't you already know?"

"Marg isn't talking about it anymore. Just real estate.
Selling the house. It's the house, the furniture, that needs to
be packed up and —" she searched for a word — "disposed of . . . Yes, disposed, that's the word."

"Ya, husbands are disposable if they're not at her
disposal. Is that right? Are those two words related or
something? I think I know what something means, then it
begins to slip away and it all starts to sound the same. It's
gobbledygook, it's pigeons shitting from the eaves. Kookoo,
kookooooo. Oh, you were expecting bird song, something
poetic. Something that doesn't shit all over your car windows. I sometimes wonder how we fucking communicate at
all."

"But Bo, I really want to know. Can you tell it to me
straight, did you get pushed or did you split?"

"With Margo what's the fucking difference? I know
you girls have to stick together! But can you get past that

one just this once? Rita, fess up, you know Marg," and looking down at her face and seeing the defensive mask that was settling onto it, he rather shrilly exclaimed, "All right, blame me, go ahead and blame me!"

"We're not dancing anymore. Why don't we sit down? This is starting to feel rather stupid. And I don't even want to think about how it appears." Rita looked around for Margo who was nowhere to be seen. "I wish you and Marg would just get off the pot and sort things out. You love each other. What's the matter with you!"

"I love her but that's not enough anymore. Maybe it never was. There are some important things that I need that I can't get with Marg. I'd gone without them for so long that I didn't even know it could be there for me. Besides Marg's too proud. And I've been her dog for twenty years but now it's over. You see that sweet thing, third table to your right, pulling at her napkin and looking at us?" Rita turned and looked at a young woman whose get-up was like prom night in the fifties — strapless chiffon, a little string of pearls around her neck. Her blonde hair was smooth and shining, it looked lacquered. She was indeed pulling and wringing her napkin and frequently turning her head to watch them. She had no drink to nurse. She had no one to talk to. Rita thought she recognized something of herself in the girl, something of course from the past, from her youth.

Bo waved to the young woman, then signaled with two fingers. At that the girl settled back in her seat and smiled, making a visible effort to relax.

"I see her."

"That's my date. And when I'm with her we don't have an argument every two seconds. My worst time with Sabrina has been in a dream where it was her body, but

Margo's head. I was asking her to marry me and Paul was grabbing my arm, hissing into my ear not to do it." He shook his head and tried to clear off the air around him as if caught in spider webs. Then he looked directly and hard at Rita. "Sabrina doesn't make me feel stupid all the time. And she's young and pretty and Margo won't forgive me for that ever. This just confirms everything for her. The worst thoughts about me she's held in reserve for just a moment like this. But things are not as simple as she would like to make them out to be. I don't care if she's young. I just need someone warm. Not stupid. Warm. Like you Rita, in another life it could have been you." He bent over and swiftly kissed her and walked away. She watched his retreating back until he sat with his date. Feeling dizzy and nauseated and more thoroughly depressed by her dance with divorce, Rita went to look for the powder room.

She was vomiting champagne into the toilet, the bubbles backing up making the experience particularly unpleasant, when the bride entered the adjoining cubicle. The bottom of her full skirt billowed into the neighboring stalls. Some of the liquid splashed onto the hem of the bridal dress. Luckily Rita had eaten almost nothing, so she was throwing up pure champagne and stomach acids. Rita's throat burned.

"I'm so sorry, Alice, I'm sick. And in more ways than one." Rita left the stall to dampen some paper towels to wipe off her friend's dress. She apologized to Alice again through the partition as she scrubbed at the hem of the gown.

Alice pulled in her skirt to have a look. "I don't see anything, although I can smell it," she said. "I would feel sorry for you, Rita, but I'm too busy feeling sorry for myself. Do you have a some change? I need a Kotex."

"Don't worry, I've got one in my purse. Here." She poked it under the wall of the partition.

"Thanks. I hate this. Some honeymoon! Paul's going to sleep on the couch. You know he can't stand me when I'm this way. One quarter of the time, he can't stand me."

"And three-quarters of the rest of the time you can't stand him. Or shouldn't. Am I right Alice? On such firm foundations are many marriages built." Rita bit her tongue, ashamed of the cynical remark she had just blurted out. "I'm sorry, Alice. PMS and dry heaves, you know, we're all victims!" she added lamely.

"That's not true, Rita, what you said about marriage. Anyway, I don't think we've ever expected the same things from a relationship. But it seems to be more than that now. I can't put my finger on it but something has changed in you lately. Although this is not the time nor place, I wish you would talk about it. You sound so bitter. You're getting bitter, Rita, real bitter."

"Am I? Well maybe I'm just reacting to what happened to Margo and Bo. I'm sorry! I'm trying to come up with an excuse. It's a hell of a way to talk to your friend on her wedding day." The alcohol was wearing off, its anesthetizing effect.

Rita flushed the toilet and hurried to wash her hands and splash some cold water on her face. She talked over her shoulder to Alice, raising her voice to be heard over the sound of running and splashing water. "Alice, I have to find a bun or something to settle my stomach, then some coffee to make me alert so that I can get the hell home. I don't know anyone here and the ones I know I'm not up to dealing with."

"Meaning Margo and Bo? Marg has disappeared. She's my Matron of Honor and she's gone. My mother-in-law is going to have a field day with that. But I don't care. Go home, Rita, if you really want to. I love you. Go home, but please let me find you a ride. You shouldn't be driving after drinking so much." Alice said as she was coming out of the stall, struggling with her full skirt to get through the narrow door. Rita turned to Alice and hugged her. Careful in the embrace not to touch the bridal gown for fear of spoiling it with her wet hands, Rita held her hands out, the wrists together, around and away from Alice's back, as if offering them to an invisible officer for handcuffs. After the embrace, Rita smiled wryly and over the blast of the hand air dryer said, "I love you too. And believe me, I'm dead sober now. There's not a drop of champagne that didn't end up in the toilet. So goodnight, Alice, good night."

Although Rita couldn't find any espresso, she managed to eat a mouthful of fruit cake and keep it down along with a couple of cups of decently strong black coffee. She left by a back door, the exit which led into the parking lot. She didn't look for Margo, nor did she speak to Bo again. Her bed at home and the books by its side, her most faithful lovers, were all she cared for at that point in the evening. It wasn't easy to find the car she had rented to drive up to the inn. She tried to remember what the car looked like. Red, it was red, but wasn't red gray in the dark? The clear night sky was brilliant and dizzying with stars. Champagne bubble stars exploding all over the universe. The moon was in three quarter profile, gibbous, with a pox-eaten, dead white face. She didn't see a white goddess in that profile. She saw Neil Armstrong and the American flag. The moonlight helped her find her car.

The drive was pleasant along the winding country road to the major highway. The road was closely lined with trees, and although she could no longer see the brilliance of the coloring of their leaves in the dark, the warmth, the fire from their hues lingered in her memory. She saw them again through their absence. Memory, the mind's eye, a vision both more brilliant and more opaque, because of shades, because of tones, not recalled. Then the maples she was visualizing turned into solidly green arbors with the purple of grapes in Nikos' mouth. A Bacchus Nikos with a wreath of vines around his head.

"I am not that man! Do I look Greek? Do I act Greek? So I button my shirts the same way. All men do! Unless they're wearing a blouse. We haven't got a chance, Rita. And it's all your fault. You won't give this relationship a snowball's chance in hell. You can't even look at me. Stop looking behind you. That's where your butt is supposed to be. Look at me! Rita will you really look at me for once. I'm not anything like that fucking Greek ass-hole you married!" That was Barry. And if she couldn't look at him then or now, she could still hear him. Not that he was right. But he was half-right. If he had really been like Nikos, or enough like him so that she didn't hear his waspish whining coming through all the time, Rita would have never let him go.

She loved the intimacy of the trees, the thick intimacy of their fellowship, their reaching out to her as she drove along. Her window was half open. She could smell green, the vegetable smells she called by that name. The wind was tugging at her hair, whipping strands of it against her face. She turned onto the highway and switched her radio on to keep alert, to keep from being swept away into the past, into never-never-again-land. Some people live more in their imaginations than in their real life. She was someone like that. She belonged in a movie where she was sure to fall in love with Spencer Tracy and be loved in return.

Rita listened to a talk show and tried not to see too

much of that white line, the one that was really broken but that would begin to swim as she drove like an endless river of white moonlight, a river Lethe, a river lethal. The broadcast was a national show and someone was calling in from Saskatchewan. The woman was caught up in an awkward dilemma. Her daughter kept confusing the term vagina with the name of the city Regina in which they lived. Where do you live little girl? My home is in Vagina. What happened to you just then? I fell off a horse and broke my Regina. Ah the confusion of the pubic and the public! Wasn't that what was wrong with the world? Men who are unconscious of themselves as part of nature, as having bodies and not just fucking bodies, walk, talk, and govern with their dicks. "Wargasm." Would a woman ever coin a word like that? Leave it to the strategic defence generals in whom we trust. All out nuclear warfare. What a thing to call it! Doesn't sound like something you want to avoid. Sexy death. Ask Dr. Strangelove. What are you repressing?

Rita played with the tuning dial of the radio until she found some pop music, the kind guaranteed to keep you awake in the body but not distract your mind. Traffic was light. It started to rain and she rolled up her window all the way to keep out the cold and the damp. She shivered, an icy sensation running down the spine. As a child Rita remembered they used to say that shivery feeling meant that someone was stepping on your grave.

The windshield wipers went back and forth, back and forth, the metronome to which she drove, as if to music, forte, con brio, as if to *real* music. Rita made good time and got home before midnight. She parked the car in the driveway and walked to her front steps, jingling the unfamiliar load of keys. Sticking out of her mail box was an envelope. She pulled it out with one hand as she unlocked the door with the other. It was an ordinary Scotch budget envelope, the kind that are grayish blue on the inside. A note was scrawled on its face from her neighbor. "Sorry, this card came to our house. It's yours. Darn mail!"

Rita felt her stomach tighten. She didn't know why she anticipated bad news.

It was a postcard of the Acropolis in Athens, the moon hanging in the sky above it was gold colored and full, the sky, cobalt blue. She turned the card over breathlessly. The numbers of the address were written in European script, the one uncrossed looked like a seven.

> Dear Rita,
>
> I write to you today to tell you that I am getting married. Irene is a good comrade and she is expecting my child. I think of you who always wanted my child. I am sorry, Rita I do not forget you. I know I gave you a great hurt. We were young and the times were complex. You gave me too much. Too much for which I am grateful.
>
> *love,*
> *Nikos*

Work was her panacea. Work couldn't be consumed by brooding. Not if she were careful. Not if she were dedicated to her job. She lifted the flap over the pocket of her navy flannel jacket and felt with her finger the two sides of the postcard. The glissade of the glossy side felt smooth and cool. The flip side was a matte surface, it had some topography, texture and depth along the border around the stamp. Her finger played with the stamp scratching at its serrated border.

Rita had read Nikos' note several times before going to bed the night before, then she had read it over her first cup of coffee, the morning paper pushed aside, still rolled. The news is what happens to you, she remembered somebody wise had once said. She read the card again before she slipped it into her blazer pocket. She only walked half way to work that morning and then hopped on a streetcar. She sat in a single seat for the modicum of privacy it afforded, among the suits and designer denims with headlines below the brow. Some displayed the flash of white thigh and buttocks of the Sunshine girl. Rita read the card again. She read it again and again as if she could expand through multiple readings the brief message scrawled on its surface.

With the first reading she had been touched. The phrase, "we were young and the times complex," had a largeness about it, a largesse, a maturity, an apparent sense of perspective. It seemed definitive of more than their own particular, small situation. With the second reading, however, she had felt irritated. It was cold. That's precisely what was wrong with the note. It was impersonal. It didn't take responsibility where responsibility was due. It sounded politically correct but it was really selfish.

She felt humiliated. The note was so slight. And her neighbor had probably read it. Not that she blamed the neighbor. It was the form that was wrong. Wrong for her. A postcard by its very nature belied their former intimacy. It didn't seem to be an acknowledgement of their love, of their past together, so much as a shrugging off. If Nikos had spent as much time writing the note as she had spent reading it, he might have been aware of the possibility of such an interpretation. He wasn't stupid. His English was still good enough to come up with a phrase like that: "we were young and the times were complex." How it rolled off the tongue, at once so intelligent and so removed from the experience. An experience that through time had acquired the clear lines of a graph, the charting of statistics for a generation.

And Rita was no longer young. And the times were simpler for her because there were less personal choices to be made. What hadn't been decided went by default. Like her childless condition. Like her life without Nikos. Her singular life.

She went past her stop and had to walk several blocks back. She pumped her arms to pick up speed, her shoulder portfolio flapping at her side. The air was cool, sweet and crisp as new-crop apples, but she felt the warmth mounting in her cheeks with the exertion of her brisk pace. It felt good, the striding motion of her legs, the renewed awareness of her heart, her lungs, her blood. Perhaps it was behind her at last. Her past. She would be free of Nikos. She *was* free of him. And from then on, whatever she would do would be not so much running away from her memories, as striding into her future.

It was a bright day. The sunlight illuminated everything. Even the litter bins, stuffed to the brim with candy wrappers and juice tins, gleamed. She jaywalked across the street, weaving in and out of traffic. She smiled and slapped her pocket. She was free. The past was "Greek" to her, indecipherable, but the future seemed clear, the future was no longer the past, needing endless rewriting, clarification, explication, however much we have to revise that past in order to live each new day.

Realizing it was getting late for work, she picked up her pace with a light jog. Her shoes were thin, the soles Italian kid, and she could feel the full impact of her weight against the concrete of the sidewalk. A sharp pain ran up along the shin of her right calf. The discomfort did not make her slow her pace. She was glad to be aware of it. She was glad to feel. She thought of the broken bones of ballet dancers' feet, how they dance on, oblivious to the pain. Cripples for beauty. The way she had been a cripple for love. No more. She felt enlightened that morning with a new kind of knowledge, not the burden of more facts, but the release of the shedding of old systems, of defunct cosmologies. Beauty is not pain. Love is not pain. She would be nurtured by what she desired, by those she loved, or *love* not at all. If she had to suffer pain, if her legs hurt as she was running up the stairs to get to her office on time, it was for a reason, a pragmatic one. It was of use. Rita resolved that she would live with no pain that was not of use.

Celeste was opening the mail as Rita dashed into the office. "*Bonjour! Celeste,*" Rita almost crowed. "*Comment ça va?*"

Celeste paused in her task. "*Ça va bien. Il fait du soleil!*" Celeste was delighted to see her boss so jubilant. A little puzzled, but delighted nonetheless, because in the year she had worked for Rita, she had watched her supervisor become thinner and heavier over the months, thinner in the body and heavier in the heart. "You look transformed! Madame, you look radiant! You must be in love, no?"

"Yes! No! My darling Celeste, that's the furthest thing from the truth. Or my heart. I'm *out of love*! I'm so happy because at long last I'm out of love!" And the two women laughed uproariously together, hugging each other with delight, pretending to polka.

"What's on the agenda for today, Celeste?" Rita continued, still laughing. At nothing. At everything. It all seemed to be a joke that day. A glorious joke.

Celeste took up the letter opener again and — posing it in rapier fashion — stabbed one of the memos on her desk, looking up at Rita with one eyebrow slightly raised in distaste as she pushed the memo over to Rita with the point of the letter opener. "He called first thing this morning, at the stroke of nine, like a vampire of the day. Not his office. Not his loathsome secretary. It was as you can imagine a big surprise for me. A big honor to be addressed by M. Bilodeau directly, himself, in person, over the phone. How the rumor machines fly. Bzz, bzz, bzz . . ."

"And so it is. The fly in the ointment. So soon. Well it was a beautiful day until a few seconds ago. I don't want to see that prick ever again! How do you get out of talking to your boss until retirement, I wonder? You know it's my own goddamn fault, Celeste." Celeste knew about the on-and-off again affair with Pierre and she also knew that it was most definitively off again, although she didn't know the exact nature of their most recent break. Rita couldn't bring herself to talk about it in detail with anyone, not with Celeste, who would have been compassionate, or with Margo, who would have been critical. The experience itself went beyond that, beyond the possibilities of compassion to soothe or criticism to shame her into a show of strength. She could barely hold the experience up for scrutiny herself. She had been hurt by men in the past and perhaps she had done her share of hurting, but with Pierre she felt defiled. But there was more to it than that. Something more or something less, something like annihilation. That experience had transposed her sense of failure, her mistakes in relationships, out of the personal realm and into a kind of war zone.

Where sex was an occupation of every sort. Where sex was conquest. Or trivializing. The rape had made her feel such self-loathing. She deserved it. She couldn't get clean. She bathed and bathed and showered and couldn't get clean. As she curled up for sleep, her arms under the sheets for security, burying herself for warmth in a house that was old yet seemed to harbor a chill, it would come back to her again and again, the taste, the acrid taste of violence along with the pungent sweetness of semen. Physical pain was not an aphrodisiac. Rita had lost her desire for sex. Pierre had cured her of men. As Nikos had cured her of romance.

However cured or not, she would have to deal with Pierre. He hadn't called her since that horrible night when he had made mincemeat of their relationship. Why did he call this morning? She wasn't up to dealing with him. Was she more afraid than angry? Or more ashamed? She had been stunned when it happened, not afraid, not truly afraid until days afterwards. In tranquility, in reflection and in her dreams, to her surprise, the violence of the act was heightened. In her dreams each night now she is running and being pursued by him, but when he catches her, when he pins her down and savagely tears her pants off, the man who rapes her transforms into Nikos.

Celeste was watching her, her head tilted quizzically, her eyes crinkled in concern. Her hair, in that neatly trimmed Dutch Boy style with full bangs across her forehead, was soft and bright enough to shine even in the office's fluorescent lighting. "Shall I call Bilodeau and tell him you're ill, that you won't be in?"

"No, you can't do that. Somebody will have seen me come in. It'll get back to him. I'm not afraid of being fired. I'm afraid of him thinking I'm a coward." Rita clenched her teeth and pulled herself up to her full height. "When did he say he wanted to see me?"

"Right away. As soon as you arrive. He didn't say anything about you being late, about you not being here exactly at the rooster's crow."

"Celeste, will you please call him and tell him I'm in now? That I'll see him in his office shortly." Celeste smiled, recognizing the slight maneuvering in the gesture. Rita was being oblique and professional where Pierre had been direct. The shoe was on the other foot. Pierre would be made to feel the pinch of high heels. Rita squared her shoulders. She was not acting out of confidence so much as buying time, time to pull herself together, time to build her defences. No. She must not defend herself, she thought. She must be prepared to pull a few punches of her own.

Rita dropped her portfolio off at her desk. She opened the case and pulled out her compact to fix her face. She brushed some powder on her nose and retraced the lines of her lips, filled in the lines as in a child's coloring book, careful not to let her stroke slip. She used a rich shade by Dior, so deep a crimson that it had the darkness of pools of blood, of the lips of the *femme fatale* in film *noir*. She tossed the tube of lipstick into the air and caught it deftly. The gold colored metal glinted in her palm. Well it wasn't exactly dangerous. It was shaped like a bullet, but who held the gun?

But she wouldn't use ammunition to kill an insect. She had the back of her hand for that. With the back of her hand she wanted to leave her mark on Pierre's face. But the unconcealed "weapons" of women, powder, not as in dynamite but as in face powder and the gleaming cartridge of lipstick, were pretty flimsy. However, it would make Pierre feel safe, talking to what was for sure a *femme*. To disarm was the only strategy she could come up with just then.

As Rita left her desk for Pierre's office she touched Celeste's shoulder lightly, Celeste who was typing away, her fingers a roadrunner-blur of speed. Celeste looked up from the document and smiled encouragement at Rita. Pinching her nose and puffing out her cheeks as if to draw in breath before plunging into deep water, Rita pretended to jump into a shark-filled pool. The pantomime amused them both, then Rita hurried off. Although she had gone to the bathroom on her way into the office only a few minutes before, Rita was so nervous she had to make another stop.

The office was in full swing that morning, the clerks trying to cope with the work they were all inclined to let slide on Friday. Tendrils of smoke drifted above the desks of the heavy smokers. The smoke was apparently the only lazy thing in the room. Everything else was in a state of frenetic activity. Phones were ringing all around.

The film board was run on an open office concept and it seemed to multiply the amount of noise geometrically. If more work was not done in that kind of environment, at least it *seemed* as if it were being done. But in a bureaucracy that sufficed, in a bureaucracy appearance was all.

Rita made her way to the executive offices, private and plush and away from the noise. There the morning seemed hushed, as if all work had been completed long ago. The atmosphere was smooth and controlled. The broad-loom was thick. Phones didn't ring, they emitted a discreet trill. Pierre's secretary was on duty behind her desk. Her hair was backcombed into the shape of a beehive. It hardly looked like human hair; it looked like a Brillo pad after all the soap has been used up. Her fingernails were long and painted hot pink. To avoid digging those nails into her palms, the woman couldn't really grip the handle of the phone. Rather it was cradled loosely between her thumb and fingers, in the crook of her hand. This was glamor as Rita remembered it in the fifties when she first teased her own hair for a dance, when she had showed off the first budding of her breasts in a Kitten sweater one size too small. Pierre's secretary would have been a young woman in the fifties.

"Mr. Bilodeau is expecting me," Rita said as she walked right into Pierre's office, not waiting for an acknowledgement or reply from the woman. The secretary merely raised an eyebrow which had been plucked out and then drawn in with a pencil.

Pierre was sitting in his office smoking, not making any sort of pretence at work. He was fingering a letter but his attention was riveted on his cigarette, his vision narrowed intensely, crossing his eyes to view the glowing ember of the smoking end.

"You wanted to see me," Rita said, standing in the center of the room as if at attention. He looked at her through the cloud of smoke he exhaled. She returned his look, directly, unflinchingly, her chin was thrust upwards. Pierre nodded and kept smoking. Rita approached the desk, then braced her fingers on its edge. She looked down at the desk and at the smiling picture of Pierre's wife dressed in a formal gown. The photograph was in black and white and signed like autographed souvenirs of movie stars: *Love always, Kate.* Pierre looked at the picture too and then he placed it face down on the desk without comment.

He snuffed out his cigarette and went to the window with its magnificent view of the city all the way to the lake: the CN tower with its red light blinking, an urban lighthouse, the lake littered with sails, and the sky, like the lake, intensely blue and with ships of its own, the white masts of fairweather cumulus.

"It's been some time since we've talked." As he spoke Pierre pressed his fingers against the glass as if something in him wanted to fly out. Rita had a nice view of his back, his jacket crisply tailored, falling as if his spine were ramrod straight and he had no buttocks. Rita felt a sudden distaste for his brand of controlled sensuality.

"I don't remember talking," she said dryly.

Pierre turned around at that and gave her a long look,

at her face, then at her breasts. He picked up another cigarette from the case on his desk, lit it, and then as an afterthought opened the case again to offer her one. He had an intense air of self absorption.

"No thank you," Rita shook her head. "What was it you wanted to see me about?"

Pierre ignored the question, ignored the note of impatience. He put one hand in his pocket and played with his change and smoked with the other. "I saw you," he said, "this morning on the street car. My Mercedes is in the garage and I spent the weekend at my sister's, her home in High Park. I know you would not expect to see me riding public transit, so of course you did not. But I saw you, although not fully, not right away. I was in the streetcar, bored with my paper, annoyed at the crowding and the din, and I saw this woman with such lovely skin. I was admiring your skin and as I turned for a last look, as I got off the car, your hair fell away. I saw the rest of your face. Ahhhhhhhh! You were reading what looked like a postcard, your lips pursed as you read. As if for a kiss. I was forced out with the crowd and I waited for you at the stop but you did not get off."

"Yeh, I missed my stop. What of it? Is that why you've called me in here?"

"No that is not why, nor to talk about your skin. I could talk about the weather, the warmth of the sun on leaves burning with the colors of their last great passion for sunlight. The summer is married love. It is green and deep and true. But this last one of autumn, this flare-up, is more brilliant than even the yellow green of new leaves. You have been that for me, the colors Rousseau perfected in his paintings of jungle, of women, entangled, entangling and rich."

"I see," but she did not see. "And some of these women in the paintings, aren't they being eaten by jungle cats? But thank you. Thank you, anyway, for the beautiful thought. I suppose I should thank you. But what is it now? Winter time, Monsieur Bilodeau? Is it no longer the nineteenth century? Rousseau is as dead as you and I, the relationship that is, so before you give me the cold shoulder, you should check the temperature readings around here for yourself and see that there is no need for fine speeches. Have you considered politics, Pierre?"

"I was trained in the diplomatic service, Rita, but as you know I prefer the arts." He smiled with malice. He saw that she was angry and for some reason it made him appear satisfied and more assured.

"I have no cold shoulders for you, Rita, ever. But what I have has nothing to do with you."

"Ever!" Rita interrupted. "Get to the point, Pierre."

"There is no point. It is all so pointless. But I did not call you in to bicker. I have enough bickering at home. I've had a belly full and I'm fed up with it. Kathleen, she keeps on, yakittyyakittyyak. I see her mouth moving but I've stopped listening. I stopped listening when she told me about the abortion. No, Rita. You must stop. You are better than that. You are not a wife. You are a friend. So I will tell you that I will miss you, very much. My request for transfer to the Vancouver office has come through. I'm leaving very shortly, nobody here knows yet. I wanted to tell you myself. I wanted us to have lunch, to say good-bye properly." He walked over to Rita where she had remained standing in the center of the room and tried to put his arms around her. She pushed him away. He seemed very surprised at that.

"So we are not friends after all. Imagine how it might

have been if I had married you. We would meet again in the courts, *n'est-ce pas?*"

"We'll meet again nowhere. As it should be. Congratulations on your transfer. That I will celebrate. With Celeste. Celebrate for what it means for me and not for you. You call me your friend, but I can't imagine anyone using someone the way you used me and calling it that. Friendship."

"What I did. I got a little carried away. But you must understand, I was devastated. I was not *myself*. I felt a pull, as with tidal waves, a great rush of energy, without anger or hatred, with something not moral or immoral because it is not of the human order but it orders us at times nonetheless, with its force, without qualms or qualifications. I just wanted to die. I tried to bury myself in you. I was beside myself, Rita, beside myself. Not there. Not in the body. Not in yours, nor even in mine. I merely watched . . . as a barometer watches."

"Bullshit. You're so full of it your eyes are brown. You don't have to visit the country to smell the cow pies. I know I'm not being very articulate. But these clichés are fired from double barreled guns, at high noon, you know, the fastest in the west. And I know how well you can rationalize in the King's English or the Devil's French. If I gave you half a chance. But I know what friendship is! I also know what love is! For this woman! What a man wants! What a woman ends up with! Love is a turkey running around in the yard in the rain, her head stays up in wonder, her mouth stays open, till she drowns. She's too fucking stupid to know she's had enough, too stupid to come in out of the rain. Well, fuck love and fuck friendship with you, if you had a heart that could grow in a relationship . . . but your prick is the only thing that enlarges . . . it seems the heart is atrophied when the balls are not."

"I've done the best I can." He threw his cigarette down still burning and grabbed Rita by the arms and shook her.

"I've done the best I can. The best! Whores, you women, you are never satisfied. You are jealous of my job; you are even jealous of my thoughts. All of you women are the same. It is your fault that I'm leaving, that I have to leave! All this screwing around! All these screw ups!"

Rita wrenched herself away. Her arms were burning from his grip. She knew they would be bruised. "If you ever touch me again, you're going to have an assault suit on your hands. If you ever so much as lay another finger on me again!" Rita was breathless with fury. Then she slapped him very hard across his face. Unexpected in its impact, her slap caused Pierre to bite his lip and a trickle of blood ran from his mouth. He pulled out a handkerchief from his pocket and dabbed at his split lip. He looked at the blood on the white linen with amusement and he gave a snort of laughter.

"So you have drawn blood. Now we are even. Now we can make our peace. Because, my woman, you yourself are not without violence, without will, and because you also, my woman, must take responsibility for what happened." Rita took the handkerchief from Pierre, walked over to the sink in the corner by the bar and ran some cold water over it, wrung it out, and then walked back to Pierre and pressed it against the small trickling cut.

"Peace, Rita?"

"Yeah, peace. I'm going to pour us a couple of drinks from the bar and that's going to be our good-bye, Pierre, the executive 'coffee' break, the ten a.m. cocktail. Let's call it a separate peace. Nothing is ever again going to be the same between us, you know that."

"Yes, Rita, I know that. And I'm not the complete

insensitive that you think I am. I know I have to make a change. That's why I'm going to Vancouver. If you can't have a change of heart, you must try a change of scene." He accepted the proferred glass of bourbon in a salute. The bourbon glowed, its light the color of Pierre's eyes, the color of semi-precious stones, topaz, tiger's eye.

Acknowledging the salute with her own glass, Rita peered knowingly into its shallow depths, "Perhaps one will follow the other."

24

Lily

MICHAEL Skelton just wanted to be left alone. Because he wanted to come and to go without arousing any attention, he had gradually increased the dosage of his wife's sedatives. But his pharmaceutical precautions were no longer effective because Lily threw her pills down the drain. And she had become very methodical about this, throwing out only the prescribed dosage. Every evening for a week, sleep went down the drain.

And Lily lay in bed awake. She listened for Michael's car again. Every night when he might be expected to come up to bed he went out instead. She heard the garage door slide open. She heard the car's motor start up. She heard the car drive out and the sound of its motor fading down the street. There was a momentary brightening of the night from the headlights at the window of their bedroom now that she kept the blinds raised. The rest she could only imagine. The rest she spent the whole night imagining.

Lily went downstairs and pulled out a bottle of good brandy, some Armagnac, with its slightly woodsy fragrance of apple which she loved. She wouldn't drink the brandy, she thought she would just take a few small sips straight from the bottle. Lily rolled the liquor on her tongue. It was thick and sweet and sharp at the same time. It burned in her mouth.

Brandy seems made to be savored in a dark room. But not alone, she thought, so she turned on one of the floor lamps in the living room and sat in front of the fireplace, which was full of black ash. She was feeling chilly but she didn't try to light the dead fire. She drank more brandy. That helped. That helped a lot. She stared at the hearth, the hearth where a fire should have been blazing, the hearth where there was no warmth. She felt that to be appropriate, it seemed a symbol for her marriage, for her cold, burnt-out life. Lily stared and she sipped and she waited for Michael to come home.

It was close to four in the morning when Michael returned to the house. He saw the light on in the living room. He quickly pulled some items from his Adidas bag and pushed them deep into the garbage. He expected the door connecting the house to the garage to burst open at any moment, he expected to hear the hurrying heavy footsteps of the police. He took deep breaths and played with the zipper of his wind breaker. The sawing sound of the zipper was calming. He kept the hood on his head as if he were cold. His breathing was louder than the fidgeting with his zipper. He stopped, held his breath, and listened anxiously for other sounds. But the house was very quiet, so quiet he could hear the clock, the refrigerator and a hurried heart-beat, his own. He tried to enter his home in a casual manner, the way any married man might, any wayward husband who has been out most of the night and does not want to wake his wife or children. The house felt unnaturally hushed, the hush of repressed breathing. He held himself back for a moment more, then he purposefully made his way to the living room, to the light there.

Lily was asleep on the couch with her head thrown back and her mouth open. The brandy bottle coddled between her thighs, she made little snoring sounds. Dressed only in a nightgown, a flimsy blue silk thing, Lily was cold. Michael could see that her arms were goosefleshed in the lamp light. He took off his windbreaker and draped it tenderly over her shoulders. This gesture woke Lily. She roused herself quickly and jumped up from the couch. The windbreaker fell to the floor. She looked at the jacket and then at the clock.

"Where have you been, Michael? Where do you go? I know you go out every night at some ungodly hour, so don't deny it!" She had been saving this up for a week of nights, for all the hours that she had been waiting and drinking, and the pressure of waiting forced the words out all in a rush, and the courage of brandy made the questions accusatory and unequivocal.

"What is this? An interrogation? Just listen to yourself. Who do you think you are anyway? You're not the police." He turned away in apparent distaste from her. "I'm going up to bed."

"No you're not! Not tonight. You're going to talk to me tonight or you're never going to sleep in that bed again. Not with me you're not!"

"With you or without you. I'm going to bed now and I'm not discussing my actions with you. I'm not a schoolboy, Lily."

"Nonononono. You've got to tell me what's happening here! I have to know. What's going on? I know it's not jogging. I don't care what you're wearing. It's more than jogging that you do. It's unnatural to go out like that every night in the middle of the night. Are you seeing someone or . . . are you randomly . . . you know . . . encounters in the park . . . are you gay, Michael? Are you screwing men in the park?"

Michael was taken aback by the accusation. At first he was simply stunned, for he'd never been spoken to in this manner, certainly not by Lily. But the shock quickly turned into rage, a cold rage he expressed in his controlled but mocking manner.

"Is that all? Is that what you can come up with? Is that all you want to know, my dear? Whether I poke men in the park? I certainly didn't know you thought so well of me! I guess I've never known what you thought. Or perhaps you have forgotten how to think at all."

"You don't care what I think, Michael, or if I think! In fact, I'm sure you prefer that I don't, because when I do it leads to these questions, it leads to tonight. Rather inconvenient for you, isn't it? Isn't that your first thought about anything I have to say?"

"Well, you've never been quite so frank, have you? Not quite the angel we make ourselves out to be, are we?" He picked up his windbreaker and turned to leave the room. Then he added, breaking his cool reserve, "Your mind is filthy, filthy, filthy!"

"Where do you think you're going? You can't just leave again now!"

"I'm going out for a breath of fresh air."

"If you go out that door now Michael, it's over. I'm leaving you. I can't live like this. I can't live with a stranger all my life." Lily broke into sobs.

"We can discuss this in the morning when you've sobered up. Go to bed Lily. I have to go out again before I really lose my temper."

"No! Now. We have to discuss it now. You don't

understand Michael, I can't stand it, not knowing you, not knowing what the hell is going on. Please talk to me."

"A discussion is not possible when you're this irrational. I don't know what you want, I don't know what it is you need to know or want me to confess." Michael said this in his exasperated and paternal manner. "I'm going out. What you do about it is entirely your own affair. Is this abuse? Are you a battered woman? What I suppose you need Lily is a *real* problem."

Before he left again in the car Lily heard him rummaging through the garbage. "My god," she thought, "he *is* insane."

25

Rita

THE plants look dead from the heat, not from the natural end of their season. As Rita switches on the light, she sees the cyclamens, limp and flattened against the terracotta of their holding pots. It's four a.m. and Rita is wide awake. Her alertness is an unwelcome and somewhat ironic side effect from seeking stupor in booze, in gin and lime cocktails.

Rita untangles her legs from the sheets, throws them over the edge of the bed. She doesn't quite recognize that the limbs belong to her; those dangling appendages seem bloated and too white. She's been having this problem, this lack of identification with her own body. Too much alcohol in her bloodstream is the cause she thinks.

Her bed is a carousel; Rita has to throw herself off. She opens the window, sticks her head out and breathes deeply. The night is not hot. It's she who is hot. Her skin feels sticky and clammy at the same time. Ah, the air is cool and damp. It makes her shiver deliciously.

Above, in the sky, the stars seem myriad and bright and overly precise. Their precision makes Rita squint as she looks up at them.

The fresh air relieves Rita's dizziness. Damp curls clinging around her brow have a soothing effect, like mother's fingers coaxing away fever. Mother's fingers smoothing father's cheekbones and eyes. Every body must be the continuation of an act of love. Or so she hopes on such a night, recovering from a binge, recovering on air which is resplendent and chlorophyll-scented.

The night seems muffled; sounds are small and furtive. Rita's not really hearing anything, but she's listening to stillness, what we call silence, when what goes on outside us is hard to distinguish from the rumblings inside our own bodies. Our brains hum on less voltage than the refrigerator, that other keeper of the remains of former repasts.

Rita scans the darkness that is not blank, but textured; the darkness is furred like paintings in black velvet and rendered in broad strokes. The so-called mystery of night is kitsch, she thinks.

The moon is setting. She can see it, too large to be a streetlight, tangled in the branches and broad leaves of the horsechestnut trees. She knows it's a full moon, even though she can't clearly make out the whole, she knows from the Sierra Club calendar she checks each day. Something in her wants to see it nakedly, right down to blanched skin riddled with cellulite.

The skin of Rita's hands, which are gripping the window ledge, picks up on the moon's cool glow. Her hands grip with more force than necessary, as if she were hanging from a precipice. But it's only two stories down to green grass, springy and uncut. Yes, it's dahlias all the way down; below there's no abyss to threaten her. The residents of the garden are benign, earthworms and the occasional raccoon performing his absolutions in the bird bath.

It's a beautiful night and Rita wants to enter it and

contain its depths within her. A poet might be able to do that, a poet-filmmaker like Bertolucci, could take in beauty with darkness, could capture with the camera both the panorama of the sun-drenched Italian landscape and the shadows on skin, all that's seen, all that's hidden, in the human heart, our history and sex since 1900.

Rita feels both dizzy and elated. She's restless. She pulls at the undershirt clinging damply to her midriff. She is dressed in matching jockey underpants: the man styling she likes, characterized by both quality and comfort. Because men know how to be in the world for themselves. And that's a good thing, she thinks. And that's what she also wants.

Her jeans and sweat shirt are in a crumpled pile on the floor by her bed. But she has trouble recognizing the clothing. They have lost the shape of her body and have been reclaimed by the spirit of the manufacturer.

She takes in deep breaths of the night air, but slowly, careful not to hyperventilate. A vein is throbbing in her forehead like a single string of a bass guitar. She feels as if she were moving through a cloud, with the sudden clearing of perception and then the obscuring haze of more mist. She feels dazed, insubstantial, undefined, like smoke from the cigarette of a man walking in fog.

To clear her head she needs something, she needs to move with her body, in her body. She goes to the dresser and pulls out a pair of shorts, a T-shirt, and some thick cotton tube socks. She dresses quickly and hunts for her running shoes which she finds under the bed keeping the rolls of dust company. The room needs a vacuum attack badly, she thinks. She brushes off the dust gathered by her knees.

The clock slides into 4:15. Rita makes her way downstairs, turning on all the lights as she goes.

Slapping her thighs, "Wakey, wakey," she cries. "Rise and shine!" Her legs barely respond. There is nothing else living in the house. The mice and roaches were exterminated before she moved in, the holes of their former homes sealed over. The poison all consumed.

Rita goes into the living room and sees the empty gin bottle, the British guard standing at attention on his side. She drains the dregs, a dribble, just enough to roll thoughtfully on her tongue. She savors the woodsy fragrance of juniper. The scent backs up into her sinuses. She twirls the empty bottle to play a solitary game. The neck stops, pointing at her. And she kisses her own hand with exaggerated relish, the clear winner.

Her wakefulness and the false dawn inspire her. She decides to run right away in the ravine, to run into the sunrise. Not to wait for it, not to observe passively, comfortably sitting in a garden chair. No, this time Rita feels that she must be part of such stirring, that she must become birdsong, that aural landscape lit from within. If you could see it, you would see that invisible red flush of oxygen racing through the blood as pure melody.

The lights she leaves on, blazing, throughout the house. She locks the door, and slips the key into the laces of her running shoe. As she stoops, she double-knots her laces. She begins by simply walking quickly, her arms pumping, her hips moving in an exaggerated fashion. There is nothing worth thinking about at the moment. There is the refreshing coolness of the night air and the quickening of warmth through her body. There is the sharp intake of her breath, as if the body were in a state of perpetual surprise. The crescendo rhythms of her heart. She moves through pools of lamp light where her running, the blur of her legs, resembles flight, movement obscured not by speed, as with the hummingbird, but by the opaque quality of the light. She weaves through the hushed neighborhood streets, making her way to the ravine.

There is no traffic to slow her pace or to make her pause. Lights from vehicles can be seen far off, on Yonge; she doesn't have to approach them, they remain the flickering images of silent film. The business of life is elsewhere, she knows, on the avenue. She has a sense of her body as sacramental, the intensified functions of her blood and breathing as a hymn to the night.

The ravine is not too dark because of the full moon and the city's own brilliant aura. The path glows brighter than the shrubs and grasses which seem to soak in the darkness like sponges. She lopes along. She imagines herself a white deer, related to the moon when it was the Roman goddess of the hunt, Diana. She feels a buoyancy as if from reduced gravity, as if she were running along on the lunar surface itself, without stumbling over what one legend claims is preserved there, in the heart's museum, everything wasted on earth, the wealth of promises, broken, of love, unrequited or betrayed, of rivers, of torrents of tears. Rita is reflecting lunar light. Rita feels like a moon of the moon.

From the ravine the moon appears imminent. Rita hadn't thought of danger, of any possible danger, but when she sees the tall dark figure of a man appear on the top of a hill to her right, a dark figure stamped on the face of the full moon, which is so low in the sky it seems to be floating on the crest of the hill, as if that man with a small step has just dropped off the surface of earth's satellite, she doesn't know why, she doesn't take time to think about it, she stops dead in her tracks and starts to run in the opposite direction, back the way she came, back towards her home.

She thinks that she's not as agile as the man. She's afraid

of running up the steep ravine. She's afraid that if she tries to make it up the slope to the street in the dark she'll trip and fall and he'll be on top of her. The night, the ravine seemed so welcoming, but she feels the change, the danger, through her body and in the footfalls of the other runner. Her pace keeps time with the rhythm of her heart, tempo crescendo. But Rita isn't fast enough. And that thought alone, flickering through her consciousness, is enough to slow her. As in dreams, where adrenaline has the opposite effect intended, instead of mobilizing, speeding up the body, it makes all movement congeal. It feels the way the freezing of a frame in film looks, stasis at the point where the runner's limbs seem not to be touching earth. Such is her speed. Such is her suspended flight. Had she precipitated this chase? What if she were to stop, turn around, and say that it was all a big mistake? Would the chase dissolve as in a dream? Would she suddenly wake up in her bed, safely tangled again in the sheets?

The man is gaining on her. She can hear his breath or the wind in trees just behind her. Her own breathing is in painful gulps, like a dog trying to lap water. The school boys from town have cut out its tongue. The dog sticks its head in the pail of water and is trying to drink. Trying to drown.

The pain, the stitch in her side is spreading, beginning to sear her lungs. She can sense the network of arteries as a burning. She staggers to a halt, slapping her thighs, jackknifing at the waist to catch her breath. As she throws her body back up, she turns her head and sees her pursuer only a few yards behind her. His stride is steady and powerful and dissolving the distance between them to the space of a breath.

Almost throwing herself into a bush in her haste, Rita tries scampering up the slope to make the street. She doesn't have any other choice. She can't outrun him. In the dark, the hillside seems as formidable as a mountain, but she is propelled by a greater fear than the fear of scratches or of broken limbs.

A bush becomes the man. He is in front of her and she tries to turn back again, but he pushes her down and she falls, rolling down the hill. She lands face down. He slides to the bottom after her. He steps over her body. She is lying between his legs. He is both dark and bright with moonlight. He bends to rip off her shorts. There is the tearing sound of cloth, no other sound. Her heart goes off inadvertently, a muffled gun. She can't speak or call out for help. She tries but she only manages to make some choking sounds.

"Shut up," he says and slaps her. "Shut up, you fucking cunt." His voice comes through clenched teeth and the strange membrane encasing his head. It is a second skin that gives his face a pieced together quality, packed and reconstructed so that it in no way resembles the original animal. Like sausage. Like Frankenstein.

A sound of silence, his sex, the darker shadow, emerges. And the moon setting over his shoulders, concentrates its light, as if for theater, on this lewd act. His sex is a wood flower blossoming in the darkness, a jack-in-the-pulpit, or other strangely fleshy vegetation. It must be some sort of hybrid of flora and fauna because of the tropism of his member for the moon. The whiteness of its staff erupts in a blood filled purple head, as if his body had been turned inside out, as if his sex had been embroiled with his intestines. And a wave of revulsion overcomes Rita, a revulsion greater than her fear.

He barks at her to stay still, but she, pressing her haunches into the damp ground for leverage, and gaining a surge of remarkable strength from the earth, or from action itself, thrusts with all of her force, with her running shoes, Nike, the power in that forgotten goddess, her name alive, and kicks the man's penis. He crumples in pain. He doesn't bellow, but he cries out, in another voice, like an animal with another smaller animal trapped inside it, like a rodent's shrill scream from the length of an anaconda.

Rita runs. Naked from the waist down, she runs. She runs on will and second wind. She runs on adrenaline and oxygen and the fever of hate and fear. Not hate, revulsion, the revulsion we feel towards species we want to deny having anything of ourselves, revulsion for slugs and reptiles, for the spineless and the scaled, for the limbless, for the cold blooded snake. She runs faster than she has ever run in her life, as if every step, every jog she has ever taken has been in training for this furious race in the dark. Her life is at stake and she turns to try to run up the sides of the ravine again. She hardly feels the flaying of bushes against her thighs and hips. She hardly feels the fire in her lungs now, the desperate contractions of her heart. She ignores it all because the man is after her. He is no longer restrained and methodical in his pursuit. He charges after her, his arms pumping for speed, reaching out to grasp the woman and pull her down. Pulling her down, flailing and struggling to get away.

Her sense of paralysis is completely gone. She fights back. She claws at his face and tears off his mask. She recognizes him and that stops them both for a moment, as if they are equally surprised.

"My god," she says in disbelief, "Dr. Skelton."

With the sound of his name he feels his fingers tightening involuntarily around her throat. His hands are covered in surgical gloves. The gloves belong to Dr. Skelton, but the hands belong to the Ripper, the Strangler. Dr. Skelton can't seem to stop them the way he has stopped them in the past, at the precise moment, the millisecond, when it is still possible to stop.

The light is blue gray, a soft focus lens. The ravine is filled with the madrigals of birds. Robins, robins, nest in the tree in his yard. His children bring the empty eggshells they find scattered around its trunk in to show him; as if he could preserve that blue which is the color of the sky brought down to earth. Accessible heaven. A blue which is the color of the eyes of the dead woman, unblinking in their upward gaze.

Eyes without consciousness are like prophets without vision, or creation without god. What do such prophets see but the end of time, so like the beginning. The doctor is on his knees, resting his weight on his haunches, before the body of his patient, his victim. Not in prayer. His skill is a false god, fallen on its face before the ark of the blue sky, the rising sun.

The intelligence which can accept tragedy, which can delight in it, cannot stomach accident. The intelligence of thumbs which create architecture and anarchy. The intelligence of his thumbs which know surgery and murder. His fingers are interlaced, his thumbs move back and forth, back and forth. He watches their motion like the swinging pendulum of a hypnotist.

With his hands folded thus, he looks as if he is kneeling on the hillside in prayer. That's what the two women think he is doing when they first see him as they run along the path in the ravine. They don't stop, but they slow their pace. They're more than curious. They're somewhat moved by the sight. It's the new day, it's having once more survived, passed through the darkness, that makes this apparent act of worship seem good even in the eyes of these women who are atheists, women without religious conviction, women who never think about spiritual matters at all. This morning the man kneeling on the hillside facing east to the rising sun makes them both think about whatever principle it might be which is guiding the universe. The earth seems to shrink beneath their running feet to the scale of a lesser planet on a map of the universe so detailed even our sun is obscured and stars are as numerous as the blades of grass.

Then they see the body of the woman, its stillness, the nudity of the hips. And the smaller of the two women cries out. And the larger woman, breathing heavily, slaps her on the shoulder and they both turn to run up the opposite side of the ravine. The ravine, the beloved natural setting, has become a trap. They run pursued by their worst fears, and the smaller woman turns her head several times and sees that the man is not following them, that the man has not moved. But the taller woman does not turn her head and she is already on top of the hill and then running into the street to flag down a car.

Michael has not heard the women, not the small one's cry, nor the hurrying steps, nor the swishing sounds of nylon wind breakers, nylon pants. Rita has not heard anything for a couple of hours. Her ears are filling with ants. A wind from nowhere, from where the spirit goes when it leaves the body, from where the angels wait and make bets on the outcome of events in the world, blows across her face and Michael feels it for the first time. He shivers. He looks intently at the body and sees what he has so fiercely been hoping for that the hope might be mistaken for prayer; he sees some movement, the fine gold hair waves as with fields of wheat, but there is no life in it which can be addressed.

He picks the body up, carries it in his arms. The threshold is eternity. How is it that the body is heavier after the life has gone out of it? When you take something away how can it come to weigh more? Such a question is not posed as scientific inquiry that morning. He concedes it to the metaphysical. Such a question is a clear waste of time, a waste like this architecture of muscle and bone he holds in his arms, in ruins.

He finds his car parked nearby and opens the back door. He lays the body across the seat. Fetching a blanket stowed in the trunk, he covers her, not for death, but as if for sleep, tucking in the blanket along the sides and under her chin. He closes her eyes and shuts her mouth.

In the driver's seat he sits hunched and rolls the window down and lights a cigarette. A deep intake of breath he hears as if it were not his own. He turns to look back at the body. There is no movement from the woman. From the corpse.

Dr. Michael Skelton opens his glove compartment and pulls out his file cards. The orange rubber band is darkly stained as if from grease or blood. He rolls it off with some distaste and begins to write. He tries to organize his thoughts, the events of that early morning, he tries to explain the accident. The greatest mind in the twentieth century has said that accident, chance, is the game god does not play.

This death he has not willed, not he, Michael Skelton. Only its many simulations. He completes the last file card, the subject, yes, now he remembers her, one Rita Chiddo, now deceased, and is writing his confession when the police cruiser arrives. A detective, a big, burly but warm-looking man in a suit, the conventional brown tweed straining at the mid-section, walks over to the doctor's side of the car. Michael does not look up from his writing so he does not see the recognition in the police officer's eyes when he looks at the body stretched out in the back of the car. Dr. Skelton does not see him blink back tears before he opens the door and yanks him so brusquely out of the car. His pen makes a slash sign across the index card.

Dr. Michael Skelton is arrested on a day that is brilliant with the sun in its last fever, with trees riotous in orange and yellow and red, color designed as if to draw our star back, by sympathetic magic, from its hurtling course towards the winter solstice.

Afterword

Anxious to find out what he thinks of my book, I call the Great One at nine sharp the next day from my desk.

"I'd like you to know that your story kept me awake most of the night," he tells me in a mock scolding manner.

"I couldn't fall asleep writing it either, although I tried," I respond, perfectly deadpan.

"Yes, I like your doctor idea," he continues, ignoring my wisecrack. "I like the man. He and I have something in common."

And when I cough at this, he adds, "In the jockey shorts department." While I wonder if he is just bragging, he gives me some of his valuable insights. "Last night as I read the story I studied it in terms of its cinematic possibilities. I think the romance with the Greek can work very well. We can shoot a few nice flashbacks, on location in Greece, to add a lot of color and a little interest to our scenes."

"But the relationship takes place in Canada, not in Greece. Greece is only referred to. It doesn't enter the story."

"But we can change that. Make it a summer romance, not a marriage. Add a beach scene and some swimwear."

"I don't think I want to do that."

"Oh, but you will *when you understand what I have in mind. I want to get to work on this project as soon as possible."* Then Peter the Great offers to discuss the details later, as he wines and dines me at a trendy little fern bar with luncheon specials, a place that offers happy hour all day long.

"You like it that much?"

"I like you *that much."*

"But . . ."

At which point my outrage should get the better of my breeding and I should begin to speak my mind: *"Well if you like THAT, you'll love the sequel I'm planning. It's called* The Perils of Good Women with Looks and Brains, (No Common Sense Though) Dependent on Men To Do Something Creative!*"*

"You must be joking! No, I've got one for you! We'll call it Feminist Bitch De-balls Innocent Handsome Producer Who Wishes Her Only Well in an Attempt to Advance Her Career!*"*

"Cute. Mine begins: 'Call me Lady Lazarus.' The rest will write itself."

"I've read a few books . . ."

"Where? In a speed reading course?"

"I can see that your wit is wasted here. You should seek lucrative employment elsewhere. Take your literary pretensions to McDonald's, why don't you! I know you can't begin a novel with 'Call me Lady Lazarus' unless it's a book about a white sea cow."

With nothing left to lose, as I visualize myself flourishing a french fry in lieu of a pen for the repartee, I follow through with the following pun. Regardless of how cheap, I find it a deeply satisfying defence: *"You* mean the one with Captain Ahab No Dick at the mast?"

Even in such a fantasy exchange I have to leave before he can punch me. What I really say after he tells me he likes me is the following: "but ... but ... I don't want a personal favor. I believe I have an interesting story to offer, a fresh twist on what is usually done."

"Have you any idea how many people approach me with their new and great ideas, with their born-to-be-film books? This is just between you and me, but because of his recent marriage to a Canadian, a certain major American novelist, I think you know who I'm talking about, is willing to offer us the rights to his latest bestseller. Even so I'm making time for you, for your idea."

So I am supposed to be humble and grateful, but I am that anyway. Believe me, I know that I have no excuse for accepting the lunch date. Showing up in a wheel chair won't help either, not in a bid for sympathy nor to deflect a come-on. And it's not as if I'm not attracted to him. We women have such role models for success — from Cleopatra to Madonna ...